ISBN: 978-0-9914463-5-3

Published by 5626 Press

for Cecil and Raphael

AND IN THE DARK

THEY are BORN

BY GARRETT FRANCIS

cH. 1

There's a note on the door. The size of a playing card, its center has been stapled, its wind-crinkled edges left free to flap in the night.

Vitri stands among the weeds that have overthrown his front lawn, squinting at the note. Save for unraveling the scarf from his nose and mouth, he does not move. He waits. He listens. For the creak of a car door. For some wild cry. For a piston to fall from any of the gutted SUVs and sedans still along the street, their tires extracted and rolled off, axles flat on asphalt. But there is nothing. No movement whatsoever. No unfamiliar scent, no sound but that of the flapping paper. Each house still stands like his: stripped of its paint, reduced to shades of sand and khaki, to patches of rot and mold. All windows: boarded. All lights: out.

Vitri walks to the front door, eyes not wide but scanning, right hand gripping the 9mm pistol from his waistband, an idea that fades as he surmounts the four steps before him and shuffles along his porch. So as not to damage the note, he pries the staples from the door with his pocketknife. He brings the paper close.

JOIN US OUT BACK

The note, Vitri assumes, is an arm of his wife's anger, but one without hands, without fingers—a stump wishing it were whole, able to reach, and grasp, and wring. A desperate reach. A miscalculated reach. A futile attempt to choke answers from a throat that has only questions.

Vitri folds the note carefully and shoves it into the breast pocket of his grey thermal shirt. Pulls the house key from his pants pocket and sighs. He anticipates that that's all there will be on the other side of this door: sighs, and statements. Months-old sighs, months-old statements. *I alone am not the cause of this world's crumble. I alone am not at fault for the vacancy of our street. I alone cannot jolt it back to life.* Blank stares from their son as the interrogation ensues, a debate of place emerging, the same debate of place that had grown stale long before the blackout.

GET US OUT OF HERE, Vitri thinks the note should've read. It's what it all can be pared down to; it's what this home has been for longer than he'd care to admit.

Inside, light breathes on the living room walls. Photographs are back on the mantle, the plastic crates from which they'd been plucked stacked near the sofa. Candles burn on the end tables and the hardwood floor, saucers beneath to collect wax. More candles are on the dining room table, beside place settings for three, empty ten-ounce glasses and ceramic plates, salad forks and spoons. Two burn on the kitchen counter, near the rack of scrubbed dishes and utensils, candlelight flickering off and on the refrigerator and cupboard doors.

As much as he prefers how it looks now to how he'd left it that morning—with clothes and debris strewn from front door to back, with soiled dishes all along the counters; the scent of sweat, dead skin and rotten food fusing with the odor of the excrement drums—Vitri, just feet inside, cannot stave off his confusion. After turning the lock of both deadbolts, his steps are slow, tempered. The candlelight plays tricks. His skin appears darker than it actually is, his beard more black than grey. There are smudges of soot across his forehead shaped like commas; there's an exclamation point on the bridge of his thin nose. What the light cannot conceal is the leaping of Vitri's eyes: from floor to table, from dining room to kitchen, from candle to candle, frantically attempting to make sense of this crossing over, from one world to the next, from the present to the past.

Vitri considers his wife's anger once more, wonders into what exactly it has evolved. Self pity. Resentment. Hatred either masked or illuminated by a scene such as this. It's as far as he allows his mind to stretch before surrendering to his senses. He inhales. Almonds. The candles. Her favorite. It's been so long; months feel like years. In shutting his eyes, he is thrust back to a scene he revisits often while out and alone, scavenging, a scene before the boy, before these dark days, a scene his memory says is the last time these candles were lit: a long, bright hallway, a half-shut bathroom door, these very candles along the sink, his wife's slender figure engulfed in steam, shampoo bubbling on her soaked hair. The Shouting Matches plays from the in-wall dock. Always The Shouting Matches. A distorted F chord. A hoarse hum before diving into the first line. She never sings along, though, not a word, not once, not ever. But she sways, and her long, heavy hair gently whips from shower wall to shower wall. And over time the sway expands into a twirl, into a glimpse of breasts and pubic hair, of calves and buttocks flexed with and by the raising of her toes, the ballet lessons she'd taken as a child paying off in the unlikeliest of spaces.

As for his part in the scene, Vitri cannot remember. He cannot remember if he keeps his clothes on and stands in the steam and watches her, if he tosses the store keys on the floor, strips, turns the music up, or down, or leaves it the same, or if he just walks out, unaware that it all can expire—the music, the twirl, the water, the light—unaware that not even his imagination will be able to place him.

But Vitri wants that. That scene. He wants this—the tidying, the candles—to represent her half of the apology. If it means they'll make love again, he'll say whatever needs to be said. He'll even tell her what he saw today, what he always sees out there— the catfish remains washing ashore, the dozens of infant-shaped blankets heaped in the alley behind the ALICO building, the naked man stumbling on the other side of the Brazos, the rings around his neck, the dark scabs from sternum to groin. If she again insists on truth, as brutal as it may be, he'll say it. He'll tell her to pack the truck. He'll tell her that half a tank of gas can get them farther than she thinks. He'll tell her it's finally time to leave Waco, that he can finally see that it just won't recover, not even in the boy's lifetime. Because he misses her. The feel of her. Her collarbone beneath his lips, her breasts in his hands. He wants to kiss her, actually kiss her, like he hopes teenagers still do, unconscious of their missteps, teeth clanging periodically, passion far outpacing form.

That, he hopes, is what these candles signal. That, he hopes, is on the other side of the door, in the back yard, waiting for him. They are waiting for him. Her. Their son. All that he is supposed to need. All that he is supposed to want. Vitri takes another deep breath. Opens the door.

Outlining the yard are lit tiki torches, lawnchairs methodically placed between them as if an audience had been expected but was running late. In shadow, two scrawny coyotes stand snout to snout, front paws plunged into a shallow hole, back paws searching for traction. He watches them. Doesn't step closer. Just watches. Their coats are gone from the belly up, remaining fur in uneven clumps along the spine. Vitri can see ribs. Can see torsos at work. Gnawing. Tugging.

But it is soundless as he watches. It is senseless. His vision blurs. Blackens. His hands and feet tingle. The scent of almonds is replaced but by what he has yet to classify. And then his vision comes back. Sound too. And he watches as one yanks on a tendon with its teeth, spreads it thin like dough. Listens to the other lap from a blood puddle. He stands like this for two seconds, for four seconds, for ten, for twelve—

—then takes the 9mm from his waistband, straightens his arm, and fires. Once, twice, flash-flash, so fast it is difficult to tell if either coyote has been hit, or if the bullets were close at all. The coyotes sprint north together, across the lawn and into another until they either fall in defeat or blend into the night.

Vitri brings the pistol back to his waist. He knows nothing can be gained by walking to that hole, but he walks there anyway. He knows a fixed gaze cannot regenerate neck and facial flesh, but he gazes nonetheless. The boy's right eye is a cavern, his cheek a canal, blood and pus smeared across the nose and jaw. The index finger of his wife's left hand has been reduced to bone. Fatty strips of cheek and forearm lay on the dirt like stray puzzle pieces.

But the coyotes did not dig this hole. They did not light the tiki torches. They did not pull the trigger of the .22 pistol in his wife's right hand.

And there it is, the only emotion that Vitri will remember processing in this moment: relief, that the boy's fingers are near his chest, the entry wound inches behind his right ear, at an angle impossible for his wrist. As if his mother had whispered for him to stare at the moon.

Vitri pries the pistol from his wife's hand and tosses it on the grass. He retrieves the nearest lawnchair, sets it by the hole and sits down. Takes it in until the bile reaches his throat, until his body begins its rejection.

Despite the volume of inanimate objects—bike frames, pots, pans, toasters, dresser drawers, phone chargers, corporate keyboards, wardrobes on wheels towering over pillaged suitcases, pants, empty hangers on bent rods, objects left by those who fled on sidewalks and public transit platforms, objects left for the stubborn to sift through— Calypso Street is clear of what Reyn has been instructed to scan for: Life.

Any sign of it is to be indicated by sounding the Jeep's horn. Honk for sedans skidding out of alleyways and onto the street, honk for tweakers squatting beneath unhinged shop signs, honk for starved Rottweilers pawing through tipped trashcans, honk for small birds falling like rain, honk for their feathered pools of blood. LOOK FOR LIFE, her mother has re-written on the dashboard with a black permanent marker, the initial characters faded over time.

Beside the phrase: HNK 1 IF FAR, HNK 2 IF CLOSE, KEEP DOORS UNLOCKED.

The small chunks of asphalt chiseled out of the street either by hand or by storm do not require the horn. Nor do the trees, bare, bark paling as if doused in bleach, nor do the shards of glass glinting near the parking meters. Here, on Calypso, Reyn has decided that IF FAR means somewhere near the riverfront, near the grey and blue buildings that once were hotels and whose foundations have since been reduced to floodwalls, should the river rise again. She'll honk twice, then, if threats appear in the dollar store parking lots, or lurk among the shin-high grass of the St. Francis campus. And all Reyn can do is hope that her mother will hear it, somewhere in that hospital, whichever floor she is on, whichever staircase, whichever wing or operating room.

Reyn has been inside St. Francis before, at the age of five, for a second opinion on the best approaches for navigating deafness. She remembers her mother as comforting that day, strong and stoic for her daughter but fragile enough for love. Eyes forward. Straight back. Legs crossed; a bouncing knee. They'd held hands that day, in the elevator, in the waiting room, even while the doctor, a gangly man with a parched scalp, glanced incessantly at Reyn's mother, then leaned back, inhaled, and explained what his examination foretold.

"   deaf   mute.   different insurance,
very little   we   do. I'm sorry."

Once home, Reyn's mother, so healthy then, so colorful—a
jade sweater with sequins, pinpoint eyeliner, sun-hugged skin—had
laid on the couch, on her back, and waved her daughter over. She
then grabbed three of Reyn's fingers and placed them on her
throat. And she'd hummed there, some slow, jazzy tune, on that
blue couch, in that unkempt living room on LaFontaine.

It's this moment that Reyn wishes she could step back into
now. She thinks she'd tidy up the living room, stack the coffee
table's stray magazines, straighten the bunched rug, tilt the
television so that sunlight no longer interfered with daytime
subtitles. She'd then approach her five-year-old self, take her free
hand and lead her into the kitchen, sit her down at the lone bistro
table and write. Let her know. That she will never hear the kitchen
sink drain. That she will never hear her father's heel-driven
footsteps, nor the sizzle of his famous crab cakes in the cast iron
skillet. That touching her mother's humming throat is not to be
thought of as a game that one day she will win—correctly
pinpointing the source of the vibration as a music student would
locate notes from plucked harp strings—but only as an exercise of
reduction: to smell, to sight, to touch and taste. She'd write that the
words and phrases her five-year-old self will soon feel swelling in
her gut, that jagged ball working its way into her throat, those

beginnings, those embers, will surface only as a written question: WHAT DID IT SOUND LIKE?

Reyn hates that she will never know what the Jeep's horn sounds like. She hates that it is this Jeep that connects her and her mother now, not that house on LaFontaine Street, nor that sofa, nor fully-functioning fingers latched to a fully-functioning throat. She hates that it is her deafness that keeps her here, in the driver's seat, while her mother scrounges for what has replaced everything that she claims has been lost: FOOD, DRINK, MEDS, WORDS.

Day in, day out, these are the items they search for. They are why Reyn spends so many hours in this Jeep, outside of hospitals and pharmacies. Of course there they'll be upon her mother's return, in her possession, all four, in spades, positioned within the duffel bag just so, atop loose syringes and those rainbow-tinted vials of Ohapila as if Reyn's mother were still trying to hide the addiction from her daughter. As if she hadn't carelessly stabbed her forearm for the past nine months and plunged the drug into whichever vein she'd struck. As if her eyes wouldn't then widen and immediately yank shut for hours, leaving Reyn, whose lessons in lip reading had come to as abrupt of a halt as everything else, to watch her mother talk. As if those conversations weren't elaborate, as if her head did not roll from side to side, speaking her daughter's name.

"Reyn."

"   Reyn   ."

It'll happen again tonight, Reyn knows, miles from here, on some rural road's shoulder. She'll point at CAN WE TALK? and her mother will point at NOT NOW and proceed to open her door far enough for the dim interior light to kick on. And she'll go on with it. She'll shiver. Her stained teeth will grind. She'll cringe when the needle breaks skin. And, once her eyes shut, Reyn, as she always does, will tap her mother's shoulder, her face, as much out of curiosity as it is out of concern, an attempt to understand the drug, the pull it has on the only person in her life. And she'll once again think to herself how sad it is to sit idle and watch someone change so drastically. She'll consider filling a syringe of her own and lying down on the back seat. She'll picture her fingers filled with denim, and digging for more, yanking, struggling to drag her mother out of the Jeep and onto the road. Driving off, leaving her there for someone else to find and claim. Some other junkie with whom she could die. Staring into the night, she will contemplate exiting this forever—the Jeep, her mother, her home—being free to choose something better, to choose someone better.

Why she doesn't act upon these thoughts is no mystery to Reyn. It's fear. Fear is why she sits in this passenger seat, scanning Calypso Street. Fear is what drives Reyn to exit the Jeep each night, and walk to the passenger side, and use her shoulder to shove her mother's legs in far enough to shut the door. Fear not of herself, nor of her mother, but the fear of being left with less than no one. She is deaf. She is dependent. A helpless parasite, she feels, that can only go as far as her host.

Survival, Reyn believes, hinges on that junkie in St. Francis, that junkie that once was a mother, a good mother who, when not leaping from job to job in pursuit of pay and benefits her associate degree from Louisiana Delta rendered elusive, made it a priority to compensate for the one instructor Monroe Public Schools issued to thirty-three disabled children; after her morning shift serving coffee—for a regional chain who, due to a last ditch effort to expand, was forced to drop its reputable benefits program—and before her night shift—at a nearby distillery she hoped would eventually have enough room for her on their marketing team; the graphics department, she hoped—she'd teach Reyn how to read, how to write, how to COMMUNICATE WITH THOSE EITHER UNABLE OR UNWILLING TO SIGN. She'd sit across from Reyn at the bistro table and mouth vowels, consonants, one-syllable words, then two, and three, and four, checking Reyn's accuracy on dollar store legal pads. She'd spend hours guiding Reyn as she copied onto those same legal pads whole passages from her favorite books, and even more hours going over the reading comprehension questions Reyn would answer and leave on her pillow for evaluation when the distillery shift ended. All of which, as Reyn has thought often, would've been better explained had her mother at some point in her life been an educator. But she hadn't. She wasn't. Zero training. She'd even admitted time and again to hating school as a child. To hating reading. And yet her mother guided her. She supported her. And, above all else, her mother conversed with her. THEY WON'T TEACH YOU TO MAKE YOUR OWN DECISIONS, her mother wrote more than once, on the rare occasion that Reyn would express frustration or disinterest, THIS WILL. Another time: YOU'RE SO MUCH SMARTER THAN I WAS, THAN I AM. And another: I'M SO PROUD OF YOU. Her mother asked her questions, but not just any question. She asked the right questions. Instead of HOW WAS SCHOOL?, she'd ask, WHAT DID YOU LIKE ABOUT YOUR DAY? If Reyn was frustrated with something, or someone: HOW WOULD YOU LIKE TO HANDLE THE SITUATION? Upon awakening, on a Saturday that she took off from work: HOW DO YOU WANT OUR DAY TO LOOK?

And Reyn wants that woman back, those questions, that concern. She wants to feel important again, important to the only person in her life. Wants her to know that she yearns for the day that they can once more cuddle on the sofa and watch Little Big Man, Reyn attentive, her mother nodding off. Wants to tell her how those reading lessons didn't work, that instead of independence they fused within her a need of approval she hoped was satiable. JUST ONCE, Reyn wants to write on the dashboard,

JUST ONCE CAN WE TALK? Just once, can they go back? Can they pass one of Reyn's three *TIME* magazines back and forth, each of them underlining not just their favorite words, but a message—circled syllables of headlines, underlined sentences, a starred slogan? Can they create a code that only the two of them can decipher? Can there be something deeper than this Jeep to bind them once more?

But she is alone. Her mother is gone. Reyn is alone, and she is sweating. She removes the cat-clawed purple and gold LSU sweatshirt her mother snatched last week from a Goodwill whose roof had caved in, and tosses it on the back seat, leaving her in the baggy white v-neck whose off-brown stains still smell of stale coffee. The sweatshirt drops to the Jeep floor, settles atop an unplanned pyramid of empty bottles and cans. Quaker State bottles, Aquafina bottles, bottles of rubbing alcohol, bottles-bottles-bottles, and eye drops, and nasal spray, those that aren't empty marked of its contents either by obvious color, or with OIL, SOAP GAS, WATER, or MED in the same black permanent marker scribbled across the dash and center console. Also strewn across the Jeep's floor, atop a rusted toolkit Reyn's mother has used only to break windows, are batteries—D, double A, triple A—torn pages of magazines and newspapers to use as toilet paper, rattier clothes than those Reyn currently wears, the occasional dry pen or stubbed pencil, assorted bandannas, one pot, one pan, a sack of brown rice clamped by a hair tie.

Because, for reasons of scope, she has tilted them at the most extreme of angles, Reyn cranes her neck to view what each Jeep mirror reflects, which is, as it has been for the past hours, nothing but asphalt, the tops of buildings. Intact ruins. She shifts in the seat, tilts her eyes downward momentarily, at her hands, at her forearms, now exposed, oily but bare, save for the smeared ink near the bone, remnants of a gel pen tattoo she gave herself out of boredom. Just her name, in capital letters. She rotates her hand, examines the clear fingernails she liked most when they were turquoise, the hints of dirt packed into her uncallused palms. Reyn hooks her fingers and thumb around her bony right wrist, paying particular attention to the overlap of the two, how her index finger is firmly atop her thumbnail. She does this every day. A tick of some sort. But she also does it because she worries about how emaciated she has become. She can run her fingers over her stomach and count the notches of her abdomen. When the rearview mirrors aren't so severely angled, Reyn can see the knots of her triceps tighten as she grips the steering wheel. She can see just how large her eyes have become.

Reyn releases her wrist only when she sees a side door of St. Francis creep open. She straightens her back, hovers her left hand over the horn. The other is over the gearshift, foot at the ready.

She has thought of this moment often, of a threat approaching, not intimidated by the horn, not turned away, but instead sparked by whatever noise it does produce, hoisted into a furious pursuit. She has pictured a man of indescribable height and girth dragging her limp mother out of these hospitals by the hair. She's wondered if she could ever leave her mother in a scenario like that, drive off and debate over when it'd be best to return. Has wondered if she has it in her to gun it over the curb, across a sidewalk and lawn, pursuing from the seat of power she does hold, feeling the quick squish of the indescribable man beneath the Jeep.

Please be her, Reyn thinks, *please be her.*

Other than glancing at the ink-covered dashboard and gauges—half a tank remains within the Jeep—she keeps her eyes on St. Francis' door. What appears first, seconds later, is an orange duffel bag, stuffed so full and rigid it looks as if it could pass for an antique trunk. Following, and nudging the duffel bag along with her shins and calves is Reyn's mother. That black stocking cap. That faded pink jacket. That struggle—in each hand are canvas bags she must've found, misshapen by objects testing their elasticity. She sets them on the grass. Straightens her back, puts her hands on her hips. Squints at the sun. Catches her breath.

###

Reyn snakes the Jeep through waves of abandoned vehicles—sedans left windowless on the shoulder of the road, pick-ups angled across each lane, a tipped semi-truck, moonlight bleeding onto its intricate chassis—eventually passing the SHREVEPORT 14 sign and reaching the most open stretch of Highway 20. And there the masked are. Men and women emerge from each treeline as Reyn accelerates, and make their way to the road, topless bodies defined, muscle and tendon swallowing what fat remains. Each face is concealed. Mustard-colored welding masks. Gas masks splattered neon. Trailing are the children. As young as three or four, as old as eleven or twelve, all facsimiles of those they follow: frail bodies, yellow masks, bare feet, spines curved in prowling pose.

For three months now, Reyn has bore witness to this, to them, this emergence. For three months, she has driven this very stretch of highway, and for three months she has looked at her mother at this very moment, and for three months she has seen the very same reaction, a placidity she has yet to understand. Her mother's shoulders do not tense, nor do her hands. She maintains her slouch. She keeps her eyes forward. Blinks. Again. Again, and again.

An exchange, that's what this is. Trade. Of pills and plastic jugs, of rubbing alcohol and peroxide, of bandages and batteries and beakers, rubber-banded bundles of tongs and forceps, baggies

18

of cotton swabs and iodine, all that currently bulks the duffel and canvas bags on the Jeep's back seat. They do not want the magazines. They do not want the brochures. They don't even want food. Medical supplies are all that the masked desire. In return is gasoline, and oil. In return, freedom is granted—to roam the stretch of highway they have claimed, to search, to resupply, to approach as they do now without the onslaught that Reyn pictures happening to unknowing passersby, a blur of yellow swarming tighter and tighter, releasing only when the intruder has been immobilized, corralled to the nearby exit ramps. In return is the only thing Reyn's mother seems to truly desire: Ohapila.

As Reyn understands it, these yellow-masked men and women are its creators. Small bands of them venture into emptied cities each day to scrape paint, rust, and aluminum into buckets that they then lug back and dump into what her mind tells her are giant black cauldrons. She pictures the rubbing alcohol dumped in next, the peroxide, the iodine, ingredients of an imprecise process, an unbalanced blend stirred and boiled for hours over an uncontrolled flame far out in the woods, consistency and color a foreign idea, some vials smooth and the color of copper, others choppy and closer to maroon. *Imprecise*, Reyn has thought, because the masked need not care; if there are more like her mother—and there are; she has seen them—there is demand. They need not travel, they need not promote, they need not risk. All will come, and all will pay, and all will return.

For three months, they have returned. Three months, and Reyn still can't help herself from sitting up just that much straighter, from gripping the steering wheel that much tighter, from feeling as if this somehow won't continue, this trade, how the masked allow their Jeep to approach. *They'll turn soon*, Reyn thinks. *There will come a day where the deaf mute and her mother are no longer needed.* Either deemed dispensable, or converted: stripped, fitted with a yellow mask, given a weapon—a claw hammer, a wrench, a hatchet, a screwdriver, a rusted knife—and then a tattoo, of the state, of an eagle, of a gator, of a family tree, a barbed wire or illegible character, any other symbol that stretches across these masked adults, these masked children, across chests and hips, arms and shins. Escorted to a tree, or ditch, or valley, shown their new home, their new life. It'll happen, Reyn is certain, because progress will deem it so.

Progress: when Reyn's mother first guided her to this outpost, there were ten yellow-masked men and women upon arrival. Now there are seventy, including the children, there are over eighty.

Progress: just two weeks ago, the masked began construction on their shelter, standing one hundred feet from the highway, between hand-sawn tree trunks. Now, it is the width of a basketball court, and it stands ten feet tall, a skeleton in place to make it taller, to add a second floor. Now: semi-lit by lanterns placed on surrounding stumps, Reyn can see that windows have been found and cut and set aside to wedge into allotted slots.

Progress: Reyn has never seen a pistol in the hands of the masked until this moment, when she pulls the Jeep parallel to the shelter and two backlit silhouettes emerge. The shorter of the two holds the pistol. He is stout despite the living conditions, and wears a yellow with black specks on its cheeks shaped like teeth. His torso jiggles with each step, belly spilling over his belt loops. The other is tall, torso chiseled, with risen veins that run from wrist to bicep, from hips to ribs. He wears a yellow hockey mask tight against his cheeks, across of which has been painted the bends and curls of black serpents. As they have done in the past, together they surmount the gentle slope leading to the road. Leaders, Reyn understands.

Progress: the gauntlet converges on the Jeep.

Perhaps, contrary to what they were instructed to do at the start of this relationship, Reyn and her mother are now to exit the Jeep. Maybe Reyn isn't supposed to shut the vehicle off. Maybe they aren't to sit, and wait for the leaders to come to them, negotiating and executing trade through an open window, squishing bags through the frame, contorting both bodies and objects. Maybe Reyn and her mother are no longer welcome here.

But, under her mother's direction, Reyn does not deviate from what has become routine. She rolls down her mother's window, then shuts the engine off. And she stares, first at her mother, who has twisted herself to reach for one of the canvas bags, and next at the tall leader, who has stepped in front of his pear-shaped counterpart and now stands feet from the vehicle. His torso looks to Reyn like what one would find beneath the hood of this very Jeep—power and torque compacted into tubes and parts, into reservoirs and wires. She stares. Even as his eyes find hers, she stares. Even as he tilts his head, as he lowers himself to her level, masked face in the center of the window's frame—she stares.

Reyn's mother hoists the canvas bag over the center console, into Reyn's line of sight. But then she stops. She looks at Reyn—two seconds, three seconds, four—until her message is clear. THAT'S ENOUGH. She then glances down at Reyn's crotch, at the weeks-old bloodstain on the driver's seat. Embarrassed, Reyn bows her head, until the stain is all that she can focus on. To her, it is the only evidence of her change since the blackout, and she is ashamed of it, of her mind's inability to control her body. *It shouldn't have happened here*, she thinks. *It should've happened in a different world, in a bathroom, on that blue couch, at a cousin's house* where her mother would be called to pick her up, and they'd drive home, and they'd eat frozen yogurt together, and they'd pass notes back and forth, Reyn's of confusion, her mother's of assurance, of encouragement.

A mother would do that. A mother would welcome her daughter into womanhood, not ignore requests for tampons or pads because NOT WHAT WE'RE HERE FOR. A former version of her mother wouldn't write that.

Reyn lifts her head when her mother reaches for the second canvas bag. The gauntlet stays put while the leaders step closer. The muscular one grips the windowsill with his right hand, which Reyn can now see has been marked by black ink—JOHN, from left to right, one letter on each knuckle. And she can see his eyes now, or some semblance of them through the mask, flickers, and then nothing. She watches her mother address him. Watches her jaws stretch. Watches her mouth. Watches JOHN take the canvas bag from her mother and, with planted feet, with so much bend in his torso, pass it to his counterpart. He then points at Reyn. Clearly points, at her.

And back to the stain Reyn's eyes go. The stain. Nowhere else. The stain that she is. The dependent. The parasite. She imagines her mother telling JOHN about her flaws, about her ears, about her tongue and vocal cords. How difficult it has been. How much time she has devoted. How much it still costs her. How she manages. How much better off she'd be if things were different. Ohapila. Back to Ohapila. Back to blackout. Back to comfort.

Reyn the Deaf.

Reyn the Mute.

Reyn the Burden.

A light kicks on. The passenger door is now open. Reyn's mother is stepping outside. Reyn taps the dashboard, fingers not aimed at any particular word, phrase, or command. Her mother turns around, skin like ash under the light, stocking cap already off, hair matted. She looks at Reyn not with malice, or concern, but with apology. *For what?* Reyn wonders. She raises her hands to ask. And then her mother's eyes dim into what Reyn interprets as a sad admittance, that where she is going, that what she is about to do, will scar them both.

Her mother scribbles her hand in the air until Reyn provides her with a pen from the center console. She leans so her wrist is flat on the dashboard and, when she is done, she caps the pen, and points at what she has written.

SHUT YOUR EYES

Reyn reaches for her mother, but it is too late—she backs her way into JOHN, into the night and, before closing the door, mouths to her daughter: "It. Will. Be. O.K."

And then there is once again darkness, and a panic eased within seconds, as Reyn swivels to see her mother open the rear passenger door of the Jeep. The light comes back on and, after passing the pistol to a skeletal man nearby, in climbs the fat man, who, as he slides to the driver's side, sends forward scents of smoke and wood, sweat and paint. Once settled, he frantically nudges his hand beneath his gut and tugs at the button of his pants. Reyn turns around. She does not want to see it, him, his, this. She has seen penises before, but only the bloated penises belonging to dead men stripped of their clothes, color nearly the shade of the alleyways and sidewalks upon which they rested. SHUT YOUR EYES. And, yet, she looks in the rearview mirror as her naked mother, on hands and knees, climbs atop the backseat, puffed eyes like strangled ovals, ribs like foothills to the valley that is her stomach. Only after JOHN follows, only after JOHN shuts the door and strokes himself hard in the darkness, only when he and the fat man are thrusting at opposite ends into her mother does Reyn shut her eyes. The Jeep bounces with the thrusts. Shakes, sways.

And Reyn's mind bends into the afternoons she'd spy on her mother, seated before the open armoire in her bedroom, sun glaring on the makeup kit in her lap. She thinks of the fear she had of being caught, how silly it'd been to be so afraid, but how much more interesting it had made the scene, how intensified it all was— the swiftness of her mother's wrist, the calm, the precision, the faith in the finished product. She thinks of all those times her mother still hoped to impress her father after his long days in that torrid kitchen.

Reyn opens her eyes. The masked men and women have advanced on the Jeep. A pair of tall men peer into the driver's side window while four others have gathered on the passenger side, hands shaped like magnifying glasses, extensions of their eyes. Ahead, there are women and children dancing, their weapons piled on the road, arms free to flail. And flail they do, as if their shoulders do nothing to connect one to the other, up-down-around, up-down-around. They stomp. Left-left-right-left-right-right. They jump, they bounce, they slap their thighs as if they are drums. And Reyn feels it. Transmitted to her are synchronized thumps and thuds that soon disband, bleed left, bleed right, left, right, left-right-right-left.

The Jeep continues to sway—continues to shake—continues to bounce.

Reyn turns around. JOHN's tattooed right hand grips her mother's breast. He no longer thrusts, but half-stands-half-sits, propped by the bent left leg upon the seat. Reyn's mother, seated now, strokes him. Fast, hard, faster, harder. Mirrored on the other side of the backseat is the fat man, masked face tilted back as if searching the Jeep's ceiling for some kind of answer. Small. Stiff. Faster, harder.

The sharp vibrations from a man open-hand-slapping the Jeep's quarter panel forces Reyn's eyes to cross into her mother's line of sight. Her forehead is damp. She does not blink. When she knows Reyn will not look away, she mouths: "Shut. Your. Eyes."

Which Reyn acknowledges. Which Reyn obeys. She turns around. Closes her eyes. Absorbs all of it. What follows are visions of yellow masks floating through the night sky, slow, then fast, then slow again, and circling, yellow masks searching for faces, hovering over the Jeep at their own will, crashing into the windshield, jabbing at tires, redirecting the headlights to a faceless crowd of half-naked men and women staring, just staring at Reyn in the driver's seat, one in the distance sculpting a mask with a blow torch, molding it to an infant's cheeks. And the infant grows, evolves rapidly before Reyn's eyes into a woman content atop a lookout tree, happy to stand outside of vehicles like this, and watch events like this, and celebrate moments like this, and stomp to moments like this, and dance.

There is a tap on Reyn's shoulder. She opens her eyes; wakes. The interior light is on. The spectators have vanished. Her mother, clothed now, but looking as if she weighs more than she ever has—shoulders slumped, unable to lift her neck—passes a bowl of stew to her across the seat. Steam rolls onto Reyn's cheeks. Within the stew are potatoes, carrots, strings of pork. Reyn turns to the back seat. In place of the canvas bags are eight meal-sized cans without labels and a bottle of rubbing alcohol. On the seat, atop the emptied duffel bag, are five large jugs of gasoline, a bundle of loaded syringes between, wrapped in twine. Before sitting in the passenger's seat and closing the door, Reyn's mother points to a note she has set on the center console, which Reyn grabs and unfolds:

THEY ASKED FOR YOU

Reyn again snakes the Jeep through the vehicles strewn across Highway 20, back the way they came. Out of the corner of her eye, she sees her mother tying off her arm with a shoelace. The Jeep reaches a more open stretch of highway. Reyn, feeling more comfortable in taking her eyes off of the road, watches her pull a fresh syringe from the bundle they'd just received, and inject every last drop of it into her forearm. It only takes seconds for the effects to take hold.

Dead eyes. A tiny grin. Soft limbs.

Reyn's mother savors it for only a moment before easing the used syringe out of her arm, untying her arm, and grabbing another one from the bundle. Reyn holds up her right hand. Waves it quickly, back and forth, back and forth.

Mom, no, she hopes it communicates. *That's too much.*

But if Reyn's mother registers her daughter's hand at all, she ignores it. She proceeds to tie off her other arm. So Reyn becomes more aggressive in her approach. She raps her knuckles on the dashboard. And when her mother, high as she is, turns, Reyn repeats the motion. She even mouths it: *That's too much.*

Reyn's mother speaks, angrily, and Reyn reads her lips: "What do you know?" She keeps on talking—talks and talks and talks— but she moves her face this way and that, to the point that all Reyn can make out are syllables. Reyn's mother then holds up her thumb and forefinger, an inch or so between them, as if to say, *I'm just going to have a little bit.*

And she isn't lying. Reyn's mother doesn't inject the entire syringe. Only a third of it. Like before, she blisses out. Closed eyes. A tinier grin. Even softer limbs. There's no way for Reyn, from where she's sitting, to detect that her mother's breathing has become labored, but it has. Until it's clear that her mother is convulsing, there's no way for Reyn to know anything has gone wrong at all.

Reyn slams on the brakes and the Jeep finally comes to a full stop beneath an overpass. Out from the driver's side Reyn bursts, running around the Jeep to the passenger side. She opens the door and stands there, paralyzed, watching her mother continue to convulse. Seconds pass before Reyn readies herself. She waits for the perfect moment to steady her mother's arm with one hand and use the other to—there it is—pull the syringe out. As Reyn unties the shoelace around her arm, Reyn's mother falls forward, toward Reyn, and out of the Jeep, crashing on the asphalt.

Reyn grabs from the glove compartment a bundle of tongue depressors. She rolls her mother to her side, takes one from the bundle and forces it between her teeth. And, she holds her.

She holds her until the convulsing subsides. She holds her as she loses consciousness. She holds her as she urinates on herself.

Reyn sits in the passenger seat of the Jeep, door open, interior light on. Her mother still lies on the road, unconscious.

Reyn stares ahead until she sees her mother start waking up, then steps down from the Jeep and walks over. Looking down from above, Reyn sees her mother speaking.

"Glenwood," Reyn makes out. "Gotta save those babies. Take us to Glenwood, Reyn. Take us there, girl." There, Glenwood—a hospital they've picked clean many, many times.

Reyn crouches and works hard to help her mother stand, summoning as much strength from her legs and torso as she can.

Her mother puts forth zero effort. Skinny as she is, her mother's dead weight is too much for Reyn and they tumble to the asphalt.

Unaffected, Reyn's mother turns to her side and falls back into a deep sleep. Reyn kneels beside her and shoves her—hard. Over and over and over. She feels a wave of rage in her sternum.

Just help me! it's saying. *Please just fucking help me.*

She doesn't know what to do with it all, this rage, where to put it. She shoves her mother once more, then buries her face into her mother's shoulder, where the wave can crest in the form of a sob.

Finally, Reyn's mother stirs. When she does, Reyn does notice from the driver's seat, but she makes no move to help her. Instead, she takes the smallest amount of joy in watching her mother struggle to push herself off of the asphalt. The sun is rising. They've been here for hours.

Reyn barely moves her eyes as her mother sits in the passenger seat and touches her hand to her head, where she'd scraped it on the road. From the pity overtaking that small amount of joy, Reyn offers her mother a canister of water. Her mother nods her thanks.

Reyn then points to a message on the dashboard. YOU OKAY?

Reyn's mother shakes her head. She points at Reyn as if to ask, *Are you?*

Reyn shakes her head. She's not. She hasn't been. She can't remember the last time she would've said she was.

Her mother points to, I'M SORRY.

Reyn nods, because she doesn't know what else to do.

Once she's done rubbing her temples, Reyn's mother points to GLENWOOD on the dash. SUPPLIES, she points to when she's met with Reyn's confusion.

JUST THERE 2 DAYS AGO, Reyn writes.

"Just drive," Reyn's mother says. Slowly. Clearly, lips and eyes and nose all aimed at Reyn. "Just fucking drive us to fucking Glenwood, okay?"

###

Back here. Back to West Monroe. Back to Glenwood. Where they were two days ago, where they were the week before, and the week before that. The same Glenwood Regional swallowed by ivy. Reyn doesn't understand why, if her mother had been at all successful on any of the previous visits, they've come back. She pictures the place stripped of anything deemed useful. Food: gone. Water: gone. Meds: gone. Just a junkie wandering through empty halls, rummaging through empty cupboards, standing in empty operating rooms.

Yet Reyn writes nothing. She steers where her mother points her, to the ambulance lane. Once parked, she unbuckles her seatbelt, and waits. For something, for anything.

But, instead of grabbing the duffel bag and exiting the Jeep, Reyn's mother blankly stares at the glove compartment and twirls her hair. Which leaves Reyn to wonder what it is she's thinking of—whether the sacrifice of her body needed to be, whether they got enough in return, whether or not they could've high-tailed it west and found an exit far away from the masked that led to a more hopeful life.

A fresh young girl is what they'd wanted, Reyn knows. A tight young girl that wears no mask. I should've been told, Reyn has thought. I could've done it.

How much could they have gotten then? Reyn has been wondering. *Ten jugs of gasoline? Twenty cans of food? Two-dozen lighters? New tires? One pistol? Permission to drive anywhere they pleased?*

Where could they be headed right here, right now, if it were Reyn who'd been in the backseat with JOHN and the other man?

And what of Reyn had her mother's actions protected? What, really? What was actually left of her to protect?

SHUT IT OFF, Reyn's mother finally finds on the dash. She taps it to get Reyn's attention. SAVE GAS.

After Reyn complies, Reyn's mother opens the door, steps out into the morning light, and slumps toward the nearest Glenwood entrance, a gaping hole in a once-automatic glass door. Before stepping through, Reyn's mother turns around. She faces the Jeep, finds Reyn's eyes, and raises her hand. Raises her thumb, her index finger, her little finger.

I. LOVE. YOU.

The hours crawl. Clouds merge in the sky, then unevenly peel themselves apart, and curl, and thin, evaporating eventually to blue.

Open on Reyn's lap is her favorite issue of *TIME*. A commemorative issue whose hard cover states, PEACE AT LAST just beneath a photograph of the USS Bataan, the oldest in the fleet, and upon whose topmost deck are men and women with their arms in the air, celebrating the end of the Iranian conflict. In the distance, miles from the aircraft carrier, is the coastline, a semi-elevated city with clay buildings aflame, thick grey streams of smoke unraveling into the sky. 19 SEPTEMBER, 2027. She has read it, several times, from cover to cover—the detailed timeline of the conflict, each and every headline, each and every block quote, each and every word of the personal accounts from soldiers, sailors, and SEAL teams, from the wives and children. None of that, however, is what keeps Reyn returning to this particular issue, the oldest in her collection of three. Words are not what keep her turning its glossy pages.

Near the back of the issue is the smallest of photographs—DADDY, COME HOME, its caption reads, and in it is a camouflaged father of twenty-five, both of his light-haired daughters in his arms, wet cheeks against his clean-shaven neck. Though she has flipped to this image hundreds of times before, Reyn intentionally prolongs the process now, one page at a time, hoping that doing so will recapture the feeling she had that first time—the smile, the joy, the empathy, the escape. One page. Another. Another. Blindly flipping. Losing interest in blindly flipping. Past an advertisement for headphones, past another promoting the *TIME* app, past a cartoon with suited men being dropped into a soup bowl of oil by a grey hand three times their size. Another, another, past the American flag, past a flavored vodka ad, two at a time, three, three, three-three-two, until Reyn skips ahead and grabs the back cover, closing the issue altogether.

She reaches beneath the driver's seat and pulls out the others. Calmly places PEACE AT LAST atop the 14 APRIL, 2029 issue, atop WHAT APOCALYPSE?, atop the enormous drill that makes the men working on it look like mice, their heads a third of the VANCE STEEL logos hugging the cylinder. She shoves it all back where it belongs.

###

3FAJ172: MICHIGAN

MFV9124: TENNESSEE

084BART: NEW JERSEY

LEV2225: CONNECTICUT

XGZK628: NORTH CAROLINA

B808B92: IDAHO

The Idaho license plate on the Ford pickup aligns with what Reyn remembers her father's last postcard looking like: mountains, beautiful mountains in a false blue, jagged and with white peaks. He'd written carefully, letters curled where they needed to be, sentences relatively straight across the back of the card. I LOVE YOU, he'd written. I'M SORRY. XOXO.

Reyn remembers the day she walked out to the mailbox and found that postcard. The earliest days of what would become the blackout. TV stations out, yes, cellular towers inoperable, yes, internet connection down, yes, but weeks before the landlines had been uprooted and heaped over asphalt, weeks before buses were hijacked mid-route by men that had just looted local gun stores. Weeks before and, yet, her mother had been voluntarily bed-ridden, quilt to chin, blinds shut. She remembers walking that postcard into the house on LaFontaine, sitting on the couch, and digesting every syllable again and again over a span of hours, thinking of how odd it was of her father to declare his love from a distance, and then apologize for the distance, how odd it was for Reyn to fondly remember his deep slouch, his crooked smile, how odd it was for her to actually miss him.

She remembers waiting days before attaching a sticky note to the postcard that said, WE CAN GO, and delivering it to her mother, who, hours later, arose, walked down the stairs and proceeded to toss the card into the kitchen sink and drown her husband's last words with the last of the tap water. She remembers the next time her mother came down the stairs, when, as few as six blocks down the street, men and women in grey coveralls and surgeon masks surrounded fled homes, putty knives in hand. She remembers her mother not even bothering to write a note, but immediately packing up the Jeep, ushering Reyn to do the same. She remembers obeying, blindly obeying, climbing into the passenger seat at twelve years old, unaware that her mother's only intention would be to drive around, unaware that on her thirteenth birthday she would be shown how to operate the Jeep, unaware that it would be the place that she'd become a woman. Unaware that, in the beginning, she would look at the license plates of abandoned vehicles and hope that whomever its owner was had somehow made it safely home amidst the chaos, with their high-powered flashlights, with quarter-sized candles in their palms. Unaware that something incomprehensible within her would turn, that she would eventually look at these license plates and think only of herself. Where they could be right now. How far out of Monroe they could've gotten.

A lone pigeon bobs awkwardly on the sidewalk, pecking at debris as the breeze tumbles it by. The way it moves hints at injury, the majority of its weight on one narrow leg. Its breast is closer to bone. When the sun hits it just right, there is a pea green shimmer on the remaining feathers, a dark red gloss to its left eye. The pigeon stops and thrashes its head in a series of diagonals.

Reyn looks at the knuckles on her left hand. REYN, they read, one large, deeply shaded letter on all but the thumb. She then stares at the hole in the glass door, where her mother entered the hospital. Not much else of the building's interior can be seen from the driver's seat; darkness, mostly, slivers of light illuminating ten feet inward, making clear only the tile floor.

Any minute now, Reyn thinks. *Any minute now*, her mother will walk through that hole, goods in tow. So many things, Reyn hopes, things they've proven they don't need, but things that'll make them each smile, that'll make them each forget, forget it all, if even for a moment. Plastic containers of peanut butter, jelly and honey anchoring the bottom of a bag her mother lifted, bruised but edible apples and kiwis between. Another bag in the other hand, this one full of toilet paper and tampons, bars of soap and bundles of books—actual books—shampoo and chewing gum. *Any minute now*, she thinks, *any minute now, any minute now.*

LOOK 4 LIFE
HNK 1 IF FAR
HNK 2 IF CLOSE
KEEP DOORS UNLOCKED

THEY ASKED FOR YOU

KEEP DOORS UNLOCKED
HNK 2 IF CLOSE
HNK 1 IF FAR
LOOK 4 LIFE

Reyn steps through that hole in the Glenwood Regional door. Once past what had been visible from the Jeep—that initial burst of light—Reyn sees that each of the forking hallways before her are strewn with bodies. Still bodies, child bodies, adult bodies, rotting bodies, black bodies, white bodies, naked bodies, bodies cut open, bodies with surfacing bones, bodies whose legs and backs and faces are pressed to the walls, a small path between bodies to walk upon, an arm here and there to step over.

The smell alone causes Reyn to vomit. Scavengers have been dragging them, stacking them, manipulating them to ensure mobility. Syringes populate the path, a few sticking out of forearms like diving boards over taut pools of grey. Once the vomiting is over, once her body allows her brain to resume its function, Reyn can't help but wonder if each and every place that her mother enters is like this, an incinerator awaiting heat. If so, she cannot fathom how her mother has done it, how she has gone so long without saying so, and has instead absorbed the assault on her senses and re-entered the Jeep looking the same as when she'd exited.

Doing her best to not look at the bodies, Reyn begins down the left hallway, which, of the two, holds more daylight. Head up, eyes up, she passes examination room after examination room, each either with its door partially open, or with shotgun holes as doorknobs. Within these rooms, Reyn can see, are anatomical diagrams, clear jars of tongue depressors and cotton balls. And more bodies. Far fewer than the hallway but three or four to each, some scattered, some stacked near, or against, the respective door.

At the end of the hallway, adjacent to a pair of elevators, is a doorway cleared of bodies, but also void of its floor directory, reduced to a rectangle of dry glue. Reyn opens the door. Dim light from the hallway seeps into the dark room, a breath long enough to see the staircase, wide enough to see that ten feet from the bottom step crouches a naked man with eggshell skin and scraggly hair the color of rust. Reyn looks to the floor. Diarrhea splatters on the tile, onto the blue and pink cloths over his feet. The man twists at the torso, rotates his gaunt face toward Reyn. Somewhere in that beard are his lips, somewhere he is saying something to her. But Reyn, only seeing the red blade of the scalpel in his right hand, lets go of the door. She sprints up the stairs, sprints-sprints-sprints, the room growing darker and darker as she goes, as she tackles another flight, her hand dragging across the wall, hoping to find a door handle. Once she does, she quickly flings the door inward and steps into a hallway just as dark, save for a haze of daylight at its apparent end, one hundred feet away. There is no time. She steps toward that light, telling herself that the bearded man will not follow, that, if he does, he will not find her, that he will not grab her with jagged fingernails, that he will not shove her face onto the tile and rape her.

As she'd done on the stairwell, Reyn extends her arm to the wall and feels her way forward, first at a walk, but then, as she becomes acclimated, stalking faster and faster and faster, fingers grazing dried splotches of something she refuses to inspect. Every few steps, she turns around, expecting a shape to break from the dark. Faster, faster, almost to a jog now, and faster, and faster, until she no longer can step, but only slide. She falls to the floor. Liquid splashes onto her neck, onto her sweatshirt. Smells of vinegar. She quickly removes her right foot from the bedpan but, in so much of a hurry, Reyn trips once more before sprinting to the hallway's end, arms locked to brace her impact with the wall.

The daylight comes from windows along another hallway. On the windows, on the bits of wall between, are red handprints, red streaks to the bottom. To Reyn's immediate right is another staircase, this one's floor directory intact. There are four floors altogether. *There is no reason to go up*, Reyn thinks, *no reason at all*. Her mother has left by now. *She is outside*, at the Jeep, *locked out and waiting. Make your way down. Hurry.* Yet, in nearing the windows, Reyn can see that the red handprints are still slick. She looks at the tile floor. More red. More streaks. More handprints.

And so Reyn follows the trail down the hallway. It grows thicker as she approaches an open door. She looks up. To the left, behind an entire wall of glass, are newborns still bundled in their blankets, color-coded by sex, some faces nearer to skeletons than others but most like mush, soft flesh caving in on itself. Untouched, in rows, elevated as something sacred.

The trail of blood extends further into the room, past the first row of babies, past the second, and proceeds into a curve, which Reyn follows. There, at the end of it, is her mother, curled and bloody. Reyn does not hurry to her, nor does she drop to her knees. But she approaches. Once there, she crouches. She examines her mother. Sees the puncture in her throat; thinks of the scalpel in the man's hand. Taps her shoulder. Places the back of her hand against her cheek. Warmth leaving her skin. Eyes, chest: motionless. Reyn pulls her hand back but remains crouched. Looks at her mother. Looks elsewhere, at the floor, at the blood, at the babies, at her feet. At the glass enclosing all of this, wondering when the bearded man will come, wondering how long she has with her mother before she's forced to sprint.

Vitri unlatches the charcoal grey carrying case his 9mm pistol came in. He takes the pistol from its fitted slot in the foam and sets it on the horizontal board separating him from range and target. Nearby is the 500-count box of ammunition he purchased earlier that morning from the Cabela's near Cottonwood Creek, its flip-top open, precisely stacked rounds reminding Vitri of the wagonfuls of straw he often sees between cities, while en route to designers, to neo-hipsters at small-town markets. Before grabbing the empty clip from the carrying case and subsequently inserting the rounds, Vitri backs into the partition separating him and the slender man that wipes his mustache after a series of revolver draws. He looks at his wife, standing adjacent, honey-colored hair pulled back, arms folded, safety-glassed eyes drifting from shooter to shooter, muffed ears no match for the shotgun blast of the husky woman at the end, in the white A&M sweatshirt, stock firmly against her shoulder. Vitri grabs a round from the top of the stack and shoves it into the clip.

"You okay?" Vitri asks, when the shooting slows. His hair is short, cropped, the fade from sides to scalp filling in. Three days of stubble have blackened his husky cheeks, his chin and neck.

Eyes on the smoke above the A&M woman, Vitri's wife nods. "Yeah," she says. "Yeah, I'm great, Vitri. How are you doing? You look tough holding that thing. Do you feel tough? Does holding that thing make you feel tough?"

"Maybe it does," Vitri says, as calmly as he can, insistent on not letting her see how much this troubles him, the way she talks down, the way she shits on everything that excites him. But he says something true. Something he accepted the week before, when he fired off thirty-six rounds behind Mel's Handguns & Accessories, walked over to Gavin, the overseeing sales associate, took off the same safety glasses he wears now, and gave him a look that said, *This is the one.* Because it does make him feel tough. It *does* make him feel strong. It makes him feel something she never could: a scream without the scream, a contained freedom slow-released through this trigger finger.

"That doesn't explain why I'm here," Vitri's wife says. The slender man, finished with his session, walks past, revolver back in its hip holster, and nods. Vitri's wife nods back.

Vitri steps closer to her. "I want you to know how to use it. I want you to be able to protect yourself."

She finally faces Vitri. "From who? You?"

"What does that mean?" Vitri asks. But he knows. He has watched her slowly pull her jeans over the bruises along her hips, the welts on her backside. Her bottom lip is still swollen from the thrust that drove her face into the dresser. He lowers his voice: "You used to tell me to do shit like that to you all the time."

Vitri's wife stares downrange, at black targets with white rings, dime-sized holes sprayed from top to bottom, side to side. "Maybe I never did it for me." She lifts her safety glasses enough to rub the inside corner of her left eye. "Maybe I never wanted it, maybe I never—"

"Well," Vitri says, "I want this. I like this." He raises an open hand and fans it as if encompassing the width of the room. "And I hope you like this too." He tries to give her the most understanding look that he can, one that says, despite his tone, he knows how distant they've become, that this tone, this conversation, is a façade, that it's only this way because he doesn't know how to tell her that he wants what they once had. "Now, come here and I'll show you how to work this thing."

Vitri's wife goes, eventually. After watching Vitri fire an entire clip at the target, she walks to him. Though she cringes as he does so, she lets him rearrange her sore hips into whatever angle he feels is best. She listens when he tells her to relax, and breathe.

Both pistols lie side by side on the bench seat of the S10, barrels pointed in opposite directions. The red backpack on the floor tips over when entering a sharp curve. Keys clang as the truck accelerates.

Vitri can't help but squint. He has not slept. He has not eaten. His eyes have been rubbed pink. Sweat has dampened the burgundy scarf he keeps over his mouth and nose. When the sun slinks behind one of two clouds, Vitri's eyes ease into an unblinking stare, forward, and with determination.

He'll run out of gas before he hits Tyler. He knows he will. He knows he will be stranded, and that he will walk through this flatland. He'll walk, alone, and he'll survive for as long as he can. He'll try, and try, and if he doesn't, so be it. So be it.

For the sixth time since leaving Waco, Vitri reaches into the breast pocket of his grey thermal shirt and pulls out a slip of paper. A note. A different note. Vitri unfolds, glances down.

872 E JUNIPER GROVE
TALLAHASSEE, FLORIDA

"Eight-seven-two, east Juniper Grove," Vitri says, his voice hoarse, a terra cotta soldier just woken, and with orders, arms and legs cracking to life, debris tumbling. "Eight-seven-two, east Juniper Grove, eight-seven-two, east Juniper Grove."

The sun has launched its pink and orange tendrils into the night. A few of the kitchen candles still burn, the rest snuffed out by the breeze stirring through the open back door. Vitri approaches, his breathing labored, and swivels through the doorframe. The boy is in his arms, cradled, but unable to fit like he once was, heavy head angled at the floor, chin pointed at the ceiling, dangling arms and legs bent like manipulated wire. Without pause, a scarf-free Vitri walks to the staircase, turns his body sideways and carries the boy up the carpeted stairs, head first, past the ascending picture frames on the wall—the first of Vitri and his wife's wedding day, tux and gown clean but each of them with cake smears along their cheeks, gobs of frosting on their fingers. The second: Vitri and his wife on the bow of the AMERICAN QUEEN, backs against the railing, overcast sky above, a calm river below. The last is of the boy and his entrance into this world, skin blotched red, wisps of damp hair across his scalp, a light blue blanket around his torso.

Once atop the stairs, Vitri, still turned sideways, carries the boy past his room, past the bathroom, and into the master bedroom, path not guided as much by light as it is by memory, by repetition. No candles burn on this second level. Only darkness, save for the slivers of sunlight jutting through the slim cracks of poorly boarded windows. It's enough to see that the floor has been cleared of clothes and shoes, of coat hangers and nails, all other things that had been thrown and ignored. It's enough to see that the bed has been made—quilt pulled tight, all pillows where they once were intended. It's enough to see the pistol case at the foot end of the bed, orange in color, and open.

Vitri eases the boy to the mattress. He rolls him onto his back. Carefully angles his arms; places one hand over the other. Then, he swiftly reaches for the pistol case, shuts its top and strides through the bedroom, past the bathroom, down the stairs, past it all, opening it once back in the kitchen.

A bore brush. Stray rounds. Gun oil. A patch holder, its patches. Cotton swabs and a cleaning rod. The only thing missing from the case is the pistol; the only thing out of place is a note, written on the back of a convenience store receipt and taped to the foam itself. Vitri peels the note off and holds it over candlelight.

IN CASE THINGS GET WORSE FOR YOU TWO.
-CARMEN

Carmen. His wife's sister. Carmen, the ginger-haired County
Clerk that loves dogs but hates strays. Carmen, the conspiracy
theorist with a government job, living in a bungalow on wheels that
she had begged an ex-boyfriend to buy. Carmen, who would refuse
to apply sunscreen to her sallow skin but who would lie under the
sun for hours on end, top off, chest down, her back appearing to
fold in on itself by day's end. Carmen, who defiantly claimed not to
drink but who would swig the better half of someone else's bottle
of wine. Carmen: Vitri's wife's only confidante. Chapter-length text
messages while stalking department store aisles for Christmas toys.
Hours-long phone conversations behind bathroom doors.

###

"Tell me something," Carmen says. It is a summer evening.
The kitchen window is open. Merlot has liberated Carmen's
tongue. She adjusts the shoulder strap of her thrift-store sundress.
"I'm only asking because I love you," she adds, "but are you happy
here?"

She sits at the dining room table but speaks at a volume that
Vitri, who is outside and tending the grill with an oversized metal

spatula, can hear her, even over his wife's opening and closing of cupboard doors. He flips the hamburger patties and rotates Carmen's veggie kabob, wishing the cumulative sizzle were louder, deafening. He pictures Carmen on mute, sitting on the sofa, mouth moving, hands as accents. He could handle that Carmen. Laughs at the image of that Carmen. Yet he says nothing. Closes nothing, flips nothing. Does nothing but check his cell phone for the time—7:33. When he looks through the kitchen window, he sees his wife walking toward Carmen, wine bottle in hand.

"Here as in Waco?" Vitri's wife asks. She tops off Carmen's glass, pours her own, then sits at the table.

"Be serious," Carmen says. "We both know you've wanted out of Waco for a long time. What I mean is here, as in your life. Are you happy with it?"

One day. That's all Vitri needs to do: stay strong for one day. Stay strong until she goes to whatever-the-hell conference that has brought her here from Tallahassee, until she goes to sleep, until she shoves the top end of that kabob in her mouth.

Vitri's wife swirls her wine glass. Sips. "Why do you ask?"

"You remember when we used to go to PopPop's for Thanksgiving? I'd bring my boyfriends, you'd bring yours, and at night, after the old fucks passed out—as chilly as it was, as stuffed as we were—we'd all pocket the leftover booze and sneak off to the bluff? We'd have the bottles empty by the time we got there? You remember that?"

"I do."

Vitri looks through the window again. Wishes it didn't bother him that his wife is smiling. Wishes he could stop himself from straining to hear what he hopes is exclusively a recollection of PopPop—a man he has only seen in a casket, grey hand over grey hand—and not Jeremy, not Chris, not some man-child that left her long before meeting him, when she was twenty-seven and he thirty-one. He moves a mound of charring meat to a cooler corner; watches the coals ignite the drippings. *Too old*, he tells himself, *for liquor bottles atop bluffs. Too old to be jealous over a time that didn't belong to you.*

"I think that was the happiest you I've seen." Carmen waits for a response, a rebuttal, something. "Look, it isn't like I'm around you twenty-four-seven, but I'm not an idiot. You're paler than I am. That new diet has you looking like a skeleton. Your eyes—"

"Jesus Christ," Vitri's wife says. She glances at she and Vitri's son, on the suede recliner in the living room, television glow on his face, floor fan pointed at his legs. "Give a warning the next time you're going to attack me."

"I'm not attacking you; I'm trying to help."

"Calling someone a skeleton doesn't seem like help."

"Because it's honest?" Carmen asks. "You want me to tell you that you look radiant? That I like the way your straps keep slipping off of your shoulders? Is that what you want to hear? Is that what Vitri tells you?"

"Not now, Car."

Carmen shakes her head. "It is, isn't it? He probably tells you every other day how pretty you are, how comfortable your sunken eyes make him."

Vitri can't help but feel pity in this brief moment of silence, for Carmen, for the malice in her tone, for her disapproval of him. He is beyond anger with her. Anger was when she drunkenly vomited on her plate after giving her maid of honor speech at their wedding. Anger was the first time she came back to Waco, when she knocked on their bedroom door at 3:00am and asked if Vitri would sleep on the couch so she could snuggle with her sister.

"Look," Carmen says, "that girl back at PopPop's, that girl up on that bluff, she spoke eloquently, and she spoke often—to me, to each of those drunken boys—about the pursuit of an extraordinary life. 'I'm going to live in Dublin,' that girl said. 'And Lisbon, and Brussels. I'm going to design evening gowns for the world's royalty, I'm going to climb over the Great Wall, I'm going to run with the bulls—"

Vitri's wife snorts. "I never said that," she says.

"Whatever," Carmen says, "Let's say you didn't. But what have you done that a younger you intended to do?"

Silence.

"When was the last time you left Texas?" Carmen asks.

Vitri flips the meat. Vitri rotates. He can't even answer that question. Years, he knows.

Carmen persists: "Do you think that's a good thing? Does that represent a high quality of life to you?" She lowers her voice, looks at the boy, then back at her cousin. "What about him?"

"Let's keep this about me, okay," Vitri's wife says.

"It is about you. Which means that it's inherently about him." Carmen gulps wine, wipes her mouth with her wrist. "I grew up here, too. I know how little opportunity there is. And I look around now, not just at you, but at everyone here, and, more than ever, I just can't understand how these people can so readily accept mediocrity. I can't understand how these people inject their children so deeply with it. Why? To feel better about their own life? To tell themselves they haven't done that bad of a job?"

Vitri sighs. He briefly picks at an ingrown hair on his stubbled chin. *Tell her she's wrong*, he thinks. *Go on, tell her. Tell her that Tallahassee is no exotic destination; tell her that Waco is no dumping ground. That he isn't either, that she isn't, that none of them are, that Carmen's words aren't welcome here. Tell her that a one-week trip to Madagascar doesn't make her a world traveler; only a single, childless woman in a job she doesn't like and isn't good at. Tell her she is riddled with false empowerment. Tell her that she's a hypocrite. Shout it all. Who cares if the boy hears? Who cares if it scares him into turning the TV off and facing this heat with his father? Do it.*

"Carmen, I—"

"I want what's best for you," Carmen interrupts, "and I want what's best for your son. If that includes Vitri, if that includes Waco, then fine. Tell me and I'll shut up."

"You'll just stop? On a dime, just stop?"

"If you can sit there, look me in the eye, and tell me that you aren't spending your days wondering if Vitri is manipulating you into accepting an existence you never intended, then, yeah, I'll shut the fuck up."

Do it. Say it. Shout.

Vitri's wife gives an awkward laugh. The laugh fades. "And what if it doesn't?"

"Doesn't what?"

"Doesn't include Waco," Vitri's wife says. "Doesn't include Vitri."

At that, Vitri grabs the serving dish from the side table of the gas grill he was given for Father's Day, into which he sets all of the hamburger patties. He shuts the grill off and, before going inside, before turning at all, lifts the largest patty he'd made and squeezes. Hamburger blood drizzles over Carmen's kabob skewer. Over the vegetarian's blackened zucchini, over chunks of onion, over the baby carrots.

When he does walk through that back door, he is greeted by both Carmen and his wife. "It smells so good," they say in heightened tones, and, "I'm starving," to which Vitri says nothing. He tosses the serving dish on the counter, grabs his keys and walks toward the front door, stopping only when his wife reaches for his hand.

"I thought we were all going to eat together," she says.

"I can't stomach that," Vitri says.

"Oh, come on, Vitri," Carmen says. "Sit down, have a glass of wine with us."

"Fuck off, Carmen," Vitri says, then continues toward the front door. He stops near the living room and stares at his son. "Hey," Vitri says and, once he has the boy's attention, points to the kitchen and adds, "it's going to serve you well in life to never, ever, listen to those cunts."

"What?" the boy says.

And then Vitri is gone, out of the house, down the steps, down the sidewalk and to his truck, too upset, too focused on escape to look at Carmen's sedan, at the orange pistol case peeking from beneath the passenger seat.

###

Vitri swerves the S10 to the right of a stray fender, then powers the truck up a hill partially shaded by grey-barked cottonwoods, a relief for his eyes that won't last for more than a mile. East, he thinks. To Tallahassee, Florida. Eight-seven-two, East Juniper Grove. He sighs. The scarf over his mouth has dampened with sweat and saliva. He places the note back into his breast pocket. *Because you do things when you're angry. You go places.* He grips the steering wheel tighter. Glances at his reflection in the rearview mirror. *You're going to Tallahassee, Florida and you're going to do whatever it takes to get there.*

Vitri lies in the middle of his bed, between his dead wife and dead son. He has shut their eyes but, like them, his hands are over his bellybutton, calm, folded, fingers too numb to fight or search for their counterpart. Slinked around his neck is the burgundy scarf. And atop his chest is his 9mm pistol. Twice now he has shoved the barrel into his mouth and twice now he has pulled it out. Thoughts continue to flood. Ooze out of his earholes, out of his nose and throat. The first time he put the barrel in his mouth, he was transported back to the store, to that afternoon when another man's pistol was aimed at his face. It was why he'd even entertained the idea of getting a pistol in the first place. He remembered the smell of the man long after that afternoon, rather than the look of him, the stale sewage on his coverall sleeves, the hash browns on his breath, the desperation of a man with nothing.

The second time he put the pistol in his mouth he thought of the first time he stepped foot in this very room. Bed gone, dresser gone, TV gone, periwinkle curtains and oak closet door, all gone. Empty. For sale. His wife's hand in his. A shirt and tie causing him to stand straighter, to puff his chest. The taste of a margarita still on his lips. Though it was nearly two years before his time, he pictures the boy there, too, sprinting up and down the stairs in his t-ball uniform and cleats, no bat in his hand, not even a glove. Nothing. But he stops. He looks at his mother and father. No smile. No frown. A gaze that just says, "What? Do something."

An audience. That's what has stopped Vitri from going through with it, from closing his eyes, nestling the barrel against his palate, and squeezing the trigger. Fear, real fear. A fear present since birth and evolving as its host does, flexing, twisting, tweaking itself over time. Over knee scrapes and heart breaks. Over lost jobs and uncertainties.

As dead as they are, Vitri wants to believe that they are sleeping, that his son will wake first, and then his wife, and that this, this moment—when they nearly bore witness to his admittance of failure—will be forgotten, placed in the wrong drawer, tucked neatly with the useless.

And so he rises. He looks once at his son, and once at his wife. Then, pistol in hand, he scoots himself off of the bed and walks down the stairs. He goes directly to the cupboard just left of the dark and silent refrigerator, on whose door, held in place by an AMERICAN QUEEN magnet, still hangs a strip of white paper, 872 E JUNIPER GROVE printed across the center, CARMEN'S NEW ADDRESS signed by his wife beneath TALLHASSEE, FLORIDA. But that does not matter now. What does is that, without one more second of hesitation, Vitri removes the gold band from his left ring finger and sets it on the bottom of that open drawer. What does matter is that he exchanges it for a small bottle of lighter fluid, a third of the way full, its nozzle layered in dust. Vitri shoves the pistol in his waistband and uses his free hand to lift one of two candles from the dining room table that, though its wick is nearly drowned in hot wax, has yet to burn out. He carries the candle to the staircase and carefully squats to the second step. Squirts lighter fluid on the edge. Tilts the candle. The flame ignites, gnaws the carpet. Smoke straws roll. Quiver. Dissipate. He rotates the candle. More smoke. And, though it struggles to spread, a flame eventually holds. Vitri stands. Watches. Aims the plastic bottle and squeezes like hell, arcing the stream up, up-up-up.

###

Vitri runs out of gas miles south of Tyler. Clouds have leaked into blue. The sun is high, searing. He needs to find shade, none of which appears to be north. No, as far as he can see, north is a continuation of this valley, a sweltering flat road flanked by fields of corn and hay that are now shriveled gray and dusty, tractor-hauled boulders between. A few hundred yards to the east are parallel treelines, trees themselves like stick figures of a child's drawing, primed to sprout sets of spindly legs and stride over this valley, over Vitri, over the truck, their leafless branches providing only a fraction of the shade he seeks.

Vitri gets out of the truck. Before walking to the passenger door, he unties the scarf. In the sun his coal black hair is tinted silver, warm to the touch. He proceeds to tie the scarf in a different fashion while walking, the main point of pressure being his forehead. He knots it behind his head and lets what remains flap down over the back of his neck. For the most part, it works, though an inch or two of flesh is still exposed, sure to be pink within an hour.

Vitri grabs the backpack from the truck's floor and unzips its largest pocket. He places the .22 pistol inside the backpack, its barrel nuzzled against two bundles of socks at the bottom. Just inches to the right, atop a Ziploc bag of almond-scented candles, and slinked around a teepee of three plastic water bottles, is a pair of unfolded boxer briefs. One metal fork is astray, as is one metal spoon, and a toothbrush with warped bristles he'd found in the cupboard beneath the kitchen sink. A bar of soap is wedged between two aluminum cans of tomato soup, flanked by granola bars in metallic green wrappers, all about to pass their expiration date. As it has been doing since he drove out of Waco, Vitri's stomach groans, tightens. It has been over twenty-four hours since his last bite, since he used his pocketknife to carve out the edible part of an apple he found near the Brazos. He should eat. He needs to eat.

Yet all he does is zip the backpack shut, and shove the 9mm into his waistband. He pats his front pockets. The pocketknife is there. The moist towelettes, securely in their wrappers. He pats his breast pocket, which is inflated by the folded note. Then, after slinging the backpack over his shoulders, Vitri shuts the S10 door for the last time, and starts east on foot, truck keys dangling from the ignition.

Vitri rests beneath a young hickory tree on the shoulder of the road whose bare limbs provide wedges of shade. His scarf is soaked with head sweat. He digs into his backpack for a bottle of water and, without so much as a thought about conservation, takes one large gulp, and another, until there are only droplets clinging to the sides of the plastic.

Vitri doesn't bother shoving the empty bottle back into his backpack, but tosses it toward the broken fence separating a hay field from the road. Outside of his own movements, and the distant honking of a lone goose, he has yet to hear a thing. Not an engine, not an ax heaving through a block of wood, not a voice, nothing. Here, though, it somehow smells more like spring, like, somewhere in those overgrown oceans of yellow and grey, some sort of flower is blooming. Lilacs. Tulips. Hydrangeas. Something whose wind-carried scent is potent enough to negate the smell of smoke that still clings to his clothes and beard.

It isn't at all what he'd imagined he'd encounter. He'd envisioned fields burnt black, downed power lines sprawling across the roads, twisting themselves around splintered, centuries-old trees. He'd envisioned gutted vehicles, limbless wanderers with teeth that had been filed to blood-stained points, somehow still polite enough to ask for something before taking, but only once. Waco, he'd convinced himself, had been a safe haven, a place one shouldn't venture too far from, a place one would regret leaving as they entered what in his mind had become a wasteland.

Not yet being proved right is what terrifies Vitri the most.

###

Three miles. Three miles, and no shelter, no homes whatsoever, just abandoned tractors he'd taken to be traps. Three miles, and the balls of his feet already are on fire, flat arches unsupported in his boots. The pain surges to his *old* shins, seems to skip his old thighs altogether and expands in his *old* lower back, *old* hip to *old* hip.

###

Fifty yards from the road is a pen of dirt and shit housing dead cattle that look like shells of themselves, their heads the same size as they'd always been but their frames shrunken, stomachs deflated. Eight in all are dead, at different stages of decay. Nearest to the road is the bull, skull at an angle, one horn plugged into the dirt.

Winded from the incline, Vitri reties the damp scarf around his mouth and nose, picturing their owner diligently feeding them early each morning, thinning their portions as things worsened, refusing to give in altogether. He pictures the farmer unable to admit to himself that what he had worked so hard for had been lost, that anything had to be saved.

Behind the pen is a small storage barn. Ten-by-ten at best, its doors open, its interior empty save for flakes of hay that wind has yet to gust out. Vitri intends to walk past the pen, to go inside that shelter, to search for anything that may have been left, to sit down, to rest, if only for half an hour. But he can't stop staring at the ruins.

###

Vitri lies in the blood-stained hole his wife dug, a static morning sky before him. A pale blue abyss. Not one cloud. He listens to the flames swallow the top half of his house. Paint sizzling. Wood popping, nails snapping free in the orange swell. It will become unrecognizable, remnants of the past strewn on asphalt, on grass, in this very hole, something for wanderers to pluck, examine, and pocket, not once considering what the completed puzzle could've looked like, the sacrifice to have it so. It is to cave on itself, structure lost, misplaced, reduced to particles hysterically searching for purpose.

Smoke floats high over Vitri, first in strands, and then in braids. He tries to breathe it in, to place in his lungs what is now blanketing the sky, swirling into a cloud whose only intention is to linger. And Vitri has seen enough.

He closes his eyes. He readies the 9mm. Opens his mouth. Edges the barrel past the roots of his front teeth. Takes a deep breath—

—and it is night, and he is upright, wearing exactly what he wears now—tan boots and all, burgundy scarf secure around his nose and mouth—and he is on a beach, a beach that, if the palm trees whose tops are aflame speak truths, stretches for miles. But there is no sound. Flaming leaves fall to the damp sand, but the branches do not crackle. Black waves in high tide eddy ashore, but there is no crash, no swirl back, rhythm only seen, not heard.

He steps toward one of the nearest flaming palms, thirty feet away. He steps again, and again, and again. Its warmth at first overwhelms him into altering his path, however slightly, boots veering him to the right of the tree.

Forward. Forward. Forward.

Hundreds of feet down the coast emerges from the black waves a woman, skin pale, luminous in the night. A journeying beacon that, when he sees her, brings Vitri's boots to a stop. He turns. Strains his eyes. Watches her spot him. He considers running, turning the other way and sprinting, spooked enough to not look back, at her, at the sand his boots fling behind him. Yet there he stays. He stays, and she advances, her steps long but calculated, birdlike, driven by toes instead of heel. Moments pass, but she does not increase her pace. Long, careful, segments of her slender body rendered visible by the glow of the palm tree nearest her. Calves he's never seen. A groin he's never seen. Narrow hips he's never seen, a slim torso and small breasts. There seems to be a smile on her face. A genuine smile. Nothing crooked, nothing concealed. But she tilts her head. Carmen wrings out her wet red hair and—

—eyes, open. Smoke cloud. Barrel out, sit-up-stand. Vitri wobbles across his backyard, coming to entirely once he is a dozen feet from the door. He looks around. At the hole. At where the grill once stood year-round.

She ruined you.

Before he enters his burning house, Vitri places the pistol in his waistband. He uses both hands to lift the scarf from neck to mouth.

Vitri hears it before he sees it. South of the road one hundred yards or so, he spots the white Suburban whose engine had moments ago idled so brutally. At its sight, Vitri, still with that damp scarf over his mouth and nose, immediately takes cover in the roadside weeds. Crouched there, he pulls the 9mm from his waistband and proceeds to watch the vehicle. Across the dirt road it's parked upon stands a one-story building made of untreated wood that does have a sign, but whose size renders it illegible from this range.

Five minutes pass. Still crouched, Vitri thinks that he should just go, just keep going on foot, east, hurry past that dirt road. *Because that Suburban isn't yours.* It belongs to someone else, perhaps some gruff man with a scoped rifle, a litter of children at home to whom he'll feed anything. In the still-idling vehicle could be dead animals, dead humans, bodies criss-crossed like mulch bags. *The gas tank is probably nearing empty. There is probably less than a quart of oil remaining. It isn't worth it.*

It isn't worth it, Vitri.

Vitri is advancing through the field toward the white Suburban. He can see now that its windows are open and, unless they are lying down, no human heads are inside. This gruff man— if it is a gruff man at all—has to still be within what Vitri can now read as *haRd WeaR*. The sign's vibrancy says that it was painted recently, above the door, in some cousin of mint green. Vitri could believe it. He could imagine it as a center for commerce, an operating establishment that exchanges screws and nails, hammers and rasps for skulls and kidneys, for sex or slaughter, whatever has become currency. A place to gain information. A place to find help. But he doesn't, and there is no way he will. *Trap*, he is convinced. *It is a trap.* Going inside HArD WeaR means pain, means a death for which he'd never ask.

Fifteen yards from the suburban, Vitri, increasing his pace, emerges from his crouch. Faster, faster yet, until he is within arm's length of the Suburban. Despite how rusty it is, how mud-splotched, its exterior smells of vanilla. He eases the grip on his pistol and peers through the Suburban's windows. No bodies, no tools, no wood. A large, unlabeled aluminum can is on the floor, a plastic spoon next to it. Hanging from the rearview mirror is a Black Ice air freshener and a thumbnail-sized picture of an old woman, her angled face confused, string tangled.

Vitri ducks on the passenger side of the Suburban when the HArD WeaR door opens and a cinder block of a man walks out. The engine sputters again. Vitri, near the front tire, waits for footsteps the still-sputtering engine won't allow him to hear. So he crouches, further and further. Looks beneath the chassis. Sees toes. Boots. Shins. He angles his arm for a clear shot.

cH. IV

Idaho will require gasoline. A lot of gasoline. More gasoline than Reyn has, more gasoline than she can stack in the Jeep. She wonders what JOHN will demand of her for it. Wonders what she can do to JOHN that her mother didn't, or couldn't. Wonders if sex is something that she can think of on the spot, rather than going into it with a scheme, if it's just something she can just feel her way through and improvise as she sees fit. Read, and react. She wonders if JOHN will give her the opportunity to do so. Imagines JOHN inside of her, JOHN trying to talk to her, and she not hearing, not obeying, JOHN becoming angry, JOHN screaming, JOHN punching, JOHN kneeing. Imagines the fat leader not handing off his pistol this time. Imagines going through with it—their insertion, her improvisation, the collective miscommunication—

only to be offered enough gasoline to get her back to West Monroe, to her dead mother.

Reyn weaves the Jeep in and out of the same abandoned vehicles on Highway 20, headlights amok in the night, left, then right, then left again. She is a mile from the masked, past the SHREVEPORT 14 sign. One-quarter of the Jeep's fuel supply remains.

Ten minutes or less. That quick. Just shut your eyes and let JOHN *spread your legs. Let the fat one in your mouth. Maybe they'll take off their masks, and maybe they'll be gentle, and maybe they'll kiss you, and maybe your first kiss will be okay.*

Maybe it'll all be okay.

She spots the first pair of yellow-masked eyes half-way-up a tree, a foot to the right of the trunk as if peeking from behind. As are the next two, and the two after that. Driving so slow, Reyn watches the eyes vanish in the night, reappearing seconds later, on the ground, as they approach the road, as they form their gauntlet. Closing in, two deep now on each side. She sees the same breasts, the same tattoos, the same long-haired boys and girls joining, the masks they'll grow into sliding up, down and across their faces as they walk, yellow hatchets and miniature crowbars sheathed in the belt loops of the denim that has been hacked to their size.

Beyond the masks to the right, the shelter comes into view. On the lawn now are pallets of wood, piles of shingles. Cans of paint are stacked and partially lit by the same oil lanterns, the same candles on the same stumps. Leaned against the shelter is a motorcycle, its tires off and nearby, accompanied by more tires, by assorted metals, all leaned against stacks of car batteries.

Think of gasoline. Think of Idaho. Tell yourself it'll be okay. Go on. Tell yourself that.

JOHN and the fat leader emerge from the structure and walk toward the road. But Reyn does not stop the Jeep. Foot hovering over the brake, she thinks, It just won't. *They won't negotiate. They won't hear you. They'll yank you out of the Jeep as if you were a doll.*

Reyn scans the gauntlet. A boy, maybe four or five years old, takes his place between two older children on the left shoulder of the road. He is the only one not wearing a mask. *They'll shred your clothes at the seams. They'll let each man have their turn.* The boy's nose is small and flat. His eyes point inward. *They'll force you to become one of them, and you'll stand here like he does, watching.*

Jeep still crawling, she wonders if maybe keeping a mask from his face is punishment. For stealing, maybe, for mouthing off, for not knowing his place. For his deformity.

Stopping will be the end.

Reyn feels a throb from the back left quarter of the Jeep. A quick bounce, a tiny bounce. A squish. Reyn presses the brake as members of the gauntlet enclose the Jeep. In the driver's side mirror, Reyn watches the masked mob huddle in the red brake light. Between two women struggling for a view, she sees a young girl lying on the pavement, clutching an injured foot, head and neck writhing. A hose unkinking itself. Screaming, Reyn knows, in agony. Screaming—at Reyn. Screaming because of Reyn.

She feels a thump from the passenger side.

Reyn turns her head. The passenger window has cracked into a spider web, thin divots extending from impact, stretching toward each corner. On the other side of that window, a sinewy woman winds up her yellow crowbar. She delivers another thump. The cracks expand. Faster, thicker, across this window, and now that window, and now that one. Chips of yellow paint embed themselves in the glass, smear with another thump. And another. The windows bend inward.

More join. Men, women, children, with instruments or fists, or both, pound the quarter panels, each bumper. One stabs the back right tire, which eases that quarter of the Jeep to the pavement. The thumps are closing in.

Do it. Go.

The mob in front of the Jeep steps aside when JOHN arrives, translucent in the light, ethereal, yellow ax gripped tight, its handle as long as his torso. He just stands there—three seconds, five seconds, seven—daring Reyn to move.

Go. Before he does.

And then JOHN lifts the ax and brings its edge down on the Jeep's hood. In it goes, and in it stays—Reyn, once gathered from her instinctive dodging of the ax's arc, watches JOHN struggle to remove the blade. Both of his hands are on its handle, a foot presumably on the front bumper for leverage. And—this incision, this wound to what for so long now has been her home—it irks Reyn. It offends Reyn. She feels it in her shoulders, in her torso, in her thighs, and shins, and feet.

Go, go, go.

She presses the gas pedal.

JOHN's face slams onto the Jeep's hood. And off they go down the road, the gauntlet giving chase. When JOHN lifts his head, Reyn sees that the right side of his mask is cracked. One plastic shard is deep into his tan-lined cheek, a slim crimson dash streaking to his neck.

But he hangs on, ax handle palmed, a grip strong enough not to just hold on, but to advance up the hood, toward the windshield. She holds a glance at his knuckles, at the J and the O, the H and the N, until bursts of pistol light fill each mirror. Reyn swerves the Jeep. Thinking it will send JOHN tumbling onto the road, Reyn stomps on the brake. While JOHN slips momentarily, he soon regains his grip, and, through the crack in his mask, gives Reyn the tiniest of smiles, dark lips curling.

I'm sorry.

Reyn presses the gas pedal. Further, harder. The steering wheel shakes in her hands. More pistols flash behind her, further away now, specks. She jerks the Jeep left, then right. Further, harder. Left again. Right again. And down goes JOHN, pulled beneath the Jeep, legs first, ax still stuck in the hood.

cH. V

Hammer sets a jar of mayonnaise on the barn floor. "Should be able to find a glob in there somewhere," he says. His voice reminds Vitri of a near-empty tube of toothpaste, remnants rolled out from otherwise inaccessible pockets; a battle for words to leave his throat. "You sure you don't want to stay in the house?"

Vitri, scarf over his nose and mouth, back against a barn wall, grabs the jar. "I'll be fine here." The light from his candle reveals blue-grey swirls of mold within the jar.

Hammer pulls a thin, folded magazine from the inside of his jacket. He hands it to Vitri. "Wouldn't want you to feel lonely is all."

Vitri unrolls the magazine. *DEEP THROAT* is its title. NOVEMBER 2001. A young brunette woman is on the cover, straddling a piano bench, ample lips parted, hands over her nipples.

Hammer backs across the barn aisle and eases his lit candle to the floor, then himself, resting his back against a support beam, then his neck, his asymmetrical chin illuminated—bashed, Vitri understood upon sight, by fists, by boot heels, by birth; a tetherball for classmates.

"My brother used to lock me in here when I was younger," Hammer says. "The first few times he did, he coaxed me in with the promise of a cigarette—one piddly little cigarette—or a can of Lone Star—again, just one—and other things, too, things a twelve-year-old thinks he wants." Hammer takes the double action revolver from his coat—the pistol he says hasn't fired for over a decade—and wiggles it as if to say it too was once a promise. He sets it on the floor, lips curling into something of a grin. "Well, once I figured out that there was no beer, and that there was no cigarette, I put up a fight. Kicked, screamed, even bit him once or twice. But it was no use. He was stronger than I was, plain and simple. He'd kill all the lights, jam a broomstick through the doorhandles. He thought it was funny, I suppose." Hammer's grin subsides. He pinches the dry skin from his lips, rolls it into a ball and tosses it on the barn floor. "Dad had already left by then. Mom's mind was on her way out. So here I'd be until morning, on the floor, against that very wall, just listening to them fucking pigs root, snort, screw, squeal. Jesus. So loud, them fucking pigs. Couldn't ever fall asleep. So I'd hum, I'd talk to them."

Vitri has no intention of commenting on Hammer's story, no intention of apologizing for what Hammer was subjected to, no intention of discussing the routines of swine. Nor does he have any intention of pleasuring himself here, in this barn. Vitri does not care. He does not want to care.

"So what I'm saying is I know how alone one can feel in here," Hammer finishes.

Yet the compassionate sliver of Vitri cannot overlook the fact that all of it—the magazine, the mayonnaise, the story, the shelter—has been handed over with sincerity, with an honesty someone like Hammer cannot fake.

"Thank you," Vitri says. He lifts the rolled magazine to clarify his gratitude.

"I'm the one that should be thanking you, Freddie."

Vitri hadn't forgotten what he'd told Hammer to call him, but hearing it once more sends his mind into a race to rediscover the ways in which he has distorted the truth. Freddie: a former police officer born and raised in El Paso. Freddie: not a good enough shot to be a sniper, but for a stretch was sturdy enough to serve as the point man on the department's SWAT team. Freddie: he has been in love before, yes, with many women—"The Rainbow," Vitri told Hammer, going on to explain: one with blonde hair; one with brunette hair; one with raven-black hair; one with fire-orange hair; one with silver hair; and one with punk green hair—but has never committed to marriage. Freddie: he has one brother, one sister, both older, both overseas, both, "In one of the Koreas by now."

Freddie: husband to no one; father to no one.

Lies. All lies. Lies that somehow led to the untying of his stomach, to licking the bowl of chicken broth Hammer served him on the porch steps, lies that led to a second bowl, lies that led to vomiting.

"Thanking me for what?" Vitri asks.

"For not killing my dumb ass." A trail of piss had stretched from groin to ankle seconds after Vitri rose from behind the Suburban and took aim. "Can't say I wouldn't have deserved it, leaving it out in the open like that." He chuckles; shakes his head.

Vitri had wanted to pull the trigger. Part of him still wishes he had, that he'd be better off, farther along, that he'd be somewhere in Louisiana by now instead of in this barn, at this farmhouse, with this man. *Take no chances. Eliminate all threats.* It's the mindset he knows he needs to survive.

But Hammer hadn't been armed. He'd surrendered immediately, arms like masts in the sky, baggy khaki jacket its sails; that slender nose, bent as if broken and left unset; remaining hair in the shape of a horseshoe, the crown of his head burnt pink and peeling; his eyes—brown, beyond scared, damp—had shrieked that he will forever be incapable of violence. Vitri had felt pity while staring at Hammer. He'd lowered the pistol, shook the man's hand, allowed him to drive, to speak as if they were destined to be friends from the start.

"I just hope HArD WeaR gets some foot traffic soon," Vitri says.

As he told it, when Hammer's able to siphon enough gas to do so, he drives around and searches scrapyards and abandoned strip malls to stock HArD WeaR, his first and only entrepreneurial endeavor. Some days, it's like he can't even find a nail; other days, it's like a scrounger's jackpot—pocketfuls of drill bits, claw hammers and screwdrivers secured in his belt loops. He has stumbled upon handsaws, upon wrenches of all sizes and colors, sometimes even an entire set. Rasps, utility belts, a plethora of chisels. Which was, at least for a moment, enough for Vitri to look at Hammer with the slightest bit of admiration, for it was he, finding the confidence after everyone else's had gone out with the light, that was looking to the future with hope, and doing something about it.

"Me too," Hammer says. "Has to. Me and Mom are low on everything again."

"I thought you said your mom was gone." The sun had set by the time they'd arrived; the farmhouse completely dark. Outside of their footsteps on the porch, there'd been no movement whatsoever.

"Dad is gone. Dad *has been* gone. Mom's just batshit crazy." Hammer reels in his laugh. "Belongs in the pysch ward, that one, but I love her. I mean that. Really do. If you ask me, though—" He pauses, leans in as if his mother were nearby, ear to the barn door, then whispers, "It's a goddamn curse." He leans back. "I'm tellin' you, Freddie, you're lucky to not have any family in a time like this. Don't have to wipe no asses, don't have no one you have to share your food with. Free to wander as you damn well please."

Vitri lets that sink in. Digests it. Lets it tumble to his gut. Can see Hammer's point, can even align it with the views of a much-younger version of himself. But he doesn't agree. Freedom and mobility, Vitri believes, are separate. Freedom, not mobility, is confusion, in having so many choices, too many choices. Freedom, not mobility, is fear in choosing the wrong place, the wrong person, the wrong route. Freedom, he thinks now, is an agent of restriction, immobility a byproduct.

"Mmhmm," Vitri says. It's all he intends to say. He believes his thoughts to be over Hammer's head, and is left in silence, wondering whether or not Hammer's statement would've been different had he told him the truth, that he'd had a wife and son, that his wife put a bullet in the boy's head, and then her own.

"Tell me, though," Hammer says. He settles in, crosses his stiff legs, candlelight swiveling as he does so. "You said you've

been in love, and with several women. What—what does—"
Hammer pauses, gathers himself. "What does that feel like?"

The question both stuns and flatters Vitri. Stuns him because, despite Hammer's apparent shortcomings, he would've expected love to surface and be fulfilled somewhere in his thirty-odd years. A coworker. A cousin. A pig in this very barn. It flatters him not just because Hammer has, as coyly as an ungraceful man like Hammer can, asked for guidance through memories, but that, within hours of having Vitri's 9mm aimed at his face, Hammer believes him—*Freddie*— to be the man to ask. Thin armor peeled off. Guard down. A desire to connect.

"It's hard to explain," Vitri says.

"Mmhmm."

Vitri stares at Hammer. Fragile. Fractured. Curious. A student on the classroom's reading rug. Something. He needs to say something. "It can be great."

Another, "Mmhmm." A nod. *Go on*, it says, *go on*.

"So many things need to align for it to be great, though. The moon, the stars, the money. You need to be assertive. You need to be sensitive. You need to stay home. You need to go places, keep things in motion." Vitri pauses. "In order for love to be great, you need to give them the world."

"Huh," Hammer says. "That sounds exhausting."

"It is," Vitri says. "It really is." And he is in a trance, lost in a memory, eyes fixed on a support beam in shadow, a dozen feet or so from Hammer. He slips off his scarf. "Sometimes you do wonder if it's all worth it, the effort, but then there are other times—as brief as they are—where those questions just go away."

"Tell me—," Hammer says, realizing that his listener's stare is elsewhere.

Vitri is on a boat. His wife is twenty feet away. "I remember watching her walk across that deck. Strapless white dress. No, wait. Red dress. Scarlet, maroon, I don't know. I don't remember. But I remember thinking that she looked so beautiful, and I remember feeling so proud, so fucking proud, of her, of me, for somehow finding the balls to pursue, for taking a risk and actually having it pay off." Her hands are in his. "And for having the opportunity to look back and think of how great it'd been, to look forward and not be scared." Vitri leans in, can smell the almonds in her hair. "I wasn't on the river that trip. I was somewhere between it, and the sun. Trees, clouds, mountains, I didn't care. Everything she said. Everything she did. It was perfect."

"Mmhmm," Hammer says. He stares. "Is this the brunette you're talking about?"

"Blonde. Straight blonde hair. Legs for days. And her shoulders—there was something about her shoulders that I loved. They were broad, but not too broad, you know? Sturdy. Strong.

But also feminine, you know?" Vitri smiles again, thinking of the way his wife's skin would tense and rise when he'd graze her shoulders with his finger.

"How good of a fuck was she?" Hammer asks.

Which jars Vitri. His eyes shift. He sits up. Scratches his beard. Feels *How good of a fuck was she?* ping-ponging from ear to ear. Squints at Hammer. "What was that?"

"I asked how good of a fuck she was," Hammer says. "You said that this was the blonde. You said she had long legs. Those broad shoulders. Sounds to me like she was built to fuck." Awaiting an answer, Hammer watches Vitri closely. Notices his eyes drifting back to the floor. Notices his twirling thumbs. Notices the elongated silence. "I was just curious, Freddie, that's all. Don't feel like you need to—"

"She was good," Vitri interrupts, eyes astray. "She was very good."

Hammer isn't sure of his place here, whether or not his best route is to ask more questions, or to let Vitri's statements stand as they do. All he finds himself doing is watching Vitri—eyes are fixed, thumbs no longer twirling, but playing their role in the pinching of the scarf, in the dragging of its frayed edges back over his mouth and nose.

"Big tits? Big ass?" Vitri asks, voice muffled now. "No. Neither. They were decent. Decent, yeah. Enough to have fun with, sure—plenty of fun—but what set her off is the kind of shit she'd ask me to do to her."

"She wanted it rough?"

"She did. Liked it from every angle. Liked it in every hole. She'd tell me to shove her face into the floor, to fuck her from behind but to keep her hands behind her back." Vitri looks at Hammer. "Powerless. She liked to feel powerless."

cH. VI

The Jeep is at the bottom of the highway's northern bank, on its side, ax still in the hood. Fluid and oil spill onto the grass. Because the left headlight has been smashed, a lone beam of light shines on the tree stumps that brought the sliding Jeep to a halt. The moon is low and bright. All around smells of gasoline.

Reyn walks to the highway, eyes wide but vision still blurred, spinning, swooping. Hair clings to the blood smeared on her left cheek. She'd felt the rest of the tires go, she'd felt the Jeep lower. She'd seen the sparks. As to what had happened next, she can't be certain. Though the road thus far doesn't reveal such a scenario, she may have flipped soon after and skidded the rest of the way. She may have even centered the immediate swerve, only to lose the battle later, when the pull had become too much for her hands to bear.

She walks on. Stops. Fifty yards from where she'd crested the hill are short and narrow rubber strips, consecutively spaced three feet from one another. They span the width of the road, no way to emerge in a vehicle unscathed. Reyn crouches, examines the strips. Each long nail, from point to strip painted red. She pinches the rubber between her fingers and attempts to lift one of the strips but to no avail. Adhered somehow to the asphalt.

She then stands and begins her trek back to the Jeep, certain that the site will soon swarm with the yellow-masked who'd given chase. Not in the next five minutes, or ten, or even thirty. But soon. She pictures dozens of them sprinting toward her, dozens that followed her on foot all this way, the ten or so miles she'd traveled, dozens with pointed weapons meant for her, to pierce her feet, her sternum, her throat. She strides back down the hill to extract what she can from the wreckage.

сH. **VII**

It'd taken an hour longer than Hammer had said it would. He'd blotched makeup across her face. He'd forced antique earrings into closed holes but, too concerned with how he was to drape the deep purple top and dirty jeans over her frail body, had forgotten to wipe the blood from her lobes. Oddly, he'd done nothing with her hair. Not a wash, not a comb, nothing. Instead, here in the Suburban, he likens it to a ship captain's wheel, jutting every which way.

Hammer's mother's hair isn't the only thing that makes Vitri uncomfortable, though; it's the acorn eyes that, since leaving the driveway, have been on him, and only him, almost unblinkingly so. As he has a few times now, Vitri, in the passenger seat, turns far enough to see her, upright in the back, childlike beneath her makeshift seatbelt. This time, he looks at her shoes. They are the color of ash, with two Velcro straps in which lint and dust have fused.

"She likes her car rides, tell you what," Hammer says. He smiles as he slows the Suburban to a crawl, passing exit ramps blocked off by accordioned semi-trucks. "Isn't that right, Ma?"

Hammer's mother moans.

Vitri turns back around. "You always take her with you?"

"Can't leave her at the house by her lonesome when there are people like you roaming around." Hammer shoves Vitri's shoulder as if they are old pals, then lets out a laugh, deep and haughty.

Which, more than anything else, depresses Vitri. He is to be in this Suburban until Shreveport, with the old woman that has been doused in rank perfume, with this giddy Hammer, this guard-entirely-down Hammer, this Hammer that has emerged from the cocoon that his self-doubt had spun. He is not at all the pants-wetting hammer he'd drawn upon less than a day ago.

"Have to admit, this is exciting for me. See, I was gonna be like you," Hammer says, "before everything went dark. Just pack all my shit up and head north, to Michigan, or whatever. Thought about it a lot."

Vitri conceals a sigh. "What's stopping you from going now?"

"You saw me piss myself," Hammer says. He shrugs. "I'm a pussy. I found that out real fast. You should've seen when everything went dark. Didn't leave the house. Sat in my room, wishing that, if this was it, if this was how the world was gonna end, that I'd somehow be the first to go, that somehow God would seek me out, and only me, and make it quick—"

"Mmhmm."

"—I even told myself that it was okay to leave Mom here to die. Said to myself that it was her time, that it'd been her time, all the bullshit we tell ourselves about death." Hammer glances at the rearview mirror, at its reflection of the woman in back. "But I didn't go anywhere. Stayed. Watched the vehicles zoom by. Watched the leaves fall. Watched all the crops shrivel up like a cold nutsack." Hammer sighs. "The day I heard the planes was, well, that was it. That was when I decided for good that I wasn't going anywhere."

Vitri leans forward. "Planes?" The last plane Vitri had seen was a commercial airliner, miles up, its exhaust cloud slashing across a clear sky. Days after the blackout.

"Yeah, planes."

"When? How long ago?"

"How long ago did I hear them?"

"Yeah."

"Couple weeks. Maybe three. You haven't heard 'em?" Hammer watches Vitri shake his head no. "Huh."

Silence.

"You really haven't heard them at all?"

"Who's flying them?"

"Fuck if I know," Hammer says.

"Military?"

"Maybe."

"Whose?"

"Ours, Argentina's, Kazakhstan's, does it matter?"

"Jets?"

"No, no," Hammer laughs. "Hell no. Old cargo planes. Cargo planes and crop dusters. Dusters have been dropping shit for months now. Pesticides, insecticides, rodenticides, all kinds of cides. You have to be able to smell it. No way you can't. Go on, roll down your window."

Vitri doesn't. He thinks of the fields he walked past yesterday, of the cattle, of walking to Florida drenched in chemicals, of coughing out organs. He thinks of flesh sliding from his skeleton.

"What about Florida?" Vitri asks. "Do you think they're dropping anything there?"

Hammer laughs. "Nothing else to kill here."

###

The Suburban rumbles east.

###

"I was what they'd call a good kid," Hammer says. "With all those promises my dipshit brother made, you wouldn't think it could be true, but I didn't even take my first sip of beer until I was twenty-three years old. Twenty-three!"

Vitri leans his head against the passenger window. Fields upon fields upon fields. The occasional giant tree dying. A paint-stripped home here and there, siding as grey as the sky, sedans and SUVs still in the driveway, some flipped, others on jacks, others not.

There are no planes, Vitri thinks.

"Mmhmm," Vitri says.

Not in Texas, not in Louisiana, not in Florida.

"That's no joke, either. And, just my luck, the whole world goes to shit by the time my palate declares that any sort of alcohol actually tastes good."

He opened a store when there are no customers. He pissed himself at the sight of you.

"I'd have to say that my favorite was this one that they call a hefeweizen. That wasn't the brand; it was the type of beer, you see. And they didn't sell it in bottles either, at least not this kind. You'd have to go to a bar, and I don't mean one of the grey-beard-regular bars, I mean an upscale place, a trimmed beard and eyeglasses type of place."

He gave you mayonnaise to stroke your dick with. He dolls up his dying mother.

"Were you a beer man, Freddie?"

Look at him.

"Freddie?"

"Whiskey." *What the fuck does he know?* "I liked whiskey."

Clouds overhead are lifting, yanked spaceward by an invisible puppeteer, remains rallying into thumbprints. To the north, however, it looks like rain. A mauve wave hovering over the distant treelines.

Vitri props his face with his elbow and hand.

"And then I had these two cousins, two cousins on her side," Hammer says. He points to his mother. "Melvin and Marvin—we called Melvin 'Haha,' and Marvin 'Giggles'—anyway, they were, as you can probably tell by their nicknames, of the prankster mold. Little hellions that couldn't tiptoe that line schools draw in the sand and label, 'suitable'. I mean, you probably know the type, being an officer of the law and all. I'm sure you ran into people like Haha and Giggles all the time."

There are no police officers. There are no courts. There are no jails.

"Well, one day, the two of them—they were inseparable, let me tell you—well, one day, they, without telling anyone, decided to drop out of high school. Just up and quit. Said fuck it all. Didn't go anymore." Hammer pauses, glances at Vitri. "You wanna know where they went? You wanna know what they were up to?"

There are no judges. There are no consequences.

"Huh? Do you?"

"Sure," Vitri says.

"Those dumb fuckers thought it was in their best interest to cook crystal meth. That's right, crystal meth. How fucked up is that?"

"Real fucked up."

I could elbow your jaw right now. I could press the barrel of my pistol to your temple.

"They never got caught or nothin' because the dumbshits couldn't even get the operation off of the ground. Something about not being able to perfect their recipe." Hammer licks his lips. "So, months down the line, they come to me—they came to me because they'd had my smoked meat before, and knew how skilled of a smoker I was—they come to me and they ask, 'Hey Hammer, how about you come work for us? We'll give you eight percent.'"

I could kill you right here. And no one would care.

"So I say to them, 'Hell no.'"

The Suburban comes to a screeching halt in the middle of the road, just before an overpass. Its brake lights shut off; its engine stays on. There are no screams. No sound at all until the driver's side door opens and onto the highway steps Hammer, arms raised. He stares through the open door. Says nothing.

"Get her the fuck out of here," Vitri says from within the Suburban.

Hammer listens. Hurries to the back door, opens it and lifts his mother out, pivoting his body so that her legs don't smack the vehicle.

The passenger door opens. Closes. Circling around the front of the Suburban is Vitri, scarf over his mouth, 9mm drawn and aimed at Hammer and his mother.

Still holding his mother, Hammer backs away.

Vitri shuts the back door and, without another word, climbs into the driver's seat. Shuts the door. Takes off.

###

East he goes, 9mm still in his lap, east, east, east.

East. That's all you need to think about.

He glances once more at the rearview mirror, at himself, at the twirling picture of Hammer's mother. He sets the 9mm on the passenger seat. Tugs the picture and its string off. Rolls down the driver's side window. Tosses it out. Leaves the window open, leaves the rearview at a severe angle. Finally smells the chemicals on the air.

Laid from treeline to treeline—across the highway—are tree trunks and telephone poles, stacked eight feet high, all of which have been paint-brushed vermilion.

The Suburban approaches. Stops. Vitri steps onto the highway. He walks north along the stack. He walks south and eventually comes back to the center once he sees there is no way he can maneuver the vehicle around or over. For a moment, Vitri puts his hands on the wood. Tries pushing the stack. He pushes, and pushes, and pushes, grunting as he does so, the pushes soon becoming punches, the grunting soon becoming screams. Once exhausted, he turns around. Looks west.

And then he walks back to the Suburban, to the passenger side. He pulls out his backpack and slings it over his shoulders as he walks around the stack, leaving Hammer's truck for the taking.

###

From the hill where Vitri stands, Shreveport is in view, mustard-colored land risen like dough around its outskirts, buildings appearing tall and robust from this distance. The air smells like sulfur. Potent. Seeping through the scarf, stinging Vitri's nostrils. With watery eyes he looks to the sky to see three sickly crows circling, obsidian feathers descending as they battle a swirling wind.

On the grass near a tree stump is the box of matches, the .22 pistol, the bar of soap. Vitri finds the can of soup he was looking for in the bottom of his backpack. He removes the lid he'd rubber-banded shut and, still standing, takes one brief, calculated sip. It tastes as advertised: like tomatoes. Expired tomatoes. His tastebuds don't fight it, though, nor does his stomach. All the sip seems to do is make Vitri hungrier. He finds himself craving a salad. Spinach leaves and halved olives, garlic-doused croutons and feta cheese, the tomatoes diced and smothered in the Greek dressing his wife fought to keep out of the house.

He takes another sip. Thinks of bacon, and melted sharp cheddar cheese, and wheat bread, a slice or two of tomato somewhere between. Then, pork altogether. And chicken. And beef. Meat he'd marinate overnight and flip on the grill the following afternoon. He takes another sip and misses the corn his wife would shuck and season, the green beans, the cauliflower and broccoli. He remembers cooking with her, the graceful routine they'd perform in the kitchen, pans in hand, swiveling around one another to open drawers and cupboard doors, lifting, dicing, mixing, shaking, exchanging smiles in one of the few moments between them that no words were needed to know what the other thought or desired.

He then thinks of noodles. Big noodles, fat noodles, wheat noodles, white noodles, noodles slathered in tomato sauce. *You will make it to Tallahassee, Florida.* Vitri stretches the rubber band from the lid to the bottom of the can, then places the can back into his backpack, forming a mound of support around it to prevent the tipping and spilling that surely would occur with his strides. *There's nowhere else.* He stands, places the remaining items into the backpack, zips it shut, then walks down the hill.

###

Vitri walks through Broadmoor Terrace, the 9mm in hand. Within the subdivision are abandoned but still-gaudy homes whose front lawns house sumacs and cedars barely toting their leaves and needles. Around the homes are shriveled yet still colorful beds of transplanted wildflowers, petals under consistent shade still pink and purple and white. *Homes of attorneys*, Vitri thinks, *officials, angel investors, physicians*. One—the same home with street-facing windows the height of hunting shacks—has three marble pillars extending from ground to roof. The next has a secluded walkway to a guesthouse larger than what the majority of Waco had called home. Two more down is a ransacked backyard greenhouse, its protective mesh torn, wilted stems drooped over clay pots. Oddly, almost as if homeowners were still lobbying for a local politician, draped over each garage door are red banners, twitching in the wind.

Entering what he may have once considered downtown, Vitri clings to the shadows. When he can't, he carefully moves at a quicker pace, something closer to a crouched jog than to a walk, using parked cars as cover. There's just too much to stand still for. Countless windows, countless buildings, countless doors, a plethora of streets. The city itself is decaying but, like Waco, it has not been thrashed. Brick buildings aren't charred, bulldozed to rubble, or left impaled by crane arms. Flagpoles are bare and bent but not down. Parking meters haven't been uprooted. Bicycle racks, though vacant, remain upright. First and second story office windows aren't blasted but are instead corner to corner with thin fractures, all glass higher intact and tinted.

Before and during the crossing of the intersection nearest the shopping district, Vitri performs a three-sixty turn, arms and eyes fixed, both hands on the 9mm. He passes shoe stores, he passes sports stores, lamp stores, thrift stores, bookstores, furniture stores, stores, stores, stores. He slows his pace when passing a clothing store—not because of the wadded jackets on the back counter, nor the navy blue briefcase leaned against the wall—for nothing but memories. He sees the empty hangers, the shelves on their sides, the vacant S hooks, the tipped racks, the stripped mannequins. He thinks of when he first took over his father's store, how the displays weren't optimized for the minimal foot traffic he was receiving. He thinks of how his wife and Carmen came in one day, before Carmen moved east. How his wife leaned on the counter and flirted with him, how Carmen, arms crossed, walked around the store alone, critical eyes behind gaudy sunglasses. He remembers how she approached the counter, interrupted, took off her those sunglasses, looked at him, and said, "You're in the wrong century here." He remembers her suggestions—the jackets up front to be nearer to the back, the fedora and bowler displays not only to be updated, but to be swapped, from one side of the store to the other. He remembers ignoring her at first. Remembers voicing to his wife afterward that Carmen didn't know shit. Remembers how over time it ate away at him, standing at that counter, imagining a new layout. Remembers how he walked around the counter, went outside, stood on the sidewalk, looked in through the glass, and thought: *Goddammit. She's right.*

Vitri examines the damage of the store before him now and cannot deny that more than an inkling of him wants to walk inside, wave some sort of wand, and take the first steps toward rehabilitation. The thought halts him, drops his arms, even, the prospect of erecting those shelves, of buffering the hardwood floors, of tagging armfuls of clothes and overloading each hook, bowing each rack.

But then there are sounds—distant sounds, southeast, but approaching. Clanks of metal. Metal on metal. Glass on metal. Thuds, pings, items shifting.

And footsteps.

Jolted from his trance, Vitri takes cover behind an aluminum garbage can still bungee-corded to a lamppost. He peeks over its rim, at the crosswalk.

Clank. Thud. Ping. Louder now. Nearer.

Vitri readies the 9mm to fire. Glances back over the garbage can. Holds.

Holds.

And holds, until one block from where he crouches, there is a girl. An unarmed girl no older than fifteen, in loose jeans and a purple sweatshirt, with dried blood across her face. In the middle of the road, walking north. Just walking, casually spinning to check her surroundings, wisps of light brown hair latching to the backpack she holds tight to her shoulders. She does not see him. She hardly even looks his direction. Nor does she seem to care at all just how loud she is, how insecure the items are within that backpack. Which should mean nothing to Vitri. Neither her bloody face nor her ignorance should concern him at all. He does not know her. She has not seen him. And those should be the only things that matter. *Walk on*, he should think. *Stay away from me. Go forth however you wish.*

Yet Vitri finds himself wanting to stand, to say something, to walk to her, grab her shoulder, turn her around, and say, "You're being too loud," or, "Stop," or, "Go home." But soon she is out of Vitri's sight, through the intersection, her noise trapped between northern buildings, faintly echoing.

Vitri rises from his crouch. His eyes stay east, until, in partial shadow, he sees a wooden door flung open. Out pour two red-masked men, facing west, facing him. Vitri crouches behind the garbage can once more.

"That way," one of the men says, his voice husky, muffled, notches above a whisper. And then there are only footsteps, ascending into a jarring series of sandal slaps on the pavement.

Vitri peers around the garbage can to see the lead man—the thinner of the two—turn north where the girl did. He is shirtless, toned, and with, from this distance, either scabs or tattoos that appear as if they are cradling his shoulder blades. In his right hand is a spiked club the length of Vitri's forearm. Limping behind is a bull of a man in a too-tight red t-shirt, gripping a rusted machete. Only when he turns north does Vitri stand, both hands on his pistol.

South, he thinks. *Go south. They are occupied. It is clear. Go south. You do not know this girl. You do not need to know this girl. You do not need to help this girl. Go south. It is clear. Go south.*

cH. **VIII**

Reyn's forehead skids across the pavement. Her left cheek, her shoulder. Within seconds, she is being flipped onto her back by a lean man in a red bandit mask, his mouth exposed. His bare torso houses scars of various sizes and length, some as wide as piano keys, others long and slim, from nipple to abdomen. He climbs atop her and cinches her torso with his knees. Tighter, tighter. Tighter.

Reyn fights it. Jerks, squirms. Blood darts down her cheek. As she tries to wriggle her hips free, the man raises his hand, that spiked club. He shouts. Reyn does her best to read his lips.

"Stop   you   cunt!"

Reyn looks to her right: a vehicle, loose papers, torn cardboard boxes, a gouged brick building, frozen in decay. To her left: a shorter man in a red welder's mask walks alongside her and stands. Grips a machete. Massages a cramp in his left leg with his free hand.

The man atop her shouts. She feels it first, his voice a series of vibrations transferred from his thighs to her ribs. Sharp. Shrill. He tightens his knees' grip even further, until Reyn's breathing becomes labored. Then he hunches over, brings his face close to Reyn's, grey neck and chin whiskers inches from her. Speaks slower.

" you don't shut up,   cut your tongue . understand me?" He turns to the shorter man. They speak. They exchange weapons.

Here, Reyn thinks. *Make sure they kill you here. Don't let them bind you. Don't let them drag you along this road. Don't let them torture you. Don't let them rape you. Don't let them convert you. No, make sure. Here. They kill you here.*

Reyn kicks her feet. Short kicks, furious kicks. She throws her fists at his arms, his shoulders and chest. She shakes her head; blood from her cheek lands on the man's bare chest. She tries to scream, to cry, but can't tell if the vibration she feels is from her or if it is from him—his open mouth, his taut neck says that he is shouting again. Quick commands, indecipherable commands, at her, at the short one. He punches Reyn's mouth with his left hand. She stops. Tongues a loose molar. Gathers. Then she's at it again, kicking, flailing, contorting her body, searching for any sort of gap to crawl through.

The shorter man drops the spiked club, limps over, and eases his way to the asphalt. Once down, he grip's Reyn's forearms and extends them over her head. Pries open each of her hands. Sets his left knee on her left palm. Right on right. Anchors her to the pavement.

Reyn continues to kick, to push, to pull. She tries to bite the man's stained hands as he grips her head, as he places his thumbs just above her upper lip and presses. Sharp pain shoots across Reyn's gums. Her efforts cease. She resumes her struggle, her outstretched shoulders feeling as if they will soon separate from her body.

The shirtless man grabs her chin. Redirects her eyes. "Open. Your. Mouth."

No.

Despite her outstretched shoulders feeling as if they will soon separate from her body, Reyn fights. Somehow frees her mouth from the heavier man's grip and snags a finger within her teeth. She clamps them tight and intends to keep them that way, no matter what.

Do it. Slit my throat. Kill me here.

She sees it coming, the shorter man's wound fist. And she can do nothing. He connects with her right cheek. Once, twice. And she is dazed, spinning, her pulse embedded in her temples. That same fist uncoils itself and reaches into Reyn's mouth, hooking its fingers to her lower lip. Left hand: upper lip. Together they pry open her mouth and, as the spinning slows, Reyn can see the man atop her move his hand to the back of the machete blade, near the tip. Even with so little room, he reaches into Reyn's mouth and grabs her tongue. He begins to cut. And it begins to gush. Bound to gravity, obeying its every rule, to the back of her throat the blood goes, more and more as he saws, and saws, and saws. There's too much; she can't swallow it all. But she tries, again and again, and can only cough. Her head jerks out of the man's hands. Blood spatters across her surgeon's face.

The surgeon backs away. Wipes his face. And she is being punched again. Two, three, four times, both sides of her head, both cheeks. Her vision begins to fade, to distort, to swirl. An oil painting over an open flame.

More blood pools in her throat. She can feel her bones resetting.

And then the shorter man's knees roll off of her palms. The surgeon goes limp, falls forward, his chest sliding onto and across her face, smearing blood into her eyes, into her hair. She cannot see, cannot breathe, cannot help but panic—flails, and tugs, and somehow worms out from beneath the surgeon's dead weight, only to emerge near the shorter man, curled on the road, hugging his stomach.

Reyn tries to stand, but falls, her brain unable to will her weak legs to do so. She tries again and falls. Once more. And then someone—some hand—grabs her. A large hand, a moist hand, a man's hand. In feeling those fingers, in assuming them to belong to yet another red mask, Reyn wriggles free, until that same hand grabs the back of her sweatshirt and lifts her to her feet. She's turned around. Though her eyes are addled, she, as the man lifts his hands to remove the scarf around his mouth, sees that he has a pistol in his hand.

Run, go, run, run.

Scarf down, he grabs her wrist. Holds her still. But she fights him. Chops at his forearm, strikes his elbow.

He steps closer. Holds her steady. "Can you walk?" she reads on his lips. When she does not respond, he wipes her face with the back of his free hand. "Can. You. Walk?"

Once more, Reyn fights. She chops. Yanks. Strikes his hands from her. Free, she steps and steps, traveling only five or six feet before wobbling left, then right. The man hurries to Reyn's side, places his arm around her shoulders and, together, they walk south, past the surgeon, who lies face down on the pavement. Feet away, the shorter man twists in pain. He points at the sky, at the buildings, at his stomach, at Reyn. Lifts his welding mask. One chalky eye, film over a blue iris, the other brown, and angry. Spit flies from his lips and tongue. Reyn feels her ears being covered by the man's hands and she blacks out—

—Reyn is on her knees, vomiting blood onto the sidewalk. No food to come up, just small pools of red under the sun. Though her hair is being pulled back she can see that the tips have become paintbrushes, dipped in red, and—

—They are in the shade, under a large green and white awning. The man has leaned her against a brick building and is now gently opening her mouth, his eyes squinted for examination—

—Reyn is flexed over the man's shoulder, head down, stomach spiraling as her eyes try to keep pace with his feet. She tries to lift her head, to see what he is walking them toward, but can only go so far until the throb takes over, relegating her instead to watching the mix of blood and saliva string from her mouth to his shoulders, to watching sweat run down his neck. There are strands of gray in the man's otherwise black beard. His nose is long and aquiline, cheekbones pronounced—

###

—Reyn is in an alley. Feet from her, the man kicks a door. He kicks again. And again. Then he stops. He looks at Reyn, backs away from the door to catch his breath. Then he is kicking again. Reyn reaches her arm toward him but cannot raise it past her ribcage. *Stop. They'll find us. Just stop.* She looks at her hands, then—

###

—Reyn is on a concrete floor. To her right is a tipped metal trashcan steadied by bricks stacked two-high on each side. There is a fire within the trashcan and, other than its immediate glow, the room is dark, nearer to purple than to black, quilts hung imprecisely over the windows and letting in slices of yellow-orange light. Loveseats are illuminated, recliners, dining tables that have been pressed against those quilts, against doors.

What the flame consumes, Reyn cannot tell, though near the trashcan is a pile of rotting wood, a pile of rug remnants, a pile of *TIME*. Atop is the bundle of syringes. Most of them have been damaged, guts exposed to air, hardened to the plastic. Reyn looks at the trashcan. Resting in the flame is a four-inch blade, its rubber handle as far away from the heat as possible. To her left is a mound of bloodstained Q-tips, an open bottle of water, an open bottle of rubbing alcohol. The man, however, is nowhere to be seen. He doesn't weave between the furniture. He doesn't tend the fire. *Gone*, Reyn thinks. *He's gone. It's time to stand. You're not hurt. Just stand up.*

Reyn tries. Tumbles. And, in doing so, knocks over the bottles, their contents converging on the concrete. When she turns herself over, there the man is, a silhouette in the nearest corner, a slim white box snug in his arm as he shuts a desk drawer and climbs over its surface. Outside of the fire's glow, his face looks so dark, his beard so full, his teeth so white. Her blood is all over his clothes, all over that scarf.

Reyn tries to stand once more. Tumbles into his arms. The man eases her back to the concrete. He watches her. Says something. Says it again. Leans in closer, says it once more, directly in front of her.

"You O.K.?"

She isn't. She knows she isn't. The throb is still there, on her tongue, in her cheekbones. Her skull feels like a compressed coil spring, fixed to burst through flesh at any second. She wants to go home. Crawl onto her bed, form the covers around her body. She wants to go to the Jeep. She wants to go to her mother.

"You O.K.?"

Reyn stares at him. Nods ever so slightly.

He nods. Says something, lips too quick for her to read. Grabs the topmost issue of *TIME*, rips its pages, tosses them into the flame. Another issue. More tearing. Another.

Reyn reaches for him. Blood spills over her bottom lip. *Stop*, she thinks. *Stop. Those are mine.*

He puts down her arm. *It's O.K.* And then he starts in on the syringes. One by one he chucks them into the trashcan. The flame intensifies, leaps sideways. Turns pink-then-red-then-purple-then-blue, contents digested in a matter of seconds. When the flame settles, the man reaches for the bottle of water and, on his knees, swivels toward Reyn. He motions for her to open her mouth. She does. He pours. Motions for her to spit. She does. He then exchanges the water for the rubbing alcohol. Repeat.

"You O.K.?"

She waits for the sting to pass. Allows the tears down her cheeks. Nods.

And, in one fluid motion, the man drops the plastic bottle and stretches to grab the knife from the trashcan. Without warning, he grabs Reyn's chin and, despite her struggle, brings her face close. He turns his left fist sideways and wedges it between her teeth.

Accepts the bite. He accepts it, grimaces, and eases the hot blade in. Presses it to the side of her wounded tongue.

cH. IX

Upon hearing the engine, Vitri halts. A small engine weaving through Shreveport for an hour now, high-pitched when throttled. The first time he'd heard it, Vitri hustled up the opposite staircase, to a window not yet boarded, and peered out into the night, locating the vehicle, a dirt bike of sorts, its lone beam of light wandering. Scouting.

The second time Vitri had heard the engine, the hustle had slowed to a jog. And now, chin to chest, he waits on the staircase. Annoyed at its persistence, he sighs as he, with the scarf over his right hand, re-grips the warm lip of the trashcan and moves it in a circular motion, stoking flakes of ash at its bottom. This is his last trip for the night and, when within seconds the engine wanes—proof that the scout has found something of interest elsewhere—he'll surmount this staircase and, anxious for fatigue to finally conquer him, enter into what he's certain was once a showroom on the second floor of this furniture store.

The showroom is small, twelve by twelve at best, with ten-foot ceilings. As Vitri enters he again looks at the torn maritime-themed wallpaper and wonders if it once represented a child's bedroom, the gold anchors and white sails something for a cribbed infant to stare at, to misunderstand and reach for. He pictures sea blue nightstands, and paintings of schooners, miniature yawls and sloops. He pictures cruise ship bunk beds pressed against the north wall, top bunk and its view of the city through three casement windows something to be bickered over by children forced along on a Sunday afternoon, children who moments prior worked as a team to spring themselves from their parents and the endless first-floor testing of office chairs and bedsprings. He pictures the room alive, warm with foot traffic, not cold and gutted, as it is now, save for end tables whose legs Vitri has snapped and piled.

Save for one bloodied girl asleep at its center, neck propped by her backpack.

Vitri sets the trashcan in the doorway, fearing that the dusty quilts he'd found and rigged over the windows with wire won't entirely conceal their presence. He quietly feeds two more table legs to the dying flame, then wads of *TIME* he'd found in the girl's backpack. He watches the varnish sizzle off; listens to the wood pop; runs his index finger over the candle wax that has solidified on the hardwood floor; runs the same finger through the lone candle's flame. Walks to the girl. Stares.

Her right cheek looks like a halved blood orange, outer ring thin and bright, interior dark and risen. Right eye swollen, brow and lash crusted red. The last time he checked her tongue was over an hour ago, after he'd lifted, carried, and placed her here. As for how it will heal, if he'd truly sealed the wound, or if it'll reopen hours from now when she tries to speak, Vitri hasn't a clue. He's never cauterized anything before. He'd spent nearly the entire trek here contemplating it and when he looks at her he kicks himself for waiting as long as he did. He thinks back to the beating she took, how it trumped the violence he's witnessed throughout his life, the four bar fights, the parking lot brawls after everything went black, watching water jugs and soap flats and generators tugged to pieces from vehicles across the lot.

He worries that what he's done won't be enough. She'll live, he thinks, but maybe not well. Maybe not like he assumes she once had.

The girl rolls onto her back, her blood-crusted left hand finding and settling upon Vitri's boot. Vitri crouches. Feels the notebook shift in his waistband. Unwraps the scarf he'd wrapped around his hand so that he can grab hers. Rolls her back to her side, in case the seal won't even last past sleep.

"Get some rest," he whispers into her ear.

Vitri walks to the right side of the casement windows and inches his face between the chilled glass and draped quilt. The sun is rising, hues of orange and pink evolving, from thin rays to slices. He used to love seeing cities in shadow, how the darkness of night could level playing fields, if only temporarily. A skyscraper no longer some symbol to be pointed out on an architecture tour, reduced instead to the rectangle it actually was, those who built it, or operated it, not hoisted to some pedestal, but asleep just like anyone else. For a long time, nighttime had brought Vitri peace. And sunrises had always delivered him strain.

Shadows below house the sound of that engine. Vitri can hear it, the scout again on the move. But not for long. Distant now, idling somewhere in the blue-grey. Vitri walks left, along the window. Stares north until, four blocks out, he spots one brake light, one headlight aimed at a white brick building. While from this distance, from this height, the bike's operator is featureless, he or she dismounts without panic and proceeds to kill the engine. Gone are the lights. Gone is the rider.

Vitri stays at the window. Thirty seconds. One minute, two minutes. He remains long enough for the sun to reject his assumption: the bike is yellow.

###

CAREFUL WITH YOUR TONGUE. WHEN YOUR BRAIN
SLOWS DOWN, JUST READ. IF YOU CAN, WRITE. THAT
CUT IS DEEP. COULD TEAR AND GUSH AGAIN. DON'T
SWALLOW ANY MORE BLOOD, THOUGH. NONE. WHEN
YOU'RE ABLE, SWISH SOME MORE ALCOHOL AROUND
YOUR MOUTH. CAN'T HAVE IT GETTING INFECTED.
BAD NEWS THERE.

WE'RE ON THE SECOND FLOOR. NEEDED HIGHER
GROUND. FOURTH WAS TOO HIGH TO CARRY
EVERYTHING. QUIET OUT THERE FOR NOW.

I HAVE SOUP FOR YOU WHEN YOU'RE READY.

- VITRI

REYN
I LIKE THAT
I LIKE VITRI
HOW'S THE SOUP?
GOOD. DOES YOUR HAND HURT?
YEAH

I'M SORRY

DON'T BE

I AM

\#

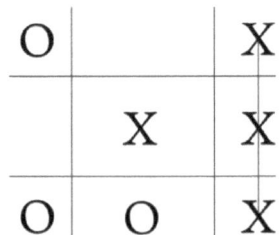

\#

YOU HEAR THAT?

I DO

WHERE YOU HEADED?

I DON'T KNOW

NOT A CLUE?

IDAHO

FAMILY?

FATHER

ALIVE?

MAYBE

MOTHER?

DEAD

I'M SORRY

WHERE YOU HEADED?

TALLAHASSEE

WHAT'S THERE?

COUSIN

ONLY FAMILY?

HAS A BOAT HE'S SAILING TO SAN JUAN

NEVER BEEN

ME EITHER

JUST YOUR COUSIN?

DON'T KNOW

WHEN?

LEAVING FOR GOOD IN A FEW DAYS

NEVER COME BACK?

NEVER

HOW MANY PEOPLE?

DON'T KNOW

ROOM FOR ME?

MAYBE

I CAN'T STAY HERE

NO, YOU CAN'T

CAN I GO WITH YOU?

WE'LL NEED MORE SUPPLIES

I CAN HELP

YOU REST. IT WON'T TAKE LONG

OK

DON'T LET THE FIRE DIE OUT

OK

There is something beyond the concealment of Vitri's lips that makes Reyn uneasy about that scarf, how its placement renders him featureless—gone is his gently aging beard, hidden are his cheekbones, high and weathered and, now that the blood no longer inhibits her vision, handsome; circled by fatigue, transformed are his eyes, the burgundy fabric of his shirt somehow extracting shades of deep brown from the center, layered instead in bright paranoia.

Even his posture changes with the scarf on. Shoulders back, spine straight, weight shifted from his heels to the balls of his feet. Ready to pounce, Reyn tells herself, ready to sprint from her and back into the world. Why wouldn't he? Why not run? Because of her he has been stuck here, in this building, not making his way to Tallahassee. Because of her, he is readying himself to stalk streets for supplies her presence deems necessary, streets he one day ago left two men to die on.

So she waits for it, the walk off, the jog, the sprint, whatever speed he adjusts his escape to. Because Vitri, she knows, owes her nothing else.

Vitri walks to her and crouches. In one hand is a pistol, this one slightly smaller than the one he has in his waistband, and narrower, the same matte black, the grip just as ridged.

He doesn't know she's deaf. She assumed he'd known when she woke to a note, assumed he'd figured it out at some point, in the night or on their way here. But it's clear to Reyn now that he doesn't even suspect it—his mouth moves beneath the scarf as he points at, presses and pulls mechanisms on the pistol. Sights to safety to trigger.

When he hands the pistol over to her, his eyes shift to the window, then to the floor. He loops his hand as if he is signaling some kind of scheme that Reyn, though she is not following, is to play a critical role in. And then, as Reyn thinks about raising her hand and writing out her deafness, without so much as a nod or wave Vitri stands, pulls his backpack over his shoulders, and walks out of the room.

Maybe this is goodbye, Reyn thinks. Maybe everything he'd written was bullshit and the pistol is a parting gift. A, "Good luck, kid."

She hopes not. She really hopes not.

Petrified of its weight, Reyn sets the pistol on the floor. She tries to stand but dizzies herself doing so. Her tongue throbs. Her cheek throbs. Her entire head throbs. She thinks of the skinned knees she never really had, the scraped elbows, the fat lips, thinks of the classmates she'd watch once she turned seven, the odd-shaped balls they'd toss with their friends, the discs, how they'd fall, and fight, and cry, and bleed. She thinks of their pain and cannot shake the exaggerated image of their collective rising, of their collective limp back home. *Home. Home*—where wounds turn to scars.

ALL WE CAN DO IS GROW WITH THEM

Reyn tries to remember the day her father wrote that. A Saturday or Sunday. She was five, maybe six. He had a moustache then, and shoulder-length hair he'd, per the restaurant's requirements, bundle beneath a hairnet, which lent to the nickname of Honeycomb, as coined by one of his prep cooks. Reyn remembers he'd just woken and was tying around his waist the grease-splattered apron he hadn't washed for weeks. And it was there, on that couch she'd so often watch those children from, he'd sat next to her and lit a cigarette. She remembers not being able to take her eyes off of his fingers, filthy as they were, scarred as they were, nicked by various knives over the years. She remembers asking about his scars that day, to which he smiled, and wrote what he wrote.

But then he pointed to his left forearm, to a curved pink line from thumb to elbow that looked to Reyn like two strands of yarn braided together and stretched taut. She remembers asking him how it happened.

MOM SLEPT WITH ZEKE REY. DAD PUNCHED A WINDOW. SO LATER, WHEN MY GIRLFRIEND CHEATED ON ME, I PUNCHED A WINDOW.

After that, he'd lit another cigarette and, instead of waiting around to answer the questions he'd prompted from Reyn, he'd kissed her head and left for work, returning home later with new nicks on his right thumb and forefinger.

Inches from the window now, quilt cocooning her shoulders, Reyn opens her mouth as wide as she can. What the window faintly reflects back at her is an engorged tongue with black swirls on the top, side and bottom. Burnt organ still warm to the touch but ribbed like tree bark.

Reyn takes her fingers out of her mouth and crumbles the specks of black grit that have clung to her fingertips. She closes her mouth, twists her neck, inspects her left cheek in the window, then her right.

How swollen, how engulfed they are in bright purples and bright yellows. The panic she works to hush doesn't allow her to understand it now, but the bruises will get worse before they get better—the swelling will decrease, and her eyes will once again approach normality; those bright purples and yellows will exhale to violet, will stretch and deepen.

Just then, through the window she sees Vitri appear, one block to the west. Out of the early morning shadows and into the sunlit street, eyes monitoring east, then west as he walks north, two hands on his pistol, avoiding piles of chipped marble, sidestepping stray shards of glass, breeze swirling debris around his calves. Once he crosses the street, he steps into an alley, out of Reyn's sight.

As she backs away from the window, part of the quilt Vitri had wired catches the center windowsill, leaving a gap through which sunlight spills onto the floor. Reyn grabs three severed table legs from the pile Vitri has made and, despite it already being hot in the room, and smoky, Reyn places them in the fire as Vitri had written for her to do. She watches the new smoke ascend to the ceiling, faint puffs that evolve into elaborate coils.

Reyn then turns her attention to what Vitri had removed from his backpack and set on the floor: four aluminum cans, three bottles of water, one pair of socks, almond-scented candles. There is a thin magazine, too, doormatting the water bottles, its front cover face down.

DEEP THROAT

She has seen that phrase before, on gas station magazine stands, and on auto-filling search engine bars. It does strike her as odd, however, that it is in Vitri's possession, that it is something he carries so close when he carries so little otherwise. Odd, but not uncommon, that he has deemed the brunette beneath the lime green letters beautiful. She sits on a piano bench, her hands masking her large breasts. Her eyes are shut. Red lips parted. Hair and torso damp. Reyn thinks that the woman cannot be older than twenty, then wonders if her mother had looked like that once, legs thick, free of surface vein, tan and smooth, if, before Reyn ruined her, she'd had a stomach just as flat as hers, breasts just as round.

Flipping past advertisements for cannabis and vodka, and several more for cologne and phone hotlines, Reyn finds more photographs of the cover woman, the first being a severe close-up of her breasts, merlot fingernails over her large, puffy nipples. Its caption: PAINTER WHITE PLAYS WITH HER TITS. The next is of Painter's groin, pink razor in hand, pubic hair no wider than an eyebrow: PAINTER WHITE SHAVES HER PUSSY. Reyn flips the page: Painter White is on her back. Reyn flips: Painter White is upright, staring off camera. Advertisement, advertisement, advertisement. Painter White's arm is reaching for the erect penis that has entered the frame. Reyn flips: Painter White's mouth is open, eyes squinted, gunk stringing across her nose and lashes, off of her chin. PAINTER WHITE GETS PAINTED WHITE.

Reyn flips back to PAINTER WHITE PLAYS WITH HER TITS. She sets the open magazine on the floor, then stands. Careful not to bump her cheek or mouth, Reyn removes her sweatshirt and tosses it aside. She has lost so much weight that the white t-shirt she has worn underneath for months has stretched so loose that if wind were to pass through the room it would flap behind her like a cape. She eases that off, too, and looks down at her breasts, squeezed by the too-small beige training bra her mother had found for her once she'd outgrown the others. She looks down. She looks at the magazine. Compares. Covers her breasts.

Reyn flips to the front cover, then swiftly kicks off her shoes and unbuttons her jeans. Gravity does the rest. She looks at Painter. She looks at herself. At Painter, at herself.

Painter, herself.

Painter.

Clumps of hair do not dwell under Painter's arms, or beneath her waistband. Painter's face is not busted. Stubble does not shade Painter's legs. Painter is not pale and narrow but tan and sculpted, a work of art created for and captured by the men who desire her. Even men like Vitri. Kind men. Rescuers, caretakers.

Inferior. That's what this exercise has confirmed. Reyn is inferior. Subjacent. Baggage left behind instead of something to be sought, if only for moments. The acceptance of this—the way it continues to burrow its way through her sore gums—eclipses her desire to be Painter White. It inflames her. She wants to rid the world of this woman. Rip her from those pages. Ball her like mountain snow, and set her into the trashcan to be slowly, and painfully, melted. Yet, without an inkling as to why, all Reyn does is gawk, and flip, gawk, and flip. Until the anger is no longer external, until she has embodied it, until she has twisted her way into becoming its incognizant carrier.

Reyn tosses Painter White back to the floor and, as quickly as they'd slipped off, she pulls her jeans to her waist and buttons them. She stomps into her shoes. With little consideration of the pain in her face, she jostles her head through the collar of her white t-shirt. She does the same with her sweatshirt. Untangles her hair. She then walks to her backpack against the wall, crouches, unzips the largest pocket, and plunges her hand in, fingers searching for *TIME.*

She wants to change the conversation she's having with herself. Wants to search the magazines for more information on San Juan, on what is to become her new home, if Vitri tells the truth, more than what the tourism ads she remembers could provide: the blue-green waves, coastal castles, and designer bottles of rum. She wants an article. A profile. Something. She wants to know so that, should he return, she can converse with Vitri about it, so she can appear intelligent about at least one thing. So she can pull her weight with at least one thing. But her hands find nothing but food cans. Plastic bottles she nudges aside. The cold metal of a small, adjustable wrench at the bottom.

Confused, Reyn extracts her hand. She looks around the room as if somewhere in its emptiness the magazines have been tucked. She turns toward the quilt-covered windows. Through the gap she'd unintentionally left, the sky is graying by the second, scurrying to black, dimming the room. The quilt quivers. She can feel in her feet a dull vibration transmitting through the hardwood floor. Tremors that tell her to stand.

And that's all she does. She does not back away. She does not walk to that window.

She stands, and she thinks: *We've been tracked.* She pictures a cluster of masked men and women—red, yellow, both—standing on the street, weapons ready, the darkness an illusion, a diversion for the rabid few sprinting the staircase, to her, to her mouth, to her groin, to her tongue. It's a thought that motivates her to sprint across the room and shut the door. She searches for a lock—finds none.

She grabs the trashcan with the intention of swiveling it in front of the door—it's too hot for her hands. So Reyn grabs the pistol. She backs away while her hands find its grip, and once ready, she stops. Takes aim at the door.

Ten seconds pass. Her outstretched arm trembles.

Thirty. *You can do this*, she thinks. *You are capable.*

Another ten seconds, another thirty. Nothing. The door handle hasn't been turned. She crouches and places her free hand on the floor, feeling for sprints, for stomps, though little can be distinguished over the tremors. Either nothing is beneath her, or everything, more of the masked than she'd initially assumed, more than just a cluster.

Eight of them, she imagines, ten of them, twelve, all for her, picturing each of the masked carrying a body part of hers down the stairs—a leg slung over a shoulder; hands cradled to someone's sternum.

Reyn waits another thirty seconds. Nothing. The tremors lessen, but only slightly. She stands. Lets her outstretched arm ease to her side. She turns to the window. It's lighter outside. Lighter, and lighter yet, darkness from before peeled back like a scab. She slithers between the quilt and the windows. A fist-sized crack is in the upper right corner, its thin veins stretching toward the sill. The grey cloud before the building shrinks, from fifteen-feet wide to twelve, to ten, narrowing itself back into what she sees now is a manhole on the street below, fifty yards or so from where Vitri had crossed. Bits of brick and marble fall to the street. Thumb-sized shreds of wood. Paper floats about.

Miles north, another grey cloud takes shape. Up it rises, up-up-up like stairs, higher than the tallest building, then higher yet, and wider, as if there are arms within to be spread, a black hug to offer the sky. Then, another rises, miles east. Another, west.

Reyn looks back to the manhole on the street below, half-expecting to see Vitri emerge. She wonders if he is the orchestrator of this. Wonders if her panic was pointless, is pointless. Wonders if this is what he spoke of from behind that scarf: "If we want to get out of the city, we have to create a distraction."

But, with the nearest cloud completely retracted, it becomes clear that there's no movement to the west, Vitri or otherwise.

Two hundred yards north, however, a dirt bike skids from an alley, across the street, and into a lamppost. At the sight, Reyn crouches beneath the windowsill. Seconds later she raises her curious eyes to see the motorcycle's yellow-masked driver stumbling in the street, dazed, searching for his balance. He falls. He pushes himself back to his feet. Falls down again. He keeps looking behind him and, after he falls once more, Reyn understands why: sprinting from the same alley are two red-masked men.

cH. X

Navy blue briefcase in hand, Vitri sprints across the street, away from the crash, and down the alley leading to the furniture store. He'd seen it unravel from streets over, through an abandoned art gallery's fogged windows: the motorcycle, the crash, the stumble. He'd glimpsed the masked. And he'd hurried, all the while wondering what for, questioning why he wouldn't flee now, why he hadn't earlier.

South. East. Out of Shreveport. Away from Reyn. To Tallahassee, alone, like he'd intended, leaving her with the means to survive: food, fire, a loaded pistol, and the false hope that he'd come back for her—the façade that, yes, there may still be wanderers capable of humanity, to go out of their way to save, out of their way to heal.

And so he'd jogged south, one balled raincoat in his left hand, 9mm in his right.

What turned him around—what spurred him back to that clothing store, to that second raincoat, to that navy blue briefcase, and now back here, to feeding briefcase and backpack through the alley window he'd broken yesterday and scraped clean with this very pistol barrel—was the fact that Reyn had watched him sign his birth name to a lie.

He pictured her tucking those words into a pocket, studying the exchange for days, too young and naïve to know how the world works, too optimistic to burn the pages, to set the damn notebook down and leave, just leave, emerging from the furniture store only in search of him.

And so his feet had slowed as the thought came full circle; it dawned on him that he hadn't at all given her the means to survive, but that he'd effectively given her the ammunition it'd take to die.

After Vitri vaults himself over the windowsill, he hurries over the floor's boot-shaped bloodstains, to the wooden staircase. He wishes it weren't guilt propelling him up the stairs, up-up-up. He opens the door into the hallway and slows his pace so as not to spook Reyn. There is a slight haze of wood smoke swirling into the hall from beneath the closed door. Vitri approaches, presses his ear to the door. No footsteps. The popping of plastic by flame.

"Reyn, it's me," Vitri says from behind the scarf, now blotted grey by the soot that had descended outside. "Reyn?"

Vitri opens the door slowly. Feet from the door is the trashcan and, beyond that, at the window and staring north, somewhere between crouching and standing, is Reyn, torso half-wrapped in the quilt he'd hung over the window. Without shutting the door, Vitri steps around the trashcan and into the room.

"Hey," he says. "Don't watch that."

Reyn shifts her weight but, still, she doesn't respond. She doesn't turn around.

Vitri steps closer. "It's okay, Reyn." He tosses the briefcase on the floor.

A gunshot rings out.

Vitri covers his throbbing ears.

Reyn turns around, pistol in hand.

"Are you fucking deaf?" Vitri yells. He watches Reyn step out of the quilt, toward him, revealing a single bullet hole in the window. Vitri's stomach tilts. His ears are still adjusting. "Fuck, fuck, fuck," he says, striding to the window.

Three-hundred yards out, one red-masked man forces the yellow-masked rider's small intestine over a parking meter, a struggle halted only when he is waved forward by his counterpart, who on his own has advanced toward the furniture store.

Vitri turns, grabs Reyn by the shoulders, and says, "We need to get out of here." Tears are in her eyes. The .22 pistol is no longer in her hand. "We need to get out of here," Vitri repeats. He crouches, picks up the pistol. Places it in his waistband. "Did you hear me?"

Reyn doesn't move. Can barely look at him. Stares at the window instead. Wipes her eyes. She, Vitri understands now, can't hear him. She hasn't heard him, not now, not last night. She hasn't heard a single word that he's said.

Still crouched, Vitri reaches for the pen they'd left on the hardwood floor and, after standing, shoves it in his front pocket. He then nudges Reyn forward, around the trashcan, to the hallway and toward the staircase. He makes her walk in front and up they go, toward the third floor, the sound of their creaking steps yawning along the walls, overpowered only by the sound of red-masked shoulders ramming the ground level door.

"Go, go, go," Vitri says to Reyn. They pass the door to the third floor's hallway.

A loud thud from below. A desk or dresser toppling over. The legs of other furniture skidding across the concrete.

"Fucking go," Vitri says. As if she were a horse, he swats at Reyn's right hip with an open hand. Again and again, and off she goes, up the staircase, to the fourth floor, until more than a few feet are between she and Vitri. Halfway up the staircase, due either to worn treads or an uneven equilibrium, or both, Reyn slips, falls, her left knee crashing into one particular step with enough force for the wood to bow beneath her weight. Within seconds, she is back on her feet and continuing up the staircase.

Another thud. Another skid. Distant now.

Vitri leaps over the bowed step and reaches the top. This door, as he'd discovered the night before, doesn't open to a hallway, but to a large, carpeted room with fifteen-foot ceilings. An old break room for store employees. Two windows on the west wall and the hatched skylight above let in blocks of overcast sky. Blotches of muted pink paint linger on the walls. There is a nook at the south end of the room housing two vending machines, each with gaping holes crowbarred above their deposit doors, coils of stripped wire spilling out like guts. And there are three tipped café tables—two in the center of the room and one tucked near that nook, in the southeast corner.

After easing the door shut, Vitri grabs Reyn's arm and leads her to one of the café tables in the center of the room. He points at the carpet behind the table—GET DOWN, he hopes it'll be interpreted as. Reyn, without hesitation, drops to her knees and inches toward the table's metal legs, body partially hidden by the tipped surface of the table. Once she settles, Vitri widens his palm—STAY. Reyn nods. Vitri pulls the pen from his pocket and crouches. Rolls up her sweatshirt sleeve and writes on her left forearm.

1 LET THEM WALK IN
2 THEY'LL WALK TO YOU
3 DON'T LOOK AT ME
4 I'LL SHOOT
5 IF I CAN'T, YOU SHOOT

As Reyn reads, Vitri pulls the .22 pistol from his waistband. He isn't going to hand it over until she nods, until she acknowledges that here, in the center of this room, she is to be bait. After she does nod, Vitri hands the pistol over, then quietly flips the café table nearest the door upside-down, onto its surface, and slides it across the carpet to the northeast corner of the room. He kneels behind the table, pistol barrel steadied on the narrow bar fusing leg to leg.

Over his breath he can hear them—somewhere below, he can hear the red-masked men. Second floor, third floor, something is rolling across the hardwood. Slowly, achingly so. Then, a door handle. A door latching. Vitri looks at Reyn, whose exhalations are seesawing his, and holds his index finger to his scarved lips. Presses his ear to the north wall.

Creak—

—creeeeeaaaaak-creak-creak-creeeeeaaaaak—

—creaks from one pair of feet, then two—

—creak-creeeaaak-creak-creeeaaak—

—the sound slows, then trails, as if they, convinced that their ears and eyes had played tricks on them, had turned around on the staircase, had given up and were ready to return to the rider they'd mutilated. And soon there is no sound. Nothing at all. Vitri looks to Reyn. Other than gingerly wiping sweat from her bruised cheek, she is still. She is calm. Eyes on the door, braced for whatever may barge through—

—SNAP—

—*Her knee*, Vitri thinks, the step she bowed, now split in two—

—creak-creak-creak-creak, the steps fast now, closer, creak-creak-creak-creak—

Vitri waves his left hand until Reyn looks his way. When he has Reyn's attention he points to his scarf as if it were a mask, then to the door. She nods. Looks briefly at her inked arm before returning her eyes to the door. Vitri grips the 9mm. Tighter now. Tighter.

The doorknob turns.

Vitri glances at Reyn. IF I MISS, he wishes he'd written, knowing what'll happen to her upon his failure. Yanked by the hair. Dragged. Raped. KILL YOURSELF.

The door opens.

The tip of the point man's Bowie knife is the first thing that Vitri sees. It creeps, it lurks, it hovers, it grows as the point man slowly moves through the doorway. And then Reyn is spotted. Vitri can see it in her eyes. Strained, scared, wanting to flee but consciously denying the desire.

Don't look at me, Vitri thinks. *Just don't look at me.*

The door opens further.

A faded brown boot comes into view. A shin, a thigh, a waist, a bicep.

"Look at her," the second red-masked man says. His voice is deep and crackly. "She's perfect, isn't she?"

The Bowie knife is twirled. Shoulders bob forward as if sea. Neck, head. One step, two steps, three steps, four—

Vitri fires.

To the floor drops the point man, to the air once more goes Vitri's hearing, to the vending machine crawls Reyn, and through the doorway hurries the second masked man, turning, turning, stomping directly toward Vitri, a sickle secure in his right hand.

Vitri fires.

The masked man drops the sickle and clutches his gushing throat. Yet he continues toward Vitri, stomping until the stomps slow to toe drags. Eight feet and closing, stomping, staggering, stomping, dragging, bleeding all over himself.

Vitri stands. He waits for the masked man to come closer. Just a bit closer. Five feet, three feet. Aims. Fires. Down goes the man's hands, buckled are his knees.

Vitri looks to the point man, who, though injured, continues to dig his fingernails into the carpet and slither himself after Reyn. Reyn, pistol still in hand, has nearly backed up to the nook now. Vitri steps over his tipped café table and hustles to the point man. He steps on the man's back. Can feel the man's groan vibrate through his toes. Presses the barrel of the 9mm to the back of his head. Pulls the trigger. Strips of mask leather adhere to the carpet.

The man goes limp.

Vitri looks at Reyn, who, backed all the way to the nook now, won't take her eyes from the body. She is crying.

"Why are you crying?" Vitri says. He can barely hear his own words. "Huh? Why the fuck are you crying?" He walks toward her now, scarf shifting with his lips, feet gaining momentum as she cowers. "Do you feel bad that these men are dead? Huh? Do you? His hearing is coming back. "That's four people I've killed because of you. Four fucking people." Vitri snatches the pistol from Reyn's hand and, in one quick motion, chucks it at the back of the point man's head.

###

Vitri stands to the side of the second-floor window, peeking beneath the quilt. A dark green plane circles overhead. Straightens its path; descends slightly. Out of its cargo bay falls a black rectangle, small when compared to the tan parachute that unfolds seconds after to slow the plummet. Vitri watches the wind take the rectangle north. Watches three red-masked men emerge from the manhole below and chase after it on foot, around vehicles, through alleys.

The plane flies east, toward a distant grey cloud falling back to the earth. It circles, straightens, descends, unloads another rectangle. It isn't until moments later, after the three red-masked men have returned and are shoving an oversized black duffel bag down the manhole, that Vitri turns around and writes to Reyn that they'll leave in the middle of night.

BORN DEAF?
BORN DEAF
CAN'T HEAR A THING?
NOT A THING
SPEAK?
WOULDN'T KNOW
SIGN LANGUAGE?

SOME. I READ. I WRITE

YOU'RE GOOD AT IT

CAN WE TALK ABOUT SOMETHING ELSE?

SURE

WHERE ARE MY MAGAZINES?

FIRE

SYRINGES?

FIRE

WHY?

NEEDED FIRE. WHY'D YOU HAVE THOSE?

MOTHER'S.

DRUG?

THEY MAKE IT

WHO DOES?

EAST. MONROE. MASKS. YELLOW

YELLOW FROM MONROE?

LOTS OF THEM

SHOULDN'T GO EAST?

NO

WHAT'S SOUTH?

I DON'T KNOW

WE'LL GO SOUTH THEN

OK

WE'LL FOLLOW THE COAST

OK

SOMETHING WRONG?

WHAT'S IN THE BRIEFCASE?

RAINCOATS

HASN'T RAINED IN A WHILE

PROTECT FROM CHEMICALS

GOT IT

WHY DO YOU KEEP LOOKING AT THE CEILING?

UP THERE, WHAT DID YOU SAY?

I WAS ANGRY

I KNOW

NOTHING TRUE

THE TWO MEN?

WHAT ABOUT THEM?

NOTHING

WHAT ABOUT THEM?

I WANT TO SEE THEIR FACES

###

Reyn and Vitri roll the trailer over first. Scars coat his shaved head, some the length of a fingernail, others as long as a soda can, the majority, however, seemingly a work of something greater—above the neck and along the crown are multiple crescents, arranged in various patterns. Off-ruby stones on fishhooks droop from each earlobe. His neck has been stained so heavily that an entry wound cannot be located. Where there aren't bloodstains, it appears as if his skin hadn't only been shielded from the sun for stretches at a time, but that for months it had been scrubbed with some bleaching agent. Veiny, bloated. Since his death, his red vest has compressed to his chest, tight enough that the center button's stitching has begun to unwind. Beneath, on his gut, Reyn sees a tattooed red hand, jagged along the fingernails, made illegible by the soaked and matted chest hair. The entire room smells of excrement, that which had been in each of these bodies still finding ways to surface.

Vitri tosses the sickle toward the door, then waves for Reyn to hover the candle over the man's face. Leaning in, Reyn sees that there is a small hole in the man's leather mask, above an eyebrow. Below are eye fissures, tear-shaped holes for nostrils, a mouth-hole wide enough to feed a small spoon through. Along the jaw and hairline, the mask is sewn to the trailer's face, stitches an inch apart at most but, as if they'd run out of thread, from right ear to chin the mask is anchored to flesh by thick staples. Vitri places his scarf on the carpet and looks at Reyn. She shrugs her shoulders. He grabs the notebook, writes.

STILL WANT TO?

Reyn nods. She wants to. She needs to. Needs to see who these people are. Believes that by doing so, some form of clarity can be had. History. Purpose. Theirs. Hers. Why they are here, dead. Why she and Vitri are alive, why she's still in Louisiana, why she has yet to put on a mask, things she's never hoped to discover by staring at a stranger's face. She expects Vitri to feel the same way, but all he does is stare at her, then at the man, his eyes sadly alert, his bottom lip between his teeth. "We shouldn't do this," the stare says. Reyn sets the candle down and asks for the notebook.

I'LL DO IT

Vitri shakes his head. He pulls his knife from a pants pocket. Points at the candle and, once Reyn again brings the flame over the man's face. He starts in on the staples, digging the point of the blade into the man's flesh, then prying, lifting from the staple's center. At first, the trailer's skin resists: it lifts with the knife; shivers with the knife; descends with the knife. Won't let go. Vitri twists the blade, lays it flat, applies his weight to the handle for seconds. Then, pluck, out it comes, bloodless and still bent around the loose bit of leather. Reyn, despite her curiosity, can only focus on Vitri's right hand, on the wounds she'd given him the night before, when he'd pressed the hot blade to her tongue. Teethmarks from knuckle to knuckle, dried blood black in the dim light. I DON'T WANT THIS TO HURT YOU, Reyn considers writing, I'M SORRY.

Having established an effective method—dig, twist, pluck—Vitri quickly makes his way through the staples. Reyn takes it upon herself to lift what of the mask Vitri has freed. She peeks beneath; glimpses long, tangled hairs. Grey roots, black centers, red tips. And then Vitri grabs her hand. Removes it from the mask, redirects his light over the man's forehead, and dives back in, slicing through four of the stitches. He cuts through more—two, three—then slides his hand beneath the loose half of the mask. Grips tight. And rips. Three more stitches out. Angrily resets the trailer's tilting head, and rips. Two more. Reset, rip, until the mask is off.

There is bruising around the entry wound. Swelling, too, as far down as the trailer's eye, reducing the oval to a slit. The other eye is open, wide open, whites strained red, the center a light purple. It is all Vitri needs to see. Knife in hand, he stands and walks to the point man. But Reyn stays. Examines the man further. A once-hooked nose whose angle has been intensified by the mask. Parched lips at a diagonal. Faint crow's feet looping each eye. He is no younger than forty-five, and reminds her of no one.

Which makes it difficult for Reyn to decipher the feeling she has when looking at the dead man. It isn't pity. It isn't sorrow. And it isn't satisfaction. She studies him for as long as she can, before it dawns on her that she must follow Vitri with the light. But it isn't enough time for her speculation to mesh itself into anything cohesive, anything detailed. She pictures a faceless woman. A fast car, something he'd tinker with. Pictures a mangy dog by his side. No, a cat. He looks more like a cat person. *Ralph*, she thinks. She's never known a Ralph. Has no basis for this. *You look like a Ralph.* And it is only in this way that Reyn feels closer to him, understanding of him, his life, the motives she thinks may have led him toward his time beneath a mask. *Ralph just wanted to feel loved*, she thinks.

Before she crosses the room, Reyn drapes Vitri's scarf over her arm and grabs the notebook with her free hand. She turns and, if he weren't leaned against the bit of wall directly beneath the window, moonlight on his hair, Reyn wouldn't be able to see Vitri. Puzzled, she walks to the point man, candlelight flickering with each step—he lies on his back, face up, Vitri's knife across his neck. His nose has been flattened. His lips are parched. He has the same earrings as Ralph, the same tattoo. There is matted facial hair, but it is blonde, wispy. There are no wrinkles on this face. The eyes are young. The cheeks are young. The point man is a boy, a tall, lanky boy with a swimmer's torso, lump half-developed in his throat.

Reyn looks at Vitri. He stares at the floor but keeps pressing his hands together, fingers waging war with one another, grappling for something, anything. *Maybe*, Reyn thinks, *Vitri knew the boy in a previous life.* Nephew, neighbor, employee, something, some role. When Vitri finally looks up at Reyn, it is with wet eyes. Tragic eyes, eyes of anger, eyes of regret, eyes of grief, and memory, and—she can place the look—Vitri is lost, utterly lost.

Reyn drops the notebook, carefully sets the candle nearby, then crouches in front of Vitri. As he tips his head down, Reyn follows with her hand and dabs his wet face with the scarf. She watches his fingers. Grappling. Allowing neither to emerge victorious.

Eventually Vitri grabs her, not with malice, but with enough strength to tug her toward him, close, within his arms, to his chest. He holds her tight, so tight, so very tight, and his hands move all over—back to neck, neck to shoulders, shoulders to arms— massaging, scratching, shifting, stroking her hair. Calming those fingers. Vitri then kisses Reyn on the top of her head. He kisses her near the temple. He kisses her on the cheek. Again. And again.

cH. XI

Vitri is flying—no, no, he isn't flying, but he isn't walking, isn't jumping, isn't running; he is seated but still soaring through the sky—ascending, knifing through clouds. He is atop something, some soundless creature he, because he can feel its flaps, knows to have wings. He lets his arms dangle, lets his fingers wander the creature's dry skin—there are no feathers; scales; stubble. He swivels his head. Tries to see through the clouds, through the extending fog. It troubles him that there is no scent on the air. Only a sound, a hummed melody, a

doo-doo-daahhh-dah-doo-doo-daahhh-dah,

and as much as he strains to listen, as much as he strains to see, there is nothing, no source,

doo-doo-daahhh-dah-doo-doo-daahhh-dah,

doo-doo-daahhh-dah-doo-doo-daahhh-dah,

a woman's voice, a raspy voice, a weakening voice, siphoned from the sky, plummeting to panic, to what lies beneath, vaulting him to reach, to itch, to gasp. And then the creature is no more, and he is falling. Falling after the voice, falling, falling, falling straight down, slow at first but accelerating past the fog, into darkness, until he, without so much as a surface ripple, is underwater, on his back, staring at a refracted moon, bloated, bright, and chambered in by thin strands of stars swinging like holiday lights in a crosswind. When he tries to roll himself into swimming position, he plunges further beneath the surface—one meter, two meters, three, that panic returning in the form of a scream, voice distorted by the water, by the soaked scarf that has untied itself, and is now stretched over his face, yanking him

doo-doo-daahhh-dah-doo-doo-daahhh-dah,

muddied by the water, and deeper now, a new voice, a voice he has never heard,

doo-doo-daahhh-dah-doo-doo-daahhh-dah,

and over him floats a rusted tricycle with white handlebars, over him floats a crumpled flashcard, over him floats his son, his dead grey feet, his legs—snug in his pinstriped pajama bottoms—then his torso, his water-shriveled face. Blood seeps from the his son's ears and spins counter-clockwise, strands of red dissipating with the wake Vitri creates with his clawing hands. But then his son is gone, past, and Vitri keeps moving, because he cannot stop, and he keeps on clawing, he keeps on reaching, because it's the only thing he knows how to do. And then, like that, his hands are granted control of the moon, of the stars, and, before he is aware of the power he wields, he wrenches them into the water until he is shrouded in white light,

doo-doo-daahhh-dah-doo-doo-daahhh-dah,

and over him floats an upside-down frying pan, over him floats a pair of black flats, a yellow sundress, over him are suds, lilac-scented suds funneling toward him as if he were a drain, lilac-scented suds outlining ten toes, dripping from a woman's smooth calves, a woman's thin thighs,

doo-doo-daahhh-dah-doo-doo-daahhh-dah,

and he stops reaching, stops clawing, stops moving altogether. Gives up. And then he is lifted. Toward the surface, toward the moon and the stars, toward the woman, her groin, her torso, her breasts, her neck—

From the metal trashcan, Reyn watches Vitri's hand twitch. Asleep, he looks so much like a child, so serene, so at ease, and adorable, legs curled, cuddled against the west wall, drooling on the cap end of his water bottle pillow, his body a respiring mound in the far reaches of the candle's glow. She feels as if she could watch him like this for hours.

Leaving the lit candle by the trashcan, Reyn tiptoes to the door, where she has set the briefcase and their zipped backpacks. She hopes that Vitri will appreciate that upon awakening, her effort, how much time she has saved by packing for the both of them. She wants him to nod, to smile. To wrap his arms around her and squeeze, and hold, and hold, and hold. For now, though, she's in search of something. She unzips the largest pocket of Vitri's backpack and, in doing so, causes Vitri to stir. She extracts an unlit candle only when he has settled, then, careful of the noise she know she must be making, she slowly unzips her own backpack and wrests out Ralph's sickle. Items in hand, she returns to the trashcan. Sits cross-legged on the floor, facing Vitri, the only man besides her father to have ever kissed her.

She knows how childish it is to think anything of it, to place weight on something that, in the moment, could be viewed by most as trivial. The man was scared. The man was angry. The man was lost. And Reyn was just the person that happened to be there. Nothing more than within reach. A band-aid. That's all. No man dreams of band-aids, of anything to mend a wound they'd never admit to having, a wound they'd rather ignore. Hours from now— when they are to walk south in silence—she knows he'll do everything he can to rid his mind of the fourth floor, her included, her especially; Reyn, whose disability had set the whole thing in motion.

Feeling so certain of such makes it no easier for Reyn to accept that, for the hours he has been asleep, all she has wanted to do is reciprocate. Kiss him on the forehead. On each cheek. Moments ago, she even lowered herself enough for her breath to move his hair, so close that she could smell the dried tomato soup on his upper lip. What stopped her, what brought her here, behind the garbage can, had been anxiety. Her stomach had spun. Her pulse had risen. Her mind had darted to an image of Vitri waking, of Vitri reaching up, of Vitri choking her. She pictured Vitri, so embarrassed, so ashamed, so clueless as to how she operated, letting go of his hold, prepping her for what she would assume was their trek to Florida, and then trading her to the masked. For a weapon. For a vehicle. For a masked woman with the body of Painter White, a specialist in the field of wounds.

Reyn straightens the unlit candle's crooked wick, then tilts it to the flame of its lit counterpart. Once the new candle holds the flame, she sets it on the floor. Brings the old candle close. Examines the layer of melted wax atop, the black burn marks across the glass, their turbulent smudges and slashes—high, low, thick, thin, jagged, rounded. Before blowing out the flame, Reyn hovers her nose over the candle's rim and takes one deep breath. *Almonds.* Warm. Welcoming. She imagines them in a small house, one burning on a coffee table during game night, another on a nightstand overlooking a set of ruffled covers. *Pillars*, she thinks. *A home. That's what these are.*

As the wax cools, Reyn, like the man that gashed her tongue, grips the back of Ralph's sickle, clambers her fingers up-up-up until only an inch or two of the half-moon blade is visible, dried blood flaking onto her fingers. She then eases the blade into the wax.

R + V

After setting her work on the floor, Reyn peels the clotted wax from the tip of Ralph's sickle, balls it with her fingers and places it in the shallow pool of wax forming in the other candle. She then rises and tiptoes to her backpack. Into the large pocket goes the sickle. Between it and *DEEP THROAT* she places R+V, but not before shoving it into a stray wool sock. There it will harden, and, she hopes, endure. Because, even if Vitri wants to forget, this, it, she and him, she wants it all to be remembered. He saved her. He healed her. He protected her. Kissed her.

Forcing these facts to vanish, she feels, would be tragic.

Reyn zips the pockets of each backpack and out of the corner of her eye sees a water bottle rolling across the floor. Vitri is awake, sitting up, eyes wide and searching, uncertain of his surroundings but becoming acclimated once more. Reyn, carrying a pen and the notebook, walks toward Vitri. But Vitri jumps to his feet. He hurries to the window and yanks the quilt aside. Darkness is lifting, an early morning indigo slipping into its place, the tops of buildings transitioning out of shadow. Vitri lets the quilt swing shut, turns around, stares at Reyn, then raises his arms in question. But all she can focus on is his crotch, on his erection, the bulge of the denim.

JUST GOING TO WAKE YOU UP

TOLD YOU NOT TO LET ME SLEEP

YOU NEEDED IT

Reyn stands behind Vitri as he crouches and examines his backpack. She waits for him to turn before presenting the notebook to him. But he ignores her. Looks past her, around her, scanning for something else to cram, anything she may have forgotten. When he finally notices the notebook, Vitri takes it from her. He jams it into her backpack, zips the large pocket shut, then asks for the pen. Once in his hand, Vitri stands. He grabs Reyn's arm, rolls up the sleeve of her sweatshirt and crosses out the instructions from before. Writes.

USE YOUR EYES

STICK TO SHADOWS

HOLD MY HAND

Heaps of dead birds on Cotton St. Bent beaks, smashed beaks, stray red, blue, and black feathers held in place by the weight of the damp, dank air. There is a dog, too, dozens of feet away, some mutt with one ear batting its weak paws at a plastic bag in front of a ravaged insurance building. Other than that, in the hours that they've been on foot, it has seemed to Vitri that the streets of Shreveport belong to he and Reyn, and the cars—cars, cars, cars, tires gone, windows smashed, hoods off, guts out—the crumbling of wood and brick chips beneath their feet one of only a few sounds to be heard.

Vitri quickens their pace. Tugs Reyn's right hand with him through a portion of Loyola's campus, adjusting his focus as the sun does, from roofs and windows to sidewalks and intersections, scanning, searching. They move like this through cemeteries and city parks, past medical centers, past museums, past hotels and libraries, past it all and out of the city.

###

Vitri leans against the QUERBES PARK sign. His clothes are heavy with sweat. His feet ache. Though on the air is a scent of vomit, the park, aside from the tipped garbage cans, is rather clean. Fences are intact. Save for white blotches on their tops the size and shape of watermelons, hedges have remained green. Tree branches are bare, soggy leaves carpeting the yellow grass, the concrete path winding through the park—dark yellow leaves, bright red leaves, semitransparent green. Vitri watches Reyn reach for one from the ground. He grabs her arm.

"No," he says, then slides the scarf off of his nose. He puts his hands on his hips and scans the area, paying particular attention to a dry water fountain in the center of the park. "Think we're safe?"

He turns to see her unzipping her backpack. Hair falls into her eyes. She brushes it away, careful not to bump her cheek. The swelling, Vitri assumes, is nearing its peak. In one day, maybe two, it will begin its long slog back to normalcy, dark purple center gone, yellow edges dissolving. It hasn't slowed her though, as he anticipated it would. Not one bit. She has been step for step with him the entire way, gripping his hand with more strength than he imagined her possessing. And, though her breathing still is somewhat labored, Vitri, having been caught staring at her, spots excitement in her eyes. For being on the move. For being here, in this park. For being with him.

"Oh," Vitri says to himself, having forgotten for a moment about Reyn's deafness. "Right."

The girl, Vitri thinks, does not yet know how to hide her feelings. Resist them. Shove them down. Concentrate them into curling toes. IS NOT THE TIME, he wants to write. HERE IS NOT THE PLACE. But he feels it, in stares such as this, in how sweaty her shy hand had been on the second floor, before dawn, before they descended the staircase. He can even see it in her handwriting now, as she sets the notebook on the surface of the park sign, how, when compared to the first sentences she wrote for him, their rigidity, their lack of both care and strength, she grips the pen as if it were her brush and the letters her paint. So focused. So round, so perfect.

THINK WE'RE SAFE?

Reyn smiles wide enough that Vitri can see the layers of black on her tongue. *All this girl knows is misery,* Vitri thinks. He takes the notebook. Looks at Reyn. Nods, then takes off his backpack. He places the notebook within it, and pulls from its side pocket a bottle of water. He offers it to Reyn.

She sips.

He sips.

Their breathing slows.

Vitri looks across the park. He feels Reyn's gaze upon him, and wishes it was as easy as just swatting it away. He slides the scarf back over his nose, then walks south, this time not bothering to offer a hand.

They come upon NEBEKE'S, an auto dealer just off of what Vitri confirms to be the corner of Southfield and Anniston. Behind the half-filled lot is a twenty-foot high mound of dirt that appears as if, perhaps for some sort of renovation, it had been intentionally placed and shaped by machine. Before walking to it, Vitri tries to signal Reyn, first with the wave of one hand, then with the flailing of both arms. But on she goes, oblivious, toward the south end of the car lot. And up the mound he walks, toes digging into the dirt, lungs labored.

Atop the mound, Vitri's scarf flaps in the wind. That same scent of vomit is on the air, stronger now that he is higher, the roofs of nearby buildings rotted and appearing as if a single footstep would turn the block to rubble.

He is surprised to see as far as he can. Four miles east, maybe more. Surprised but pleased at what he sees: beyond sequential mounds of dirt like the one he stands upon is a large bridge arching over what he knows to be the Red River, sunlight glaring off its skeleton. The river itself, from this distance, looks nothing like a river at all, but, rather, a crater. A direct drop off from the east and west banks. The faintest trickle at the bottom.

He focuses once more on the bridge, and wonders about the bridges further south. He doesn't know if they're wooden, but pictures them as such, their footboards snapped—or, rather, snapping as they cross. He pictures himself trudging through the bottom of the river, backpack held above his head. Pictures himself improvising some sort of raft for Reyn.

We cross now, he thinks.

He looks down on the lot. Nearest to the street is a row of wounded hybrid vehicles that, like the subsequent rows of sedans and SUVs, extend two hundred feet south. He hadn't noticed it before; couldn't have so close to the ground—each vehicle's roof is marked with one red M, some painted by can, others by brush.

Alert, Vitri pulls the 9mm from his waistband and stumbles down the mound, making his way to the middle row once on concrete, searching for Reyn through cracked windshields. Halves of hoods have been sawn off, batteries lifted entirely, pistons and gaskets strewn about, leftover, discarded. The engine of a Sonata is missing, the air filter of an Elantra. And still, no Reyn. Vitri drops to the pavement and looks beneath each sedan. Then, each hybrid, all four tires of every other gone, rolled away. Nothing else. Oil stains. Washers.

Then there is the sound of a dreary car horn. Again.

Vitri stands.

Again.

He scans the lot for the sound. Aims his pistol at nothing in particular.

Another honk, this one quieter, lighter.

Vitri rotates his body toward the sound, toward the back row, the southeast corner of the lot. There, in the driver's seat of a dented silver Jeep sits Reyn, one hand on the wheel, the other dangling out of the shattered driver's side window. She waves at Vitri. Even has the audacity to smile.

She was trying to be quiet, Vitri tells himself as he jogs to the Jeep. He pictures two or three red-masked men sprinting from across the street and into the lot, searching with malicious joy for the origin of such noise.

She was trying to be quiet, she was trying to be quiet, she was trying to be quiet.

By the time he reaches the Jeep, Reyn has leaned over and opened the passenger door for him. At first he refuses to get in. Makes a waving motion with the pistol instead that he assumes Reyn will take to mean, WE NEED TO LEAVE. The thought, however, never seems to cross her mind. When she isn't waving him in, Reyn is pointing at the dashboard.

160

Vitri surrenders. He quietly shuts the door after climbing onto the passenger's seat. Once in, he looks all around the Jeep, at the critter-clawed back seat, at the dirt-caked floor, in the glove compartment, the only artifact in the vehicle being its manual. Then he stares as wickedly at Reyn as he can, for as long as he can, a look he hopes will communicate what he feels: YOU'RE FUCKING THIS UP. But the girl isn't to be broken. She smiles. She points again at the dashboard.

LIVED IN JEEP WITH MY MOM FOR A YEAR

WHY?

NOWHERE ELSE TO GO

LOTS OF PLACES

MOM DIDN'T THINK SO

WHAT DID YOU DO?

SEARCHED. FOOD, WATER, GAS, SYRINGES.

DRIVE US OUT OF HERE, KID?

I COULD

ALWAYS WANTED TO TEACH SOMEONE

KIDS?

NO

NEPHEWS? NIECES?

NO

WIFE?

NO. WE NEED TO

Way east are engines, loud engines, gas engines, small engines, roaring engines, high-pitched, piercing.

Louder now, higher now, louder, higher, nearing NEBEKE'S. Vitri palms Reyn's head and presses it down, until she, taking the hint, balls herself beneath the dash, ankles hooked around the pedals. Then he too tucks himself, as far as a grown man can, chin in limbo between the glove compartment and seat. He looks at Reyn as she, beneath the steering wheel, somehow turns herself around, eyes now inches from the driver's seat. Vitri holds his finger to his mouth. BE QUIET.

The engines are closer now, louder. Vitri counts three of them, distinct if he strains to listen, the lead engine sounding like a cross between a moped and a chainsaw, high but snarling when slowing or cornering. The second thumps low like a chopper, one twist of the throttle sounding as if it were grinding asphalt, arcing it behind the vehicle like a waverunner would seawater. Vitri looks at Reyn, who has shoved her arm beneath the seat. Her arm wiggles; metal clangs.

Vitri grips her arm. Points at his scarved face, then to the window, and it seems to be enough to scare her still.

While the sound of the first two engines fade, one lingers, and it hardly sounds like an engine at all to Vitri. It sounds instead as if it is hovering, the sound he'd expect to hear if one were to place industrial sized magnets just feet apart. And it isn't going away.

"Why we stoppin'?" A boy's voice over the sound, a pubescent voice, cracking.

A woman's voice: "How the fuck you expect to drag those reds out them holes from here?"

"We need some juice." Gruff but somehow neutral, patient. "D'you rather be sittin' duck in the city?"

The woman, rasp fading: "I'm gonna cut that dick off later if I find out you're just pissin'. Old as shit man, swear I'll cut that dick off." There are three loud clangs then, scrapes, the sound of metal being severed. Twenty feet from the Jeep, thirty at most.

The boy: "Hurry up, Crow."

Vitri waits for the scraping to stop, then peeks over the Jeep's dash. Through several windows appears a distorted Crow, elbow deep under the hood of a chardonnay-toned hybrid. He is a shirtless black man in torn, faded-yellow pants and, when he lifts the battery from the car, Vitri can see a yellow mask on his face—a hockey goalie's mask, with a jagged hole cut around the mouth. Vitri dips his head when Crow turns toward the Jeep. Reyn attempts to rise and, again, Vitri palms her head. Forces her still. Forces her quiet.

When he peeks over the dash again, Crow is walking north, between the hybrids and sedans, toward the woman and the boy, who sit upon what at first glance appears to be a motorcycle—height, shape, the two large wheels. It is sleek. It has been carefully painted bright yellow. The handlebars appear to have been swapped out for an assortment of control sticks and levers. Pedals rise over each footguard. Visible beneath the bike's frame are car batteries, four of them in all, and lined with yellow lights.

The woman: "You satisfied now?" She sits in the sidecar on the left. The boy sits in the sidecar on the right. Like Crow, both are shirtless and wearing modified yellow hockey masks, some seemingly unified faction, the only glaring difference between the three of them being skin color. Strangely, neither woman nor boy face forward. Both are pointed backwards in their sidecar, assault rifles mounted for their use. Behind them—nearer to the front of the bike—are stationary riot shields bent at sharp angles.

"Yip, sats'fied," Crow says. He hands the just-removed battery to the boy.

"The fuck m'I supposta do with this?" The battery is larger than his head.

"Make room," Crow says.

"I got some room over here, honey," the woman says. She stands, leans over the bike, her breasts swinging in front of the boy's face. Seconds after she takes the battery, Crow, straddling the bike, accelerates the three of them west, away from the lot, all origins of sound drifting north.

Vitri looks at Reyn and nods, then lifts himself back onto the passenger seat. Upon receiving approval, Reyn plunges her arm back beneath the driver's seat. Vitri opens his door and steps out onto the lot. Looks east. At fractions of the bridge. At the route he now believes they should give up on. The bridge is no secret; more yellow-masked people could come from the east at any minute.

South it is, he thinks. *South we go.*

He looks back at the Jeep. Reyn crawls over the center console and passenger seat. Once on her feet, she shows Vitri what she has found: a flashlight, no bigger than her hand. She clicks it on, revealing a white beam dulled by daylight.

Vitri nods. Squints at the street. "That's nice, Reyn," he says.

SOUTH, south for hours. Away from distant gunfire, out of the city's reach, into and across suburbs, past an airport with no planes or cargo, SOUTH, across desiccated creekbeds, where they eventually stop for soup and water, Vitri's eyes always east, SOUTH, off of the roads, into thinning forests, dried up bayous, even, swamp grass waist-high and feeble, ash beneath footsteps, merged into the grey and brown and yellow, SOUTH, until the sun sets, until night falls, until dew comes.

###

Vitri watches Reyn jackknife through the brush. Nimble, quick, gripping her backpack's straps, ducking beneath branches, glancing back every few steps, eyes in the night like two white buttons on a black shirt. She wants him to watch. Wants him to see her take the lead. Wants him to reconsider her.

"Slow down," he wishes he could say to her. "Stop trying to impress me."

Yet he is impressed. Pleased. And not just at how thus far he has underestimated her capabilities, her drive, but more so at the fact that she is not as thin as he'd originally surmised from the bagginess of her sweatshirt. He has to strain to see it now, but an hour or so ago, when, in the day's waning light Reyn forged ahead, he noticed a tightness of her jeans he hadn't before. Taut against the backs of her thighs. Shifting waistband halted at, and by, her developing hips. Enough to think her older than he did upon finding her. *Fourteen*, he thinks. *Maybe fifteen*, and accelerating now, taking charge, forging a narrow trail for him.

Vitri stops for a moment when what he thinks is a spooked squirrel leaps from a nearby tree and onto the forest floor. He listens. To the twigs Reyn's feet snap ahead. To the rustling of the squirrel. And, before he continues, he hears the jangle of metal to his left, the pitter-patter of the squirrel bounding over hollow wood. Then it is gone, and Vitri only hears Reyn's steps, distant now, fading. He pulls his scarf down. Wipes the sweat from his cheeks and upper lip. Takes the flashlight from his pocket, clicks it on, white light hovering over the copper-tinted pine needles at his feet. Looks ahead, where he last saw Reyn. Slowly aims the light that way, hoping for her to see it, to turn back. When she doesn't, Vitri, knowing that Reyn will eventually look for him and see that he hasn't kept up, begins aiming the light elsewhere, searching for the origin of that hollow sound. He shrouds a trio of gouged tree trunks in light, gashes not made by saw teeth or bird beak, but a drill of some sort; several deep, thumb-wide holes line the trunks from left to right.

Vitri cautiously rotates the light over more matted weeds, more trees, more grey, and brown, and yellow. And then, in a small clearing no more than twenty feet from where he stands, he sees it: the white light shimmers off of a ground-level door latch. He squints. Steps through weeds, toward the clearing. Stops. Shines the door—fresh wood stained amber, a thin layer of dirt over top. A rusted latch.

Still no Reyn. No footsteps. No twigs.

It's a trap, Vitri thinks. He pictures a wire-rigged shotgun. A metal spike driven to his gut by hydraulics. Masked men and women sprinting to the sound. So he stops. Shines its perimeter, shines all around, keen on locating the trigger. Sees nothing. Hears nothing. Thinks only of going back to the trail, of finding Reyn. He clicks off the flashlight and begins to do just that, turning around entirely, stepping through untouched weeds, stopping only when his right shin strikes something thin but sturdy, something immovable, stopping not because of how it feels, but because of the sound it creates, the quick burst of air.

A tree branch snaps. Detaches. Falls to the ground. The door is fired off, eight feet into the sky, sparks trailing, leaving only a quick-to-fade afterglow on the hole's rim.

Vitri draws the 9mm before the door crashes. Clicks on the flashlight. Aims both at the hole as he backs away, awaiting what comes next. But there is nothing. Nothing from that hole, nothing from beyond. A silhouette, a sound, for seconds there is nothing. So, flashlight still on, pistol still drawn, Vitri turns and locates Reyn's matted trail. Resumes his path. Sidesteps along, pistol still aimed. Further. Further.

And further. His mouth goes dry. His eyes water. He wheezes—soft at first, but harsher now, phlegm in the back of his throat layering itself. His vision fades. He stumbles forward. Falls to his knees. His torso constricts, searching for more than water to send up and out. He crawls. Forward he crawls, leaving the dropped flashlight, the 9mm. Forward. Forward.

Between his attempts at breath he can hear it: liquid dripping onto the leaves. Chemicals spilling from those gouged trees. Bitter on his tongue. Sour. Sharp in his lungs. But he crawls and, as he does, the wheeze evolves into a cough. *Crawl*, he thinks, *go, go-go-go, crawl, crawl, fucking crawl.* Twenty feet from where he fell. Twenty-five.

Thirty.

Thirty-five.

palm trees, a calm gulf, his wife slipping off a pink bikini, sashaying like a ballerina across white sand, toward him, towards their home, alone atop a gently-sloping dune, their son waving from a second-story window,

doo-doo-daahhh-dah-doo-doo-daahhh-dah,

Reyn appears alongside Carmen and, at first, she is smiling, her face no longer damaged but full, cute, bronzed skin, cleaned teeth. But her smile soon fades. Trees appear, branches sawn, tops rounded like recently amputated arms,

doo-doo-daahhh-dah-doo-doo-daahhh-dah,

liquid spews from the trunk, onto Reyn, onto his wife, who falls to her knees and vomits onto each grain of darkening sand, torso locked, skin peeling, and Carmen is smiling, watching and smiling, smiling so wide, laughing now with Reyn's wounded tongue

###

Water on his forehead, water on his cheeks, water on his lips, on his chin, beading to his neck. Vitri opens his eyes to see Reyn crouching over him, raincoat hood up, eyes wide, sweat on her forehead, left hand tilting a bottle of water. Her right hand is on his chest, rising and falling as he does. After setting the bottle nearby, Reyn helps Vitri sit up, then clicks on the flashlight, guiding the light over the notebook on his lap.

YOU O.K.?

Vitri inhales. Exhales. Wipes the water from his face. Bends his knees. Wiggles his feet. Feels how soggy his groin is. Can smell the urine. Takes a deep breath. Nods.

CAN YOU WALK?

Vitri's mind begins its clamber back to cognizance. Questions flood. *How long have I been here? Are you hurt too? Has there been anyone else?* When Vitri reaches for the notebook, Reyn pulls away. She points to:

I FOUND SHELTER

And then once more to:

CAN YOU WALK?

Vitri shifts his legs again. Bends his knees. Wiggles his feet.
Nods. As soon as he does, Reyn sets the flashlight on the ground,
places the notebook into her backpack, then, facing Vitri, extends
her arms. Once Vitri latches on, she anchors her weight to her
heels, anticipating a harsh tug toward the ground, a grasp at her
forearms. But, soon enough, and with effort from both parties,
Vitri is on his feet. Wobbly, but okay, upright and walking in the
dark—one step south, two steps, three. Reyn catches up. Places the
9mm in his hand. Bounds ahead, turns, walks alongside him,
smiles. For one-hundred feet they walk like this, she encouraging
him as if he were a toddler.

One-hundred feet becomes one-hundred yards. Two-hundred.
Vitri's wheezing eases. His legs loosen. Reyn turns, leads him under
trees, through clusters of brush her feet have already trampled
over, the occasional mole hole of moist soil caught in the white

light Vitri aims at the ground. Reyn increases her pace as they angle southeast, down a gentle hill that leads to several more. Up-down, up-down they go for two minutes, three, a stale note of pine on the west-blowing breeze.

Before they reach what Vitri believes to be the last hill, Reyn turns. She watches his feet, his shins, his thighs, and he hates that she does.

She then plugs her left thumb into the night sky, eyes quizzical, awaiting a response. As he walks toward her, Vitri nods. He wheezes, but holds his thumb up and does his best to shoo her forward.

"Stop checking on me," he manages to say.

Reyn then crests the last hill, leaving Vitri to watch her waist disappear, her back, her shoulders, her neck. Down a twenty-five-foot decline she goes, into what Vitri, as he approaches, sees is a U-shaped clearing, trees on all but one side.

In the center of the clearing stands a dark one-story building. Thirty by eighty. Several doors, several small windows, a parking lot to the south with a large sign overhead, text facing the adjacent gravel road. Vitri's assumption that it had once been a hotel of some sort—at the least, some remote cabin, a bed and breakfast—

is confirmed as he works his way down the hill and the numbers above each door become visible. #1, #3, #5, all odd numbers painted on its northwest side. He clicks off the flashlight once he sees that the windows have been boarded. By then, just when he feels she must be flagged down and alerted to the fact that someone else must call this home, Reyn, thirty or so feet in front of him, walks along the north side of the building, to the east, then turns and is out of sight.

Reyn's legs are partially lit by the caged red light above the seafoam door of #8. #6: yellow light. #4: purple. #2: green, each bulb free of caps, bottom ends instead coiled in copper wire. Stapled tight to the wall, the copper wire from each eventually straightens and, fed between the wall and their respective door's hinge, continues inside to copper bowls of nails, screws, washers, other chunks of metal.

Having spent nearly ten minutes in #8 earlier, she knows there are three more red lights on the other side of the door. A television, a table snug against chintzy green and yellow wallpaper. There is a bathroom. A cracked porcelain tub, a rusting showerhead, a toilet without water. She knows there's one armchair, and one small bed.

When Vitri appears, Reyn's smile fades. The scarf is back on, tied tight. His pistol is drawn, gripped by both hands as he walks toward her. Not once does he lower that pistol. Not once does he glance at Reyn. Not once does he notice her waving arms, her shaking head. His eyes shift instead from the easternmost woods, to the half-lit patches of cement, to the door of #8.

Repeat. Repeat. Repeat.

Until he nudges open the door and Reyn is left to watch him storm in, the pistol's definition a blur, appearing instead as an extension of his hands, his hands and arms an extension of his chest. He proceeds to probe the room. Tousles the quilt. Aims at each corner. Peeks around the bathroom door. Then, he looks at her in disgust. Waves her inside and, as soon as her feet are out of range, slams the door. The copper wire fed through the doorframe fractures. The red light outside of #8 goes dark.

As Reyn sets each backpack on the bed, she is nudged aside by Vitri, who, having shoved his pistol back into his waistband, frantically unzips and tears into Reyn's backpack. Out comes the notebook. Out comes a pen. When he is finished writing, he tosses the notebook onto the bed.

WHAT THE FUCK ARE YOU THINKING?

In the red light, Reyn watches Vitri rip the scarf from his face. Watches him gulp from a plastic water bottle. Watches him pace the room. There are creases all over his face. Above his eyebrows, on the bridge of his nose, rippling across his forehead. Frustration.

And Reyn is confused. *You are no longer on the ground*, she thinks. *We are no longer in the woods. There are four walls. We won't need to start a fire. We won't have to waste a candle, nor the batteries of the flashlight. There is warmth. There is warmth, and I saved you. What more do you want?*

WHAT DID I DO WRONG?

She offers the notebook to Vitri as if it were a porcelain ornament she'd broken, eyes down, unable to help herself from flinching as Vitri yanks it from her hands. She glances at him as he reads. Watches him sigh. Watches him rub an eye with his left hand. When he sits on the bed, Reyn scoots as far away as she can, holding the pen out for whenever he is ready.

SOMEONE LIVES HERE

HOW?

LOOK!

WE'LL LEAVE WHEN THEY WANT US TO

WON'T GET THE FUCKING OPTION

WE'LL BE SAFE HERE

NO BACK DOOR. NO SIDE DOOR

THERE'S A FRONT DOOR

THAT'S WHERE THEY'LL ALL BE

THE MASKED?

ANYONE

WE'LL BE SAFE HERE

YEAH?

I WAITED. I WATCHED. YOU NEVER CAME. I WENT

BACK

AND?

NOTHING

DIDN'T SEE ANYTHING?

NO

DIDN'T SMELL ANYTHING?

NO

DID YOU HEAR ANYTHING?

Guilt no longer resides in Reyn's body. No, no, this is anger. This is rage. Her hands twist into fists. She picks up the notebook and throws it across the room, then kneels on the bed and shoves Vitri in the back as hard as she can, the first, the unexpected, being the most effective, Vitri's torso tilting sideways. *Fuck you*, she wishes she could shout. *Fuck you, fuck you, fuck you.* But Vitri braces himself. Tightens his core until Reyn's actions morph from shock to annoyance.

He shoves Reyn back. Once. Hard. Down she goes on the bed, wounded cheek crashing into a risen spring. She feels something in her throat, a tiny ball of energy evolving, expanding into something that can no longer stay, into something that she rolls its way up and off of her tongue. And then Vitri's hands are on her neck, fingers wrapped around that ball, pressing, pressuring, doing their best to cut it off. When it is kneaded away, so go his fingers. So go his hands.

Seconds later, Vitri is off the bed. A dejected Reyn lifts her head high enough to watch him retrieve the notebook. As he turns around, Reyn, ferocity now tainted by terror, scurries as far away from him as she can, to the narrow headboard. When he is finished writing, Vitri walks toward the bed, ignorant of how Reyn braces herself for a blow. Sets the notebook next to her. Grabs a pillow. Plops the pillow on the floor, at the food-end of the bed. She waits until he lies down to read.

I THOUGHT YOU COULDN'T SPEAK
I CAN'T

Without rising from the bed, without even craning her neck to spot his exact location on the floor, Reyn tosses the notebook in

Vitri's direction, then the pen. She hopes the spine nicks his chin, gashes it, leaves some sort of blemish, a bruise, a scab, a scar. In a matter of fifteen seconds, up the notebook comes at her, pages still bound but awry, altering its flight. Then comes the pen, tumbling through the air, end over end.

SCREAM AGAIN IF YOU SEE ANYTHING

An hour passes.

Reyn adjusts, carefully buries her face into the pillow, back into the faint scent of cinnamon. This room belonged to a woman, she has thought for a while now, a woman that, based off of the strength of the room's remaining scents, left not that long ago. She pictures a rugged woman with curly hair, but isn't sure why. A rugged woman still valuing hygiene. A rugged woman surviving here alone, spending her days rigging light fixtures. Reyn pictures a refrigerator in one of the other rooms, a freezer the rugged woman stored underground, full of meat, the last of the strawberries she'd bartered for, a cantaloupe she'd stolen along the way.

Reyn misses cantaloupe. Misses watching her father pare cores with knives he'd taken from the restaurant. Misses opening her jaws wide and sinking her teeth in that soft orange flesh.

###

Another hour comes and goes.

###

Reyn, back pressed to the headboard, slurping soup she has taken from Vitri's backpack, rotates her eyes from the ceiling to the window. As muted as the red interior lights of #8 are, as tight as the boards have been nailed over the lone window, in slivers Reyn can see the sun yawning itself awake. Layers peeled. Black to dark blue, dark blue to grey, lighter, and stretching lighter.

She is uneasy about the start of a new day, the previous unraveling entirely unlike what she imagined. She'd pictured the two of them side by side while slogging through Shreveport, boarding Vitri's cousin's boat as one. Stopping not just when hungry or hurt, but just to stop, to converse, to plan, to laugh, to smile. Carrying on, at the very least, as friends.

She wants to wake Vitri up. Wants to ask him, CAN WE? CAN WE BE FRIENDS? She wants to know what happened in the woods. Wants to know whether or not he can confirm her worry, that her being deaf, that her being young, and sheltered, that it all has made it that much more difficult to read someone like him. She wants him to explain why she continues to imagine San Juan as a sliver of paradise. Wants him to tell her what that kiss meant.

Thinking of it in such terms reminds Reyn of her mother, that time she'd written, A KISS MARKS THE BEGINNING OF SOMETHING. NOT THE END. And then: A RECIPE CARD, NOT THE WARM TRAY YOU PULL OUT OF THE OVEN.

Which now, and at that time, rings to Reyn of her father. Her mother had written it for him. About him, his tendencies. Of course she had.

Based on physicality alone, Reyn still wonders often how her father had been capable of capturing the attention of so many women. Forty pounds overweight. Filthy. Scarred, and with little desire to change any of it. But, as Reyn knew, something about him was charming.

While she couldn't be certain that others found it charming, she found comfort in his posture, how, when he wasn't sitting or lying down, everything seemed to open up—shoulders back but lax, hands either on his hips or clasped behind his waist like a soldier told to stand at ease—as if it were an open invitation to approach, to judge if one must. Because judgment wouldn't make a damn bit of difference in how he conducted himself.

It could also have been in the way he touched people, the warmth one could find in a man who would hold you like he did, snug and secure, or in the security one could extract from his right thumb—always rubbing, never still—massaging a neck, the top of a hand, a shoulder. For all Reyn knows, her father could've possessed the sexiest voice in Monroe. He could've whispered often, leaned in close and tickled his listener's ear with propositions, with promises of some long-winded, multi-border adventure they'd never take.

However he'd done it, Reyn, from age twelve, up to the night preceding his departure, had watched her father walk those women back to the house. Amble, really, down that half-lit sidewalk, at 2:00am, sometimes 3:00, after the bars had closed. Passing a bottle back and forth. Taking pulls. Colliding into one another and smiling about doing so.

It had been one woman per week at first, on Thursdays. Within four months, one became three: Tuesday, Thursday, and Saturday—at the conclusion of each of his night shifts.

Reflecting on that first time, Reyn can't remember why she'd already been awake at such an hour, if she'd been reading, if she'd been writing, or if it'd just been one of the many nights that she'd lain in bed, eyes open, conscious brain spending its most unsettled hours leaping from past to future, from future to past. What had anchored her to the present that night, she'd soon discover, was the flickering of light outside of her window. More than that, there was movement of that light: back, forth, back, forth across her window, in and out, in and out. So she'd risen and walked to that window. She'd pried two blinds and peeked out into the night. She'd seen her father's black work pants at his ankles, his splattered apron draped over his shoulder. One foot on the grass, one on the sidewalk, hips thrusting into the woman who braced herself against the base of the streetlamp. She remembers the woman's hair—auburn under the light—and she remembers glimpsing the woman's eyes—wide, then closed, then wide again, either in pain or euphoria, neither of which young Reyn had the capacity to describe or decipher—and she remembers how two or three minutes later, up their pants went. They'd smiled. They'd laughed. They'd hugged. They'd snuggled not unlike she and her father would and then they'd sat upon the grass and shared a cigarette. They'd stood, and they'd kissed, and that was it. Off she'd gone, down the sidewalk, and in he'd come, with his bottle, more than happy to sleep blanketless on the couch.

Reyn remembers the short black woman that'd had the most colorful strands of beads swaying in the night, deflecting off of her chin and cheeks. She remembers the paperthin Nordic-looking woman, her straw-colored eyebrows and hair. The Latin woman who didn't seem to want Reyn's father to do any of the work, but bent over in the same spot as the rest of the ladies, wrapped her arms around that same streetlamp, and drove her backside into him.

She remembers the night that Mr. Hirsham, a fifty-something single father of four, walked to the end of his driveway in a mauve bathrobe and, if Reyn had read his hand gestures correctly, asked her father and some young brunette with her paisley skirt flipped up to stop, to which Reyn's father responded with the tossing and subsequent shattering of a dark liquor bottle.

She remembers the round-faced coworker whose black-framed glasses fell off of her face and onto the sidewalk, the left lens popping out, crushed by a footstep moments later.

She remembers them all. Their smiles. How often they brought each cigarette to their lips. How long they held the hug. How, afterwards, before her father would send them on their way, they'd all look at the house, eye every window not with concern or confusion, but with promise, as if what they'd just done was being filed away as a building block, as if their entrance was one day imminent.

Reyn remembers never seeing any of them more than once. And she remembers never confronting her father about it, never asking, WHY?

There was another night that Reyn, becoming rather bored with her father's routine (he was out there again, with a woman Reyn hadn't been interested enough to look at), and rather hungry, walked down the stairs, into the kitchen. And there her mother sat, at the bistro table near the back door. In the dark. Cigarette glowing enough to see the how far tears had streamed before being wiped away. Initially halted by the image, Reyn eventually walked past her mother. Flipped on the light over the sink. On the verge of tears herself, she grabbed a pad of sticky notes from the counter, and a pen.

I SHOULD'VE TOLD YOU SOONER
I'VE KNOWN FOR A LONG, LONG TIME

Which confused Reyn. Immediately, she wanted more. Answers. Truths she knew would only stoke anger, and guilt. *Why haven't you stopped him? Why aren't you out there? Why haven't you said anything?*

HOW LONG?

Reyn's mother glanced at the question. And that's all it was: a glance. She then peeled the note from its pad and crumpled it into a crooked heap. Grabbed the pen. Wrote small.

HE REFUSES TO BRING THEM INTO THIS PART OF HIS HEART

She stubbed out her cigarette. Continued.

HE LOVES US. WHAT HE DOES OUT THERE WON'T CHANGE THAT

Reyn's mother rose from the table. Rubbed her eyes. Adjusted the disheveled collar of her grey t-shirt, then stepped toward what from that point forward would be openly known as her bedroom, and only hers. But Reyn wrote, and Reyn followed, grabbing her mother by the arm and placing in her hand the night's final question:

ARE WE GOING TO LEAVE?

At which Reyn's mother smiled. Smiled and shrugged her shoulders, though not in what Reyn would classify as confusion, or in a manner fueled by the unknown, but in a manner of certainty. "Look around," her mother's shoulders said, "I can't."

Lying on #8's bed, Reyn feels as if she should've walked outside that night. Walked outside, interrupted her father, just grabbed his arm, brought him inside, and instructed him to enter that bedroom and kiss his wife. Something that said it was over. That all of it was over. That released her, that sent her in her own direction. Because Reyn's mother was incapable of moving on without someone else saying to her, "Go."

Addict, Reyn thinks of her mother. *Addict*. Not to that house. Not to comfort. Not to Ohapila. *Addict*: to Reyn's father. *Addict*: a willing participant in the transformation of person to tool, to pawn, to something to be shoved around, used, misplaced.

Addict, Reyn thinks of her father. Addict: to sex, to cigarettes, to the chase of sex and cigarettes, whether the journey be short and void of obstacles, or long, country-wide and tumultuous. Addict: not to his daughter, not to their house, not to his wife. *Addict*: above all, to himself.

And what, Reyn has wondered often, could this possibly say about her? What does the acorn say about its tree? Was her entire path laid out before birth? Has she been doomed from the start? Can a trait be reversed simply by recognizing the trend? Can it?

Can it?

I am no addict, Reyn thinks. She sets the soup she has been sipping on the nightstand. Crawls to the food-end of the bed. Watches Vitri sleep. *I am no addict*.

Half an hour passes.

###

Reyn can feel the bedsprings recoil as she pushes herself off of the mattress. Once on her feet, she peers down at Vitri, asleep. On his back, neck twisted to the side, mouth open. Chest, heart: rising, falling, rising, falling. It pains her that Vitri won't make clear to her what he wants. The only thing that he has made clear is that he doesn't want her.

And so she is going to leave him, just like this, in peace. Do them each a favor, and journey into the still-rising sun alone, toward Idaho, toward that flawed father of hers, as risky as it is for a deaf girl like her to do so alone. She knows that Vitri won't be concerned enough to request an explanation, but if he were to wake, and scramble, and present the notebook and pen with a look that asked why, Reyn would write: THANK YOU. For saving her from the red-masked. For doing what he could to heal her. For showing her more of what it is she does and does not want.

Secure in her plan, Reyn, as stealthily as she can, walks to her backpack and bends over to pick it up. It's at this moment that Vitri stirs—not because of Reyn, but because of something else, something soft enough that he sits up with only mild urgency. Yawns. Swipes balls of green-grey gunk out of his eyes. Runs his fingernails through his greasy hair. Stands. Stretches his neck. Rolls his shoulders. Reyn, aware of his state now, unzips her backpack and begins to pull the notebook and pen back out of her bag.

Before she can, Vitri, feet planted, motions for her to stop. His brows furrow as he turns more of his attention to the door. From what Reyn can tell, there is nothing of note. There are no shadows beneath. There are no tremors. No jiggling of the knob. Just a door and its deadbolt. That is all.

Then, slowly, Vitri bends to the floor for his scarf and backpack, slipping each to what have become their natural resting spots on his body. He also grabs his pistol, readies it to fire, and rises as slowly as he'd bent, ears still attentive to the door, eyebrows still angled in confusion. With his free hand, he motions for Reyn to stand, for her to put her backpack on, and then, for her to go to the door. Which she hesitantly does, tiptoeing past him, stopping only when he places his hand on her shoulder.

Vitri takes one step to the left of the doorframe, then tries to explain to Reyn what he's hearing. PEOPLE, his free hand says. PEOPLE TALKING. Vitri imitates what he wants Reyn to do: stand where she is, turn the knob, pull the door open as quickly as possible, and hold.

Reyn nods. Puts her hand on the knob. Waits for the pistol to once again become an extension of Vitri's hands, of both outstretched arms. Waits for his look.

Vitri nods.

And when he does Reyn turns the knob, yanks the door open—pinning herself between it and the wall, the only things in her line of sight being the bed, the television, the bathroom door—and holds. There's a flash, a crash of sound that follows, ending quickly enough for Reyn to feel Vitri's boot scrape across the door sweep, a slight careen into dawn. Seconds later, another flash. The sound waves from Vitri's pistol embeds in her skin. Then, she sees a hand—his hand—reach around the door, presumably for her, waving her out of the corner. Tentatively, Reyn steps out and around, until Vitri can grab her sweatshirt. Out of #8 she is pulled, toward him, toward a thin black man with stiff silver hair lying on the pavement, clutching his shoulder. His eyes are shut. Mouth open, teeth clenched, interstate-like wrinkles up, down and across his bare arms.

No more than ten feet from the wounded man stands two more men and one woman, all elderly, all with their hands in the air, all shivering. One of the two men—wearing a thin grey t-shirt and bent horn-rimmed glasses—blinks back tears. The other's skin looks like a used coffee filter, soggy and creased. The lone woman, in a baggy white t-shirt with a red AMERICAN QUEEN over an image of a riverboat, refuses to look up at all, focusing instead on her equally baggy pants and open-toed shoes.

Vitri is yelling something. Reyn can feel it through his fingertips. He is pulling her south. Three yards, four yards, across the burnt lawn, Reyn's feet failing to fully comprehend the situation, slow to match Vitri's long strides. Ten yards, fifteen yards. Reyn looks back to see the three huddled around their wounded, speaking to him, caressing his cheek. They do not give chase. They cannot give chase. *They are harmless.*

Reyn wrestles her hand free of Vitri's and, expecting him to react—to tackle, to shoot, to shout obscenities at someone, who, even if she could, would not listen—unzips her backpack, extracting from it two cans of tuna. When she turns back around, Vitri is twenty feet ahead, pistol still in his hand, waving her forward. She wants to deliver those two cans of tuna. She wants to write to them how sorry she is for what just happened, to pen THIS WAS MY FAULT, BUT THIS WAS NOT MY CHOICE, to lend any kind of helping hand.

But she stares at Vitri. She stares and she doesn't know what she sees. Stares and doesn't know what she wants to see. She stares and wishes she knew why she feels compelled to set the two cans of tuna here, on the ground, rather than to deliver them, and, more importantly, why—maybe it's her body's instinct to survive, maybe it's her heart's inability to accept rejection— she can't choose communicating with the elderly over the man striding south without her. *Addict*, Reyn thinks. And she drops the cans.

###

Late morning. Sun nibbling through fog as it climbs, a breeze stirring. South again, Vitri leading, twenty yards ahead of Reyn, pistol still out. More woods, more birds startled from bare branches into the sky, more dried creekbeds, more yellows and browns and dull greens. A squirrel, skinny, heaving its heavy tail across scattered leaves. In the distance, a three-legged deer, still alert, still determined to evade the slightest threat.

WHY DID YOU SHOOT HIM?

Reyn looks up from the notebook to see that fifteen yards from her, and closing, is Vitri, scarf off, pistol in hand. *Run,* she thinks, *run now, anywhere, any way, to anyone.* Yet it is that same fear that keeps her still, that pulls the string that produces the twitch in her thigh.

At first, all Vitri does is examine her. He squints at her bruised cheek. Thumbs her lips apart to view her tongue.

And Reyn is shaking.

After placing the pistol in his waistband, Vitri asks for the notebook. Plucks the pen from her hand.

TOLD YOU WE WEREN'T ALONE

THEY WERE HARMLESS
NOBODY IS HARMLESS

Before a confused Reyn can reply, Vitri takes the notebook back. He at her as he hands it over. Takes out his pistol. Resumes his pace.

HURRY UP. WATER AHEAD

There is—the woods Reyn and Vitri walk through eventually lead to what was once a winding shoreline of sorts. Mounds of displaced gravel. Sawn stumps of oak and ash. It smells here of stale transition, from a harsh winter to a late spring, surrounding trees, shrubs and grass playing catch-up. To the north, one hundreds yards from where Reyn and Vitri stand, is a riverboat tipped on its side, captain's deck pointed south. Water runs where it can beneath the boat, through its multiple decks, its blue-trimmed windows, trickling into what the river has become: a soggy six-hundred foot crevice layered like a robin's nest. Dried grass woven with roots and twigs.

Vitri steps toward the riverboat. Reyn follows, eyeing the shattered rocking chairs and wooden tables that have fallen from the boat's promenades. An inverted porchswing is still chained to a lower deck's overhead pipe. The red paddlewheel on the boat's stern looks to still be relatively intact, neither the breeze or weak current enough for it to rotate. Closer now, Reyn pictures the boat upright, operating at full tilt, the river high, the decks populated by men and women, eyes peeled for wildlife but, in finding none, resorting to observing the wake the crew creates. The two large black pipes would be flapping steam into the sky instead of lying like two broken chess pieces, snapped the second they hit the ground. That paddlewheel would be turning, turning so fast, and it would be so bright in the sun, just painted, the boat's sides too, a glossy white instead of an off-grey, covered in the soot and silt of a river bled dry.

AMERICAN QUEEN, Reyn can see now it once was called, white lettering on the black hull. MEMPHIS, TN. AMERICAN QUEEN from MEMPHIS, TENNESSEE. She is parallel with Vitri now. He does not move. He does not blink.

Vitri's wife sits on a porchswing outside of the River Bar & Grill. She wears a lavish scarlet dress, thin straps taut against her collarbone, tied behind her neck. A matching shade of lipstick has smeared onto the rim of her martini glass. Beside her is a white plastic mask that, if worn, would cover cheek to cheek, from upper lip to eyebrow. In her sight is a churning paddlewheel and, beyond that, St. Charles, Missouri, a city prepared for night, the neon lights of boutiques and taverns barely visible in the fading sun. She can hear the honks of cars and buses miles off. Above her is the faint jetstream of an ascending seven-thirty-seven. Sunlight bends through trees plugged into riverbanks, growing large and strong and crooked from competition. The river is high but calm, the boat's wake gently slapping the shore. She watches this. She listens to the flags on the top deck flap in the wind, then takes off her black heels and sets them next to the white mask, feeling as if, in doing so, she will maybe appear less bewildered, more sure of herself.

Fellow AMERICAN QUEEN passengers mingle nearby, speaking low but emphatically about the strength of their cocktails, the weather forecasts they've studied on their cell phones, the relatives of theirs in Minneapolis that intend to show them the city once the boat docks. Crewmembers in radiant white calmly scurry about, refilling drinks, asking the passengers how they are enjoying their trip. All smiles, all teeth, all likening it—the mystique of the river, the design of the boat, the company they keep—to a fairy tale.

Emerging from the propped wooden doors of the bar and grill is Vitri. His hair is cropped short, his face shaved clean. The dark blue polo shirt he wears has come untucked from his khakis. House whiskey sloshes in his short glass as he walks to his wife, slowly, an anxious hand in his pocket, mauling the thin lining that this very action has already loosened. But then he stops. Feet from his wife, he stops. He looks at her. He studies her. He loves this woman. He wants to hug this woman. Despite where this discussion is bound to go, he'll want to stay with her on this porchswing, and he'll want to kiss her, and he'll want the two of them to watch the river tonight.

"You had to bring that up *here*," Vitri's wife says. She doesn't address him with her eyes. Takes a sip from her martini instead. Watches the paddlewheel. "Just had to."

Vitri sets his wife's mask and heels on the deck so that he can sit on the porchswing. "You would've reacted differently had I asked you in the car? In the living room?"

Vitri's wife still has not looked at him. She keeps her eyes on her glass.

"Well," Vitri says. He sips from his drink and looks out to the river. "It's out in the open now."

"It was out in the open before we even got married. You made sure that it was." She finally looks at her husband. "Didn't I tell you then that kids were the last thing I wanted?"

"People can change."

"Didn't I tell you how scared I am?"

"You did." Vitri watches his wife sip her martini. He loves how the lipstick smear on the rim of the glass bothers her, how, because it does, she immediately smoothes it out with her thumb. "You've never told me why, though, why you're scared."

Vitri's wife sighs. "This isn't the same world we grew up in, Vitri." She waits for her husband to ask a question. When he doesn't, she continues: "We've pissed the earth off real good, for one. But kids just want their screens. That's it; that is their life. Don't give me that look. You know it's true. You've seen it. You've commented upon it how many times? The only reason they want this, anything like this—" she raises her free hand as if it can, and does, encompass the entirety of the scene, the river, the sun, the air, "—the only reason they step out into the world is so that they can make whatever they see on their screens real. They join a gang online. 'Huh, let me see what that's like.' Next thing you know they're packing dad's gun into a backpack."

"You don't think our parents thought we'd ruin the world? You don't think they were scared?" Vitri places his right arm around his wife's shoulders. "We'll raise our kids differently. They'll work at the store as soon as they can. They'll hike. They'll see mountains. They'll ride their bikes instead of buying dumb trucks."

"They'll be shunned." She leans forward, away from her husband's consoling arm. "If that's the plan, we'll be keeping them from the world. And by the time we no longer can do that, they'll be shunned, Vitri. How cool is it to have your parents as your best friends? How healthy is that?"

"Mine were."

Vitri's wife sighs. "Not the same thing."

"Why? Because my parents were first-generation?" When his wife doesn't answer, Vitri continues, "They'll have us. And they'll have your parents. They'll have my parents."

"I wouldn't want any of them involved." Vitri's wife gulps the rest of her martini. The expression on her face says it was a struggle, says that she knew better than to say such a thing.

"Okay then," Vitri says. "Jesus Christ. I don't know what you want me to say. I really don't. But I want a son, and I want to have that son with you. I want you to be his mother. That's what these rings mean, isn't it? That together we'll bring something into the world? Something new, something that has an opportunity to thrive?"

"'Something new' doesn't have to mean a human, Vitri."

Silence.

Footsteps along the deck. Chatter from the fellow passengers. A butter knife clanging a glass; a toast being made.

"One son?" Vitri's wife asks.

"One son."

"Just one?"

"Just one."

"No girls?"

Vitri laughs. "I can't even handle you."

Vitri's wife smiles. Watches the river. "This son, what does he look like?"

"I don't know," Vitri says. He shrugs his shoulders. He thinks for a moment. "Fat, skinny, tall, short, blonde, brunette, it wouldn't matter. None of it would matter."

"And what if he was born disfigured? What if he came out of me with only one foot? What if he had Down syndrome?" Vitri's wife swivels her body so that all of it—her chest, her legs, her eyes—are facing her husband. "What if he was deaf? Or blind? What then?" She lets her questions linger. "Because, if we were to have this son, if were to give life to this Roy or Billy or John, that's what I'd want, Vitri. I'd want him to have something that would always alter the rules of the game. I'd want him to know from the start that the world has no good plans for him." She waits for his eyes to shift. Watches him nibble his lip. "A mother isn't supposed to want that for her child, is she?"

Somewhere inside the River Bar and Grill, a violin begins playing. *Doo-doo-daaahh-dah-doo-doo-daaahh-dah*, low, slow, sorrowful strings. A trumpet joins in, a trombone, a saxophone, percussion, until low and slow turns into high and fast, swinging, stringing into melody. The other passengers, the crew, all the smiles file inside, some of the women already swaying their drunken hips into their partners' groins. Vitri and his wife remain on the porchswing, neither appearing as if they intend to rise, eyes not on each other but directly in front of them. The paddlewheel. The river. The sun.

The AMERICAN QUEEN's riverlorian, a stout man with shaggy hair named Hank, begins closing the propped doors of the bar and grill. In doing so, he sees the couple on the porchswing. "Come on, you two, the ball's starting," he says. His voice reeks of feigned excitement, an act, a veil over the disdain he has for such events, the regularity he plays in them, the ignorance it induces of the reasons he feels anyone should board this vessel. "I have your mask right here." This is true. In his right hand he carries one black plastic mask.

"Thanks Hank," Vitri says, "but it's too nice out here tonight to pass up."

Pleasure stretches across Hank's face before he says, "Have a good one," and closes the doors, a smile that shows how refreshing it is to him to see someone more enamored with the natural offerings this boat can provide than they are with such a charade.

For an hour or so more, there, on the porchswing, Vitri and his wife will remain, silently, and blank, reserving their energy and emotion for when they stand and walk back to their suite, for when they throw themselves into one another, her face pressed against the wall, his hands so tight around her thighs that welts—the only physical wounds of the night—will remain for hours. Ten months from that moment, nearly to the day, a healthy son will be born. And, in six years, Vitri will be alone, on a cold floor, and naked, the memory turned to nothing by a flicker of light.

Eventually, and without signaling to Reyn, Vitri turns away from the AMERICAN QUEEN and walks back south, taking giant strides along the shore, peering at the enveloped river. He grabs an oblong chunk of wood and pokes the top layer, dragging grass and pine needles aside. Reyn walks behind and watches Vitri press the tip of the wood down further, into the second layer, which, in a matter of two seconds, snaps shut on the wood. Vitri pulls the chunk of wood out. On its tip: a bear trap, clamped.

Reyn watches Vitri toss it all to the ground, then grab another chunk from the gravel. As they walk south, Vitri drags more and more grass from the top layer of the river, exposing the occasional putrefied carp or catfish. Several more traps—bear, fox, coyote. Thirty or forty feet later, Vitri, struggling to accept that they cannot cross here, furiously tosses that chunk of wood as far east as he can, then presses on. Reyn follows several feet behind, looking back from time to time at the AMERICAN QUEEN.

cH. XIII

Piles of wood flank Vitri's feet. Chunks of all sizes. Enough to last the night. Yet Reyn, crooked arms overflowing already, continues to search the shoreline for more. She is frightened enough to practice avoidance. Vitri knows this. Understands this, but does nothing to ease her fear. Seated on a tree stump, he swivels to watch her bend, and crouch, her jeans inching further down her hips each time she does so. He sips the last of the tomato soup, then fills the empty can two-thirds full of water.

"Truth is, Reyn," Vitri says. He grabs a chunk of wood and, with it, shifts the burning logs. Flames leap from one log to the next, burning dark green for a few seconds before settling on orange. Blue-grey smoke spurts into the air. "I shot that man—I pulled the trigger without knowing who or what it was. Truth is, Reyn—" He sets the soup can in the gap he has created on the fire's floor, atop of and surrounded by glowing coals. He grows more comfortable with the idea of talking aloud, to everyone, and to no one: "—I haven't stopped thinking about him since we left. I'm worried that I killed him." When Reyn turns and approaches, Vitri averts his eyes from her.

Reyn unloads her armfuls of damp wood onto Vitri's piles, then half-circles the fire to sit on a shorter tree stump. Vitri watches her struggle to remove the raincoat, sweatshirt lifting while she does so. A glimpse of hip flexors. Flat stomach. Ribs. Bellybutton. Strung tight. He watches until she settles, until he can feel her eyes on him. He looks away. Watches the fire. Pokes the flame. When his eyes drift back to her, he cannot tell what her face is saying: wounded yes, scared, quiet, humbled, on edge yet still somehow optimistic, lips curling into the tiniest of smiles, some unique blend of resiliency he wishes he had a camera to capture, something that seems to say, "Throw what you want at me. I'll move forward."

In the picture, bruises would be mended, and cuts. He'd ask her not to wear makeup, but to pull her hair back into a ponytail, to get those strands out of her eyes and off of her cheeks.

WHEN WATER IS HOT ENOUGH, I'M GOING TO WASH UP

Vitri shows Reyn the message, and then reveals the boxed bar of soap he has pulled from his backpack. Reyn nods.

BEING DEAF DOESN'T MEAN YOU DON'T HAVE VOCAL CORDS

Reyn reads again. Nods. Nods as if she knows, as if she has always known but has opted for silence. She hands the notebook back. Stares at the fire.

HEARING YOURSELF TALK ISN'T ALL IT'S CRACKED UP TO BE ANYWAY

Reyn smiles. Motions for the pen.

WHAT DOES YOUR VOICE SOUND LIKE?

Vitri says, "Blah, blah, blah" and "Waco, Waco, Waco" over and over, each time slower, dragging out the words, splicing syllables never intended to be there.

LOW, DULL, BORING
FIGURED

Reyn smiles as she hands Vitri the notebook. Seconds later, she is on her feet and walking behind Vitri. She takes the scarf from his neck, then gently places her chilled fingers around his throat, fanning them from clavicle to larynx, searching for a sound.

"You don't want to do this," Vitri says, fighting the tingling sensation escalating in his groin, up through his core. He shuts his eyes, trying to think of the last time he has been touched like this. So gently. So curiously. *Over a year,* he thinks. *Well over a year. Well before the blackout.*

A bonfire in their backyard, his wife, tipsy from wine, taking a seat on his lap. Stroking his cheek as if it were the first time they'd ever been that close, able to be intimate among a small crowd.

As if she were through untangling the intricate coding of his throat, Reyn takes her hands off of Vitri. Back to the short tree stump she walks, smiling, sore cheek stretched as far as it can go. Back to the notebook.

THERE ARE LAYERS. DEEP, QUIET. IT'S NICE
THANK YOU
YOU'RE WELCOME

As the flame eats its way through different chemicals on the wood, it transitions from orange to dark blue. Accompanying the shift are several muted popping noises that sound like a tongue exploring its limitations—teeth, cheek, lips—click-clacking as if hard-shelled pockets are heat-sensitive and bursting. For Vitri, it is a welcomed noise, something to erode the awkward silence, the brief moment of nothing between he and Reyn. No writing. No shared gaze or glance. He instead eyes the soup can, hoping that the process can be reduced to mere minutes, that steam will soon struggle into the sky.

YOU WANT TO WASH FIRST?
I DON'T NEED TO

Reyn hands the notebook back and shrugs her shoulders. She guides loose hair behind her ear. Props her undamaged cheek with her palm. Anxious. Contemplative.

IT'LL MAKE YOU FEEL HUMAN AGAIN
YOU GO FIRST

Vitri reads. Nods. Rises. Grabs the boxed bar of soap with one hand and extracts the soup with the other. Around the fire he walks, and into the woods, twenty feet in, past wilting shrubs, past thin grey brush, to a tree stump he places the soup can upon. He looks back. Confirms that his body will be at least partially covered from Reyn. Proceeds to remove his boots and socks, setting them aside in their respective pairs. The big toe on his right foot is bent, and purple, and swollen, but he does not know why, cannot pinpoint where the injury occurred, or how. If he'd felt the pain previously, only now when he can see it does it become obvious. On the bottoms of his feet are popped blisters, dead skin like wrinkled bedsheets.

He removes the raincoat, the sweater, the grey t-shirt beneath, and, for the first time in days, looks at his bare torso. Pale, irritated, nipples soft, thumb-sized rashes glowing red, chest and belly hair matted. With how loose his pants have become, he spots sea green surface veins running through his abdomen and over his hips. He hasn't seen such veins since he was fit, and nineteen, and preparing for a cannonball into the community pool. He straightens his back, puffs his chest, eyes the veins at different angles. Feels his mind tiptoeing toward the last day he, the boy, and his wife put on their swimsuits. Nine months ago. The summer had turned hot. So damn hot. Their neighborhood: abandoned. Hope: fading.

"We can't just sit here," Vitri had said to his wife. He dripped sweat as he sat still.

"I've told you that more times than I can count, Vitri." Vitri's wife: exhausted. Sleepless nights. Almost a week without bathing.

"Finding something to do nearby to pass the time and moving thousands of miles away are not the same thing," Vitri said. "We can't just wither away in this house all day, every day. There's still a world out there."

They then asked the boy what he'd like to do. "Anything you want," they said. He emphatically opted for swimming. "Swimming it is."

Six doors down they went, to the Kendricks', one of many longtime neighbors who'd hightailed it out of Waco in the first weeks of the blackout. They walked across the front yard, Vitri ahead of his wife and son. He told them to stay put as he let himself in through the pool's gate and approached the pool ledge. The water had mostly evaporated, down to shin high. Bobbing in the shallow water was a litter of kittens. Calico fur, orange fur, pure black. Vitri hurried to grab the nearby net so he could fish them out, then—

Vitri fights the memory. Curls his toes into the forest floor; feels leaves crumbling in their vise. He lifts the soup can from the stump and dunks his fingers into the water. Brings his fingers to his left armpit, swipes up, down, across. Then the right. Then his face and neck and hair. Applies soap until suds run from his head to his chest, and down, to his waistband, where it soaks through to his underwear. He shivers. Tingles. Shuts his eyes. Breathes in the cool scent of the soap. He unbuttons his pants and proceeds to scrub the left side of his penis, the right, the top, the tip.

###

Stop it. It's a man with his shirt off. He has shoulder blades. He has a spine. Reyn stares at the still-evolving flames. Rubs her fingers along the goosebumps that, no matter what she tells herself, won't go away. *Stop it. That man hates you. Don't look at him. He hates you.*

When she gives in, when she finally does look at Vitri, his back is arched. His eyes are skyward. His right arm is chicken-winged and moving in rhythm—backward, forward, backward, forward, backward, forward, until his pants drop to his ankles and he stumbles to a tree trunk, left arm extended to prop himself. Reyn stands. Cranes her neck not in wonder, but in worry, that, like last night, he soon will be on the ground, in need of water, in need of rescuing. But then his right arm moves faster—backward-forward-backward-forward. He shivers. His back eases. The arm stops. He bends over. Pulls his pants up. Looks back. Sees Reyn. Stomps into his boots and, in one quick, imprecise movement, grabs all that he has temporarily discarded—the shirt, the sweater, the soap, the can—and walks toward the fire.

Reyn sits on her stump. Keeps her eyes on the flames until Vitri, still shirtless, is feet from her, pouring more water into the soup can. After setting the can back near the flame, Vitri puts his shirt on, then the sweater. He pulls from his backpack another pair of socks and, once he has slipped them on, one almond-scented candle. To light the wick, he straddles the fire and inches it close to a low-burning flame, water dripping from his hair and chin and onto the coals.

Once back on his stump, Vitri holds the candle close to his nostrils. Then, as if just realizing that Reyn is still there, across from him, he looks at her and smiles. Smiles wide. His face is different now. Relaxed. Eyes open, but drooped just so, loose, free. He sets the lit candle on the ground and reaches for the notebook.

I FEEL LIKE TAKING A WALK

RIGHT NOW?

BEST TIME

OK

GO WASH UP. I'LL WAIT

From shoulders to thighs, Reyn is panicking. She does not want to go for a walk. She does not want to wash herself anywhere near his view. What she wants to do is sit right here, on this stump, look Vitri in the eye, and shake her head no. He hovers over her, arms extended, handing over the cold soup can and the bar of soap. "Go on," his eyes say, "go ahead."

With little hesitation, she takes the items and, sloshing water as she does so, hurries to the treeline, looking back only to determine where she needs to go in order to be entirely concealed. Only when there are two modest oaks directly between she and Vitri does she set the soup can and soap on the ground. She intends to leave them there, to not touch them, to just stand here, counting the seconds as she kicks loose leaves, dabbing water on her face and hair before returning to the fire, feigning it all. Plans that, when peeking around the tree trunk, seem as if they would be successful—Vitri is occupied, eyes shut, candle beneath his nose—but plans that disintegrate as Vitri finds Reyn's eyes. Reyn turns. Backs herself against the tree trunk. Removes her shoes and socks. Yanks off her sweatshirt, tosses it on the ground. Dunks her fingers in the soup can, swipes her armpits first, and quickly. The tops of her feet, between her toes. Then her neck, cold water drizzling to her chest, soaking through her t-shirt and bra. More water. A scrubbing of her hair, of her face.

That's it, Reyn thinks. *That's enough.* Before she puts everything back on, she once again peeks around the tree trunk—only to see Vitri storming toward the woods, toward her, working to unbutton his pants as he does so.

She wants the pistol in her backpack. She wants RALPH's sickle. She wants to run. And she does. Barefoot, she does. She takes off, away from Vitri. Ten-fifteen-twenty feet before looking back, before seeing Vitri stagger to a halt before falling face-first into the dirt. Reyn slows. Waits to see if he'll push himself up, push himself forward, to the side, push himself somewhere.

But there he stays, his back rising, falling, rising-falling, quicker and quicker. Wary of this being some trick, some strange way to lure her to what she is convinced is her death, Reyn continues to watch Vitri.

Rise-fall, rise-fall.

Waiting for either his body or his will to expire. For moments Reyn stares, until, overcome only with what she could classify as pity, she slowly approaches, questioning each step, batting *Leave him* and *Help him* between her ears. When she is within ten feet, Vitri stirs. Barely rolls himself over. Upside-down, he searches for Reyn. Locates her. Tries to wave her over. Reyn stays put, watches his hands, judges the severity of this, whether or not the man once again deserves her assistance. Steps closer. And closer. Sees him motioning for what she interprets as, "water," a request she decides she can accommodate.

Keeping as much distance as possible between she and Vitri as she does so, Reyn walks to the soup can she left, grabs it, and returns to Vitri, setting the soup can not in Vitri's hand, but nearby, within reach. She backs away. Watches him clamber to the can, watches him tilt it, watches the water splash on his face. She crosses her arms. Glances from Vitri, to the fire, and back, wondering not whether she could help him get there, but if she should, a question answered by the pain in her tongue. *Get him to the fire*, she thinks. Reyn steps closer. And closer. *Then leave. Get him to the fire, then leave.*

Reyn slides her hands beneath Vitri and helps him roll to his stomach. Grabs the back of his sweater, anchors her weight to her heels, and helps lift him to his feet, quickly side-stepping herself beneath his arm before his quivering becomes severe enough to drop him back to the ground. Together, they turn around, Face the fire. Step forward. One step, two steps, three, Reyn feeling his breath as they do so, feeling his pulse, feeling through his arm the words he is trying to say. She glances at his mouth: "I'm lonely, Reyn. I've been so lonely."

Vitri points to leaves and grass off the edge of the tree line. Nods as if it is where he wants to be left. And so Reyn obeys. Helps him there. Waits for him to lift his arm from her shoulders and descend. But the arm is never lifted—as Vitri goes down, so too does Reyn, falling on top of him, flailing, writhing, but going nowhere. And then he rolls on top of her and she can feel his words on her ear, can feel his lips on her neck. She squirms, because she doesn't want his hands on her breasts. She shoves and kicks, because she doesn't want them unbuttoning her pants, doesn't want them slithering beneath the elastic band of her underwear.

cH. XIV

Vitri's fingers search for the grip of the 9mm. He draws the pistol but he does not aim it. The scarf is over his nose and mouth. His eyes are forward, squinting into the grey dawn light. Five hundred yards ahead, atop a gradual slope, are buildings. Buildings just built. There is the faint echo of hammer and nail, the occasional glimpse of an unmasked man walking alongside the structures. Vitri steps forward, the initial blend of confusion and terror quickly morphing to intrigue. But he soon stops once more. Watches. For moments, just watches. Listens to a small engine start. Turns around.

Reyn wakes naked and alone, fresh blood on her teeth and gums. Flakes of her tongue tickle the back of her throat. Dead grass sticks to her hair and back. Untended for hours, the fire is now a stunted heap of blackened wood.

She sits up. Slides on her underwear. Clasps her bra. Stands. Walks into the woods to retrieve the rest of her clothes, not once craning her neck, not once looking for Vitri. Because, sometime in the night—while beneath him, or while pulled close to his chest—she'd told herself to expect this.

As she does now, Reyn had thought then of the last time she saw her father. Actually saw him. Smelled him. Watched him. Wanted to hug him. She remembers that he'd risen earlier than usual for a breakfast shift, where she suspected he'd angrily flip pancakes, beat eggs and catch burnt toast with ceramic serving plates.

INSULT TO MY TALENT, he'd written to her once, on a similar day, to which he followed with: ONLY + IS HAVING AN ENTIRE NIGHT TO WASTE.

More often than not, she knew, this was a lie, Reyn's father returning home immediately after his shift, exhausted, unable to stay awake for dinner, choosing instead to lie on the living room floor, apron still on, hands laced over his gut.

There was something about night shifts, she knew, that invigorated her father, ignited him to give that street lamp a second purpose.

Yet, on the night she last saw him, Reyn remembers her father walking into the house sometime between six and seven, half-turned and smiling, leading through the doorway a petite woman with straight purple hair. She, too, was wearing an apron and she, too, smiled and she, too, looked at Reyn. And she waved. Which confused Reyn. Never had she seen this woman. Never had her father insisted upon her, or any of them, entering the home he shared with his daughter and wife-turned-roommate.

Though her mother was not in sight, Reyn, if she knew her as she thought she did, pictured an empty desk. An open back door. An overflowing ashtray on the rotting deck.

In that moment, however, Reyn, as cruelly as she could, waved back. Stiff hand up, stiff hand down. Because she was supposed to hate this woman. Regardless of hair color, regardless of clothes, posture, smile or frown, she was supposed to want her out of here, this *slut*, this *whore*, this *bitch*. Out, she was supposed to think, *get out of this house. Stop hurting my mother.* She was supposed to hate her father. *Pig. Scoundrel. Prick. Asshole.* Four words fluttering in her mind, but so intangible were they, so elusive, unable to be communicated by her even if grasped by a searching hand. There was just so much joy in him, something he'd openly transmit to Reyn when around, something she thought foolish to look at, to feel, and then deny, carrying on either in anger or envy. The best she could do on that night was look away. Ignore as much as possible—an abandoned tactic when Reyn, lounging on the sofa in sweatpants, caught out of the corner of her eye her father's pointing finger.

Don't, Reyn thought, *no. Just don't. Don't bring her over here. Don't leave me alone with her. Don't put me in that position.*

She waited for the inevitable, for the two of them to enter her line of sight, for her father to frame the purple-haired woman as if she were a prize he'd won at a carnival. For the purple-haired woman's mouth to flap a futile introduction. She waited. Five seconds. Ten. Twenty. She waited until caked dust pirouetted from the staircase's railing to the floor, until she could see the stairs bow under her father's steps.

When Reyn looked back at the front door, there stood the purple-haired woman, clutching her purse, anxious eyes on her black server sneakers, unsure of what she was to do, unsure of what was to happen next, the likelihood of this work-fling amounting to anything, whether or not Reyn's mother would emerge from a bedroom or closet with a knife or screwdriver. The image was enough to spur concern from Reyn. Not that her mother would do such a thing but that perhaps Reyn, too, was partially responsible for the purple-haired woman's anxiety, lounging there on the sofa, standoffish to the lonely woman at the door. A knot of sympathy began to swell in Reyn's stomach and, though she could opt to leave the living room altogether—sprint upstairs, to her father, to her bedroom, or outside, to her mother—within seconds Reyn was waving the woman over.

Registering as brown from a distance, Reyn could see that the woman's eyes, now under light, were closer to burnt orange; *a perfect complement*, Reyn eventually thought, to that hair, to those dark eyebrows, to that silver hoop through her bottom lip. Despite the odor of fried food, Reyn could smell the melon-scented perfume on the woman's wrists as she sat down. Faint, but noticeable. Despite exposure to splattering grease and fluorescent bulbs, her skin was smooth, and glossy, presumably prioritized ahead of her stained teeth when it came to hygiene. As she sat down, the purple-haired woman pulled from her purse a notepad the size of her hand. Then, a pen. She smiled as she wrote.

I'M FAYE

Aside from thinking the name pretty, and fitting, Reyn believed Faye's handwriting to mirror her physical appearance, both choices and genetics. She either didn't believe in, or was incapable of, straight lines, even the vertical line in her I curved, elegant.

I'M REYN

I KNOW. YOUR FATHER CAN'T STOP TALKING ABOUT
YOU.
WHAT DOES HE SAY?
TELLS ME HOW SMART AND PRETTY YOU ARE

Reyn pictured her father weaving around dishwashers and
prep cooks, chatting up his daughter. She pictured him on break,
puling out his cell phone, waving the servers behind the line to
show them the pictures of her reading, the pictures they'd taken
together—at the zoo, in front of the lion exhibit, at the very top of
a ferris wheel. In doing so, Reyn's cheeks began to tingle, to warm.
Flattered that the words SMART and PRETTY had been used but
embarrassed, with wonder, at the prospect of CAN'T STOP
TALKING ABOUT YOU.

WHAT ELSE?
HOW THOUGHTFUL YOU ARE. HOW GLAD HE IS THAT
YOU'RE MORE LIKE YOUR MOTHER

Faye must've seen Reyn's worry over the matter, or felt it,
understood it enough to smile as she asked for the pen back.

ALL GOOD THINGS, SWEETIE. ALL GOOD THINGS

In which Reyn found immense comfort. The warmth left her cheeks. A grin took hold of her lips and eyes.

DO YOU LIKE WORKING THERE?

HATE IT

WHY?

YOUR FATHER IS THE ONLY ONE THAT TREATS ME LIKE A PERSON

Though Reyn asked for her to elaborate, the request was met by a shoulder shrug from Faye. And, from there, their conversation took a nosedive when it came to substance. Faye's favorite color was, unsurprisingly, purple. She was twenty-six years old. Originally from New Orleans. Mother to one calico tomcat. Filler. All filler. Faye knew it was. Reyn knew it was. But, as Reyn saw it, it was the best thing to happen to her in that house for a long time. An informed outsider had entered, sat down, and had been patient enough for ten minutes of written small talk—an effort that made Reyn feel as if she had a friend outside of these walls. An effort that, when Reyn's father descended the last stair and turned toward the living room, doused her heart in sadness—this, Reyn knew, would be the only time Faye stepped foot in this house.

What made Reyn so certain was something beyond his slicked hair, beyond the clean-shaved face, beyond the khakis, beyond the tucked plaid button-up and dark brown loafers. It wasn't even his smile. It was in how Faye's smile mirrored his. Absolute joy, a reciprocal joy that neither Reyn or her mother could share with him. An understanding that need not be spoken, written, or realized pants-down at a lamppost. As if he were a model at the end of her runway, Reyn's father stopped near Faye, and playfully placed his hands on his hips before performing a spin. He looked at Reyn. Exchanged words with Faye. He then asked for the notepad and pen, passing it to Reyn once he was through.

WANT TO GO TO THE MOVIES?

Reyn wanted to. Wanted to nod her head, leap from the sofa, sprint upstairs, change, and sprint downstairs, to her father, to Faye, to the car, into the theatre, where she would watch them, and only them, not needing subtitles, not needing narration of any sort, inference and intuition more than enough to make sense of what was in front of her.

Before Reyn could do any of that, before she could even nod, her father turned. Faye turned. And there, between them, walking through the dark dining room was Reyn's mother. Slowly, arms crossed, mouth moving, eyes scanning the three of them. Guilt panicked within Reyn, shoulder to shoulder, waist to throat. She watched Faye snatch the notepad and put it back into her purse.

Saw her father straighten his back and puff his chest. Watched calm turn into chaos. Strained necks. Overworked jaws. Stamping feet. Screams. Arms and hands structuring individual arguments, deflating all others. And Faye, eyes down, more than just her feet guiding her to the front door.

Reyn eventually did sprint upstairs, to her room, but only to watch Faye and her father walk hand-in-hand down the street after Reyn's mother chased them off of the yard.

When her father didn't return the next day, or the next, or the next, or the day after that, Reyn knew that he was gone.

Gone, gone, gone.

And, each day afterward, she forcefed herself the idea that he and Faye were in love, that they had mutually realized that love, and that they'd ran off together to celebrate that love, to prove that love, to consummate that love.

All good things, Reyn thought. Revisited. Justified. Clung to. A thought, however, that would be disproved when, months from then, days after her mother drowned the Idaho postcard, they'd stop at a gas station that had within days of the blackout been sucked dry and Reyn would spot a purple-haired woman slumped against an overflowing dumpster.

Faye had died wearing a violet leather jacket and white pants. Bootprints were up and down her legs. Burnt orange eyes for all to see.

It isn't a mystery to Reyn why she thinks of Faye now. Her thighs ache. Saliva and wind have made her neck and nipples raw. Shards of pain stretch from groin to abdomen as she steps toward her sweatshirt.

You have been raped, she thinks, *used, abandoned, trampled.* A ginger-colored squirrel parked on a low-hanging branch seems to watch her as she dresses. *You allowed this to happen.* The box of bar soap has been shredded by the squirrel, the bar itself nibbled, corners rounded, flies, beetles and whatever else staking their claim. *Never again.*

After stomping into her shoes, Reyn turns to see Vitri sitting by that charred wood heap, atop a tree stump. Backpack: on. Scarf: on, and tight. Pistol: in his waistband, bulging both the thermal shirt and raincoat. Eyes: down. Thumbs: twirling.

Grab your backpack, Reyn thinks. *Grab the fucking backpack and leave.*

She fights through the pain in her groin in order to stand straight. Forces herself to the heap, staring at Vitri as she does so, unsure of what she and her body are expressing but hoping with every ounce of her that it will be interpreted by Vitri, should he have the nerve to lift his eyes, as something between rage and disappointment. She walks directly to her backpack and hoists it over her shoulder, intending only to obey the thoughts of *leave, leave, leave.* But when Vitri rises from that tree stump and steps toward her, the thin film of reluctance is torn by the same fury she felt before JOHN went beneath the Jeep. And that fury urges her to unzip the largest pocket of her backpack. It takes her fingers, wraps them around the nearest weapon, around the handle of RALPH's sickle. And it points the blade at Vitri. Dares him to take just one more step. *Just one more step.*

Whether it is the mere sight of the blade, or what it is he sees in Reyn's face—the enlarged eyes, the flared nostrils, just how tight she is holding that thing—Vitri stops. He holds up his hands. Takes a step back. And another. And another, until he rediscovers that tree stump. They stare at one another, Vitri changing posture only when Reyn breaks eye contact. He holds up his right hand, shapes his fingers as if they were holding a pen, scribbles in the air.

No. You had your chance. No.

He scribbles in the air again as if his initial message weren't received. But it was. Loud and clear. Reyn knows what he wants to write. He'll write what his deflated eyes put on display: I'M SORRY. He'll write, and she'll read, and he'll expect her to forgive, to forget, to provide him with what he thinks he needs. *No. Never again.*

Yet, she wants that SORRY, wants to see how difficult it is for him to write it, wants to see him acknowledge how he has mistreated her. Needs to see that. Needs to feel that, as small of a victory as it may be.

So she sets her backpack down. First exchanges the sickle for the pistol, which she holds loosely in her left hand as she plunges her right hand back in for the notebook. Still crouched, she hurls the notebook at Vitri as hard as she can. The pen follows, just as fast. She stands, watches Vitri pluck the pen from the ground and situate the notebook on his lap. Notices how easily the words bleed onto the page.

THERE'S A TOWN. THIS SIDE OF THE RIVER. TWO
MILES SOUTH

Reyn reads. Lifts her eyes. Lowers them, reads once more. Contemplates stowing the notebook and backing away, pistol aimed at his throat so he won't follow. She looks again at his eyes. *He wants to say it.* She shoves the pistol in her waistband, reaches for the pen. *He's going to say it.*

THAT'S ALL YOU HAVE TO SAY?
PEOPLE THERE. NO MASKS. BUILDING SOMETHING.
HEARD AN ENGINE

Reyn draws an arrow to THAT'S ALL YOU HAVE TO SAY? She delivers the notebook, steps back, re-grips the pistol.

I WANT YOU TO GO WITH ME

Reyn circles THAT'S ALL YOU HAVE TO SAY?

THEY'LL HAVE A PLACE FOR YOU. THEY'LL HAVE
FOOD, MAYBE BOOKS
THAT'S ALL YOU HAVE TO SAY?
DON'T CRY

She wishes she could help it, wishes she were stronger, wishes she could force the tears back to her eyes, wishes Vitri would sit back on the stump, wishes that he'd stop writing and walk on, *leave*, walk on, *go away*. But on he walks, toward her, arms extended so she can read.

I'M SORRY

Vitri steps closer and closer, until he is three feet from her. He holds the notebook steady. Studies her. Five seconds. Ten seconds. He slowly tosses the notebook to the ground and reaches his hand toward her. Reyn swats his forearm away. Grits her teeth. Raises the pistol. Shoves the barrel into his chest and walks him back to the stump. She motions for him to sit. She wipes her eyes and, without turning around, retrieves the notebook.

###

South. South again. South, for just a bit longer. South, for the last time, along the shore, under a clear sky, Vitri in front, Reyn forty yards behind, raincoat on, pistol in one hand, a stick in the other, unable to quell her curiosity of the traps she'd seen the day before. She pokes, she prods, she swipes dead grass and pine needles off the surface. A dozen feet from her, a kingfisher dives into what had been the river, its beak slicing through the topmost layer. But that is all. There it stays, spindly feet twitching, then motionless.

###

Reyn drops the stick. Carries herself forward, grimacing with each step. She hates this. Hates this shoreline. Hates this river. Hates that she's walking south. Hates that she still holds the pistol. Hates that she doubts she'd even use it. Hates that, at any given moment, she can turn around and walk north, or veer west. She hates that she hasn't, that, for upwards of two miles now, she has allowed herself to be led to what could be a lie. She hates herself.

There is no town, she thinks. *You fucking idiot. You have no idea what you're walking toward. You have no idea what you're chasing after.*

Reyn stops. Right there, she just stops, and sighs. She watches Vitri continue south. *You have no idea.*

She takes a deep breath as she watches Vitri, the smell of mold breached momentarily by something faint but sweet, berry-like. Forty-five yards are between them now, fifty, his eyes on the gravel, shoulders somewhat slumped. She wonders if he notices the absence of her footsteps, and continues anyway, or if he has decided that now is as good of a time as any to let her go. Fifty-five yards, sixty. Sixty-five. Reyn looks west. Woods. Thicker woods. Thicker trees, straighter trees, healthier trees than she has seen in some time, sickly grey and yellow leaves punctuated by small green ovals and spades, a path begging to be made through the budding fescue. She looks east, across the sludgy river. Trees, sure, but with space between, moderate clearings, gradual yellow hills rolling into faint shades of green.

There is enough distance between she and Vitri now that Reyn could blot his body out with a raised thumb. *I hope you get to where you need to go, Vitri,* she thinks. And she means it. She can't do this anymore. She won't. As she turns, she slips the backpack from her shoulders and shoves the pistol in the largest pocket. Facing north, feeling lighter, feeling weightless, she begins upshore at a quick pace, and with long strides, ignoring the pain in her groin and abdomen, digging into the gravel, shoving off with power, with optimism. To what, she isn't certain, but she intends to return to nothing—the rolled Jeep, her dead mother, that home on LaFontaine. Emotional suicide, she knows. Steps back. And so forward she goes. Fifteen yards. Thirty, thinking not of where she will go, but of what it is she needs to find, a search immediately stifled by the sight of three masked boys cresting a hill across the river.

Three boys. Northeast. Three boys, all with blue faces, blue legs and bare torsos, one tall and slender, one shorter and stockier. The last, trailing behind, stands no higher than Reyn's waist. For reasons unclear even to her, she does not run. She does not seek cover. She doesn't even tighten her grip on the pistol. She just stands there, watching as the tallest, carrying a shovel, no more than forty feet from their side of the river, starts digging a hole. The stocky one stands nearby and swings a white cylindrical pail to and fro, swaying either to something Reyn cannot hear, or something on repeat between his ears. The shortest boy twirls, then hops, then jumps, stopping only when his blue mask falls off and is swept away momentarily by a gust of wind. She watches him chase after it, bend over, pick the mask up with his left hand, place it back over his face and return to a standing position. She watches him notice her. Watches him raise his right arm, the stump she now sees it to be, amputated somewhere near the elbow. Watches him wave at her. Back and forth, back and forth, back-forth, back-forth, until turning to the other boys, who, Reyn sees now, are pointing at the sky. Without so much as one more glance at Reyn, the small boy sprints toward the other boys. The tall one lifts a stack of inch-wide silver circles from the ground and places them in the lone pail they'd brought. Over the hill they all then sprint, out of Reyn's sight. Only then does she look up.

At first, there is nothing. Clouds, high and swollen. One small bird skimming the western treeline. And then it is there, one large but quick shadow moving over her, over the river. A red and yellow plane flies low, flies northeast, a mist spreading from its tail, descending, arcing as the plane does, over the hills, over the trees. It circles southwest, releasing more of the mist as the initial supply reaches the ground, smelling, and tasting, to Reyn like some stale relative of vinegar. As she follows the plane with her eyes, she spots Vitri, sprinting the shoreline, fifty yards from her and closing, a sight that urges her to take off her backpack and dig for the pistol. Vitri slows to a walk. Plugs his fingers into the sky. Looks back, looks up, looks at Reyn as the plane approaches once more, and then waves his arms, waves his hands, all toward the western trees. He pulls his scarf down. Waves. Shouts. She reads his lips:

"Go! Run! Go! Now! Run!"

###

As it dives low, the plane's engine is so loud that Vitri cannot hear himself scream. He can only feel it, those long strings of sound from throat to armpit, dissipating when Reyn sprints to the woods, when he stops shouting, when it gives way to a chain of coughs. Though he struggles to maintain a straight line, Vitri follows Reyn, the blur she has become that not even a squint can focus. Forward. Forward. Forward, gasping for air between coughs. Forward, until he stumbles beneath trees. Until he is on his knees. Then on his cheek, pine needles sticking to his lips. He massages the earth with his fingers. Listens to the plane fly back and forth. High and low. Near, far. He shuts his eyes.

Vitri wakes on his back. Reyn stands over him with an uncapped water bottle in her hand. As soon as she sees that he is awake, she proceeds to drench his face with what water remains. He sits up. Spits. Smears water over his face. He figures he'll try to stand then but, when he sees that Reyn has sat on the ground, feet from him, notebook on her lap, there he stays, wiggling his legs awake, awaiting another swoop from the plane. Hears nothing. Sees nothing.

YOU'RE WEAK

Vitri nods. He nods again when Reyn waves the notebook in front of his eyes. Reaches for the pen but resorts to watching her write when she yanks it all away.

YOU'RE WEAK

"Yes, I am," Vitri says. He reaches for the notebook and pen once more. She pulls away. Writes hard, writes fast. In the days they've spent together, he hasn't seen her this driven, this certain, and though a part of him is impressed, he can't quiet the part of him that wants to rip the notebook and pen from her grip.

IS THERE REALLY A TOWN?

"Yes." Vitri nods as he says this. Convinced he's capable to move, Vitri pushes himself off the ground, progress stymied by Reyn, who rises and points at him. YOU SIT DOWN, the gesture says. I'M NOT FINISHED. Vitri does. And, like he'll do when they resume their trek to the town, when Reyn won't be able to stop turning her sight east, across the river, he is left only to think of what he'd say if she'd just pass the fucking notebook.

I MADE A MISTAKE. I NEVER INTENDED FOR LAST NIGHT TO HAPPEN. I NEVER INTENDED FOR ANY OF

THIS TO HAPPEN. I NEVER WANTED TO HURT YOU. I'M
A BETTER PERSON THAN THAT.

He'd write that her pointing the .22 pistol at his chest
reminded him that he'd done this before, that he'd driven away
someone like her, driven her to take her life and the life of their
son.

He'd write that he'd driven her to this, driven her to this
anger, to this hatred, and that it should've never gone this way. All
of them different variations of something he's already written, and
something she's already read, and something that won't repair a
goddamn thing: I'M SORRY.

WE LEAVE ONE ANOTHER AT THE TOWN

Vitri reads. Nods. Watches Reyn put away the notebook and
pen, stand, and offer him her hand. Once on his feet, he tightens
the scarf over his face, then stumbles forward.

cH. XV

Four buildings populate the west side of the town's lone dirt road. Marked in white paint on rotting plywood, feet above fruit pallets serving as doors, from north to south: McPHERSON's PUB, McPHERSON's HARDWARE, McPHERSON's CLOTHING and McPHERSON's ACCOUNTING, all constructed with bricks of varying color—dark red specked white, yellow-chipped blue, a green one here, an orange one there.

Between each building are narrow, two-foot-wide alleys cluttered with step-ladders and five-gallon buckets half-filled with what Vitri, drawing closer and closer, hand on his pistol's grip, confirms to be mortar. The road itself, though it dead-ends with cattails and tree stumps twelve feet after McPHERSON's ACCOUNTING, houses nothing. No debris, no gutted vehicles, no bodies, nothing but dirt, the occasional divot from which a boulder has been removed.

Walking alongside the fronts of each building, Vitri passes windows of all shapes and sizes—some tall, skinny and towering, some squared just larger than a postage stamp, others as long as his hand but as wide as he is tall. All are intact. Smeared, yes, with fingerprints, the sporadic palm, but clear and glared enough by the sun that Vitri has to press his face to the glass to peer in.

Barstools of varying heights are scattered within the pub, turbulently surrounding the mismatched café tables anterior to a bar of brick-supported plywood. Atop the shelves behind the bar are mason jars filled with clear and amber liquids. There is a four-spout tap.

The hardware store has hammers on hooks, cardboard shelves bowing beneath various tool belts, power drills and handsaws. A drill press seems to guard the door.

Inside McPHERSON's CLOTHING are separate displays of laceless sneakers and boots, dilapidated sandals. The two mannequins toward the back sport faded ball caps whose brands are illegible. Draped over their necks and shoulders are silk scarves and faux leather belts.

The east side of the road is scant in comparison, one modest brick building appearing lonely but somehow stout, equipped with a thick glass door and accompanying windows to its right and left.

McPHERSON's THEATRE, its sign declares and toward its doors walks Reyn.

Vitri watches her stop and gawk at the posters hanging in each window. *Citizen Kane. The Man Who Shot Liberty Valance.* Action stills. A black and white Orson Welles gripping a podium. An armed Jimmy Stewart. He watches her resume her stride, and though he cannot pinpoint what triggers it, something in Vitri shifts. The whole thing shifts. Replaced is the river with the distant cityscape of Waco. Gone is the gravel; beneath him is asphalt. Beside him is his truck. The theatre is reduced to a one-story schoolhouse, the glass doors of which capture a fogged reflection of his son's curious face. One month ago. The last time the two of them were alone.

"He asks about you," his wife had said the night before, bundling herself in a quilt before lying on her and Vitri's bed, beside their sleeping son. "About where you go."

"What do you tell him?" Vitri asked, situating his own makeshift bed on the carpet.

"I tell him what you tell me." She then rolled to her stomach. Laid her cheek on the pillow with no apparent intent to respond.

Vitri sat on the foot-end of the bed. He placed his hand on her covered calf. Contemplated telling her what he'd done that day after she yanked her leg away. That, like many other days, he'd driven to the junkyard and, as quietly as he could, switched out the half-filled excrement drums for emptier barrels and five-gallon pails. That, as he scooped out canned peas with his fingers, he watched the sad Brazos flow around a Geo Metro impaled by the sharp edge of a downed log. That at dusk and from a distance he watched a single file line of people enter a church. That within moments the church was aflame. That the only person that exited was a woman that flung herself to the ground and rolled.

"Which is?"

"Nothing," Vitri's wife said. "I tell him you do nothing. Just like we do nothing."

"You can't tell him that."

Vitri's wife rolled back over, her eyes barely visible in the dark. "What else would you call it?"

"Surviving, that's what I'd call it."

"No. You wait, Vitri." She said this with an ease that signaled to Vitri that she'd ran the thought through her mind over, and over, and over. "That's what you do. You wait for the world to tilt back to normal. You wait for people you know to return." She rolled back over. "You just do it in a different part of town than we do."

Vitri began tallying the hours he'd spent in thought, the afternoons at Cameron Park, sitting amongst the tall grass and weeds, feet from where he'd proposed to her, the mornings he'd attempt to siphon gas from the same cars on the same streets, in case gallons had magically appeared overnight, how he'd sit on the curb after one or two and feel sorry for himself, pity evolving to guilt, guilt evolving to worry, worry to—

He woke his son early the next morning. Staved off his own anxiety as he led his son to the truck and did his best to demonstrate how he wanted him to lay on the floor, tucked beneath the glove compartment. Drove to the rural schoolhouse, something Vitri justified was both new and familiar to the boy. Felt pride in how his son, despite the amount of dust, treated each and every abandoned object with respect—the reams of paper, the books, the calculators, the rulers, the chalkboards.

And Vitri felt joy, in how, on the drive home, his son, tucked beneath the glove compartment, giggled at each pothole Vitri rumbled over with the S10. And Vitri laughed, and Vitri swerved, and the boy giggled harder, and Vitri laughed harder, and they both seemed to, just for a moment, forget all that had—

Vitri is forced to re-enter the present when Reyn tugs at the doors of the theatre, causing its locks to rattle, its glass to jiggle. She tries again, and again, and again, leaning her weight back, back so far.

Stop, he thinks. *You're being too loud. Stop.* He wills his legs to move. Walks across the road, to her. Fifteen feet away. Ten. Eight.

"Hey!" a voice from behind Vitri. A man's voice but cracking, low to high, bass to tenor. It's a voice that hasn't been stretched this far in some time. "Take your hand off our fucking door!" Footsteps follow the voice, gravel embedded between treads.

Vitri grips the 9mm as he turns, slowing only when he sees that it not just one man, but two, fifteen feet apart and walking toward the theatre, arms outstretched, pistols aimed. One is auburn-bearded and in a loose white tank and blue jeans, the other clean-shaven and wearing camoflauged cargo pants and a black baseball cap. Behind them, the door to McPHERSON's ACCOUNTING is open.

Reyn continues to tug.

"Tell her to stop," the black baseball cap says, voice deep, heavy, and smooth, rolling off his tongue with the subtlest of southern drawls.

Vitri reaches out to Reyn. Taps her on the shoulder. She turns around and, upon seeing the two men, juts her arms into the sky. *Two*, Vitri thinks. Two bullets left in the 9mm. Maybe three. *Enough*, he thinks, *enough if well-placed*.

The two men stop in the middle of the road, twenty feet away.

"Toss out the boom stick," the bearded man says. "Toss it on the ground or, we shit you not, we will shoot."

There is no hesitation. Vitri tosses the 9mm to the dirt. Looks at Reyn. Her hands are still in the air. Her eyes are fastened to the ground.

"Smart man," the bearded one says. Later, Vitri will look at the man's thick head of hair and think of high tide, it looking like some rust-colored wave crashing on his right ear. He keeps his pistol aimed as he closes the gap between he and the black-capped man. The tattoos on his shoulders have faded to grey and are crisped over by peeling skin.

The man in the black cap shoves his silver pistol in his hip holster. Approaches Vitri. His eyes are two hazel stones dropped in a still pond, wrinkles rippling down his cheeks. "What color are you?" he asks, grabbing Vitri's scarf. His hand smells of shaving cream. There is a nick along his upper lip seeping red.

"What color?" Vitri asks.

"Yeah, motherfucker, what color are you?" The bearded man presses the barrel of his pistol to Vitri's temple.

"Aggression's the obvious answer, isn't it?" The man says to his partner. He takes off his black cap. Squints into the sun. Rubs his hand over his thinning scalp. Puts his hat back on. "Jesus, back off a little, would ya? They're complying." he says to the bearded man. "Pick up his gun." Seeing that his partner has obeyed, he then reaches out his hand. "What's in the backpack?"

Vitri slowly slides the backpack from his shoulders. "I carry the weapons," he says. Without looking at Reyn, he adds, "She carries the food."

The man in the black cap unzips Vitri's backpack and inserts his hand. "You're the armory," he says to Vitri, "and she's the diner. That's cute."

The bearded man shoves Vitri's pistol in his waistband. Stares at Reyn. "Bullshit," he says. Steps toward her. "Give me that fuckin' bag."

"What did I just say?" the man in the black cap says. "Calm. The fuck. Down." He shoves Vitri's toothbrush into the front pocket of his cargo pants, returns the backpack to Vitri, then proceeds to graze his hands over all of Vitri's pockets, the only sound that of paper crumpling. "Just pat her ass down." He finds Vitri's folded knife. Places that into a different pocket. "You heard the man—they ain't masked—so stop being so damn disrespectful."

Crouched to Reyn and ignorant of his partner's shaking head, the bearded man pats down Reyn's shoulders and torso, hips and legs. He points at the bruise on her cheek. "He do that to you, sweetheart?"

"Her name's Jane," Vitri says.

"I asked her, not you," the bearded man says. His smile is ear-to-ear, but crooked, the right side of his face dominant, the left less flexible.

"She can't respond," Vitri says. "Didn't hear you either." He nods at Reyn. "Deaf mute."

The bearded man stops. Backs away. Looks at Reyn as if she were a defective toy to be boxed up and shipped back to its manufacturer.

"Daughter?" the man in the black cap asks.

Vitri nods.

"Who did that to her face?"

"Two masked men."

The man in the black cap nods. Crosses his arms. Anchors his weight to his heels. "Color?"

"Red."

"They can do a number," the bearded man says. "Still. Pretty girl."

"What's your name?" the man in the black cap asks.

"Pete."

"And where are you two headed, Pete?"

"Florida."

The man in the black cap goes to talk, but cannot find the words. He opens his mouth. Two of his teeth have decayed to grey. Closes his mouth without a sound. He turns to the bearded man. "Hear that?"

"I heard 'em." The bearded man spits on the gravel.

###

"Florida's gone, Pete," the bearded man says, who introduced himself as Ogden moments ago. He leans over a map of North America he has unfolded atop the metal desk on the southern side of McPHERSON'S ACCOUNTING. From panhandle to gulf, a large black X signifies the state's demise. The Great Lakes are shaded in. A third of Canada. The northern three-quarters of Mexico. All of the northeastern seaboard.

"Gone?" Vitri says.

Ogden straightens his back. Folds his arms. Shakes his head. "You ever see pictures of the drill they supposedly used to dice up that asteroid?"

Vitri nods. Recalls the covers of magazines, video clips of newscasters climbing into a space simulator. Remembers how absurd he thought the ensuing panic was, the urgency to buy products that, if an asteroid of that magnitude did hit, the consumers wouldn't be alive to use. Remembers comparing it at the time to the Y2K scare he lived through as a kid. Thinks now, albeit briefly, of how much his eyes had aged from one to the next.

"They wheeled that motherfucker in, lined her up at the border and let her rip. Never seen so much goddamn dirt chewed up in my life. Piles of it," Ogden says. "Mountains of the shit."

Vitri, flanking the map, looks at Bass, the man in the black cap, who sits in a leather office chair behind an identical metal desk. "You both saw this?" Vitri asks, careful of how much disbelief he reveals in his tone.

Bass nods at Ogden.

Ogden points at a small tattoo halfway up his forearm, the two ascending jets faded with time and sun, more like ravens than jets at all. "Air National Guard," he says. His voice slips into imitating a superior's orders. "'Gear up. Report to route whatever-the-fuck.' That's all we did: patrol the goddamn roads with our rifles, redirect the curious, send them on their concerned way." He pauses. "We heard the drill, sure—fuckin' thing sounded like it had the power of a thousand chainsaws. Shook the whole fucking earth. But none of us thought anything of it until we saw those mountains of dirt, until they told us to move north, to new roads. See, they hauled that shit miles north of the border. Dumped it all. Created some kind o' wall. After a while, we didn't hear it anymore. Couldn't leave, though. God no, we couldn't leave. 'Stay put,' they said. 'Job ain't over.' So we stayed."

Vitri glances at Reyn, who stands alone near the western wall, peering down the narrow hallway that leads south. He watches her gaze at the magazine clippings stapled to the walls. Centerfolds of long-legged brunettes, snippets of petite blondes with perky breasts. She leans down to inspect the three plastic crates on the hardwood floor, one overflowing with canned goods, another with syringes, some empty, some not, looking just like those he'd pulled out of her backpack following her beating from the red-masked men, those he'd emptied into the trashcan fire. The last crate contains a pile of assorted masks. Leather, plastic, even metal. Red and yellow, green and blue.

"Martinez was the one that saw the drilling from the air," Ogden says. "Watched its pieces pulled across the gulf. 'Tugboats the size of Connecticut,' he said."

"Martinez was a pilot," Bass says. "*Is* a pilot." He grabs a jar of Vaseline from the windowsill and sets it in the top drawer of his desk, then fiddles with the loose back of his chair. He waits for something from Vitri, for anything, a nod, a question, a laugh. "You think I can't see 'bullshit' written all over your face, Pete?"

"I," Vitri starts, throat noosed by the words he hopes can justify his expression, "I just—how long ago did this happen, the drilling?"

Ogden scratches his bearded chin as if it will help him articulate what his memories are whispering. "Eight months, maybe nine. Me and Martinez, well me and Martinez—"

"Where is he anyway?" Bass asks. He stands. Adjusts his belt. "Should be here by now."

"Martinez ain't no marathoner," Ogden says. "You know that." He adjusts his posture as if he were intending to elaborate upon the story of Florida.

"Well, we can't finish that cellar without him, can we?"

Vitri thinks of the planes. Of cargo being dropped. Of chemicals. Of this Martinez at the controls.

"He'll be back soon, Bass."

Bass, looking out the open front door as if Martinez will suddenly appear, says: "Soon isn't good enough when you're behind schedule." His tone shifts, from one of authority to one of anger, to jealousy even, at the notion that Ogden has had the floor for so long. "One day we're having our shit stolen by those blue fuckers, the next we're—"

"That was one goddamn time," Ogden interrupts. He shuts his eyes momentarily. "One time."

Bass looks at Vitri. "This bastard," he says, "one day, hmm, a month or two ago, decides it's in our best interest to start trading with those kids—you've seen 'em, right? Boys, blue masks? Four or five of 'em just across the river?"

Vitri shakes his head.

"No shit?" Bass looks at Ogden, who, seeming to know where this is going, leans against the nearest wall and crosses his arms. *Go on with it*, his posture says. *Get it out of your system.* "Well, one day, when me and Martinez are gone lugging gas God knows where, all of 'em come here." He points toward Reyn, toward the narrow hallway. "Because Ogden's lazy ass is napping in the back room, they startle him when they pound on the door. *Boosh-boosh, boosh-boosh, boosh-boosh.* And Ogden, as he tells it, says he got up, rifle in hand, ready to blast whoever the fuck was there. But when he opens the door, there they are, carrots in hand. Radishes. Even goddamn broccoli."

Vitri nods, though he, having not heard a person verbally go to these lengths since Hammer, processes little. *Slow down*, he thinks, overwhelmed by the voices, the words, the rapidity, the rambling, the conjuring of pointless memories. Wonders what it is that drives a person to open up to a stranger, whether it's a desire to fill the silence, or if they think the feeling of isolation can be hidden behind mountains of words. Because he can see loneliness in both Ogden and Bass. He can hear it. They've heard these words before; they've spoken these words before; these words are at once what keeps them feeling lonely and what makes them feel loved.

"And Ogden sees no problem with it. Thinks, 'Hmm, those veggies look pretty damn tasty,' and, I mean, I can't fault him for that. Not at all. They *were* good. And eating these days is a crapshoot. But as Ogden's doing all this, as he's handing the kids some chunks of wood, some nails, whatever, the smallest little bastard's across the street, climbing in and out of the goddamn theatre and—"

"—Stealing reels," Ogden interjects. "Armfuls of those silver cans."

"So," Bass continues, annoyed, "It takes five minutes or so for Ogden to realize it's going on at all. When he does, off go the three that were standing in front of him, just bounding down the shore there, tiptoeing across that river on that support we spent three weeks on."

"I got his ass though, didn't I?" Ogden says to Bass. He looks at Vitri. "Snatched up the little fucker, brought him back here."

"Cut his arm off." Bass straightens his right arm and motions his left hand as if it were a cleaver, slicing where ulna meets radius. "Wasn't very clean either."

"Didn't need to be," Ogden says.

Vitri looks at Reyn. Wishes she'd stop touching those masks. Silence.

"He died then, the boy?" Vitri asks. He feels like he is at the store again, behind the counter, letting customers talk, stoking their conversational fire with questions he doesn't need the answer to.

"I see him every now and then," Ogden says. "He just does his own thing, really. All of them do. Wander around, grow their food, dig their holes—"

"These ones wouldn't hurt a fly if it landed in their palm," Bass says. He nods to Reyn. "Not at all like the savages that did that number to her face."

"Savages," Ogden says. "That's what those reds are. Fucking savages."

"Yes, yes they are," Bass says. "Good to have for war, though. Kicking the shit out of the yellows as we speak."

"Yeah?" Vitri asks.

Bass nods. "You bet."

In silence, the three men watch Reyn by the crates. Until Reyn notices their gaze and stands.

"Marines and SEALs locked down the internationals," Ogden says from behind the McPHERSON's PUB bar. He carries over two mason jars—one of dark beer, one of light—and sets them in front of Reyn and Vitri. "Us? We were posted at local airports. Sometimes regional."

"Thank you," Vitri says to Bass. Then, to Ogden: "Why airports?"

"The blackout, as I'm sure you noticed, threw everyone into a tizzy," Bass says. He watches Ogden step back behind the bar and grab two shot glasses and a bottle of bourbon. "Sounds like you were one of the smart ones and stayed home, but, for the first few weeks or so, wave after wave of people would drive to the airports. New Orleans, Orlando, Birmingham, wherever the fuck else, there they'd be, assuming they could barter for a flight, that, with as little as a few dollars that would become worthless within hours, they'd be able to bribe some pilot into taking them out of the country." After Ogden sits down, Bass grabs the bottle of bourbon and pours himself a shot. Downs it. "And, well, there Ogden would be."

"Orders were simple: protect the airport." Ogden follows suit, takes a shot. "If people drove up, were civil in asking us questions, we'd tell them to fuck off and go on their merry way. And they would. Nobody really put up a fight. But if they came in numbers, if they approached aggressively, orders were to take them out. Neutralize them."

"And if they somehow broke through the lines," Bass says, "if they reached an aircraft with someone competent enough to fly the damn thing, that's where Martinez would come in."

"He'd circle all day. Make his rounds. Refuel. Make his rounds, refuel."

Vitri sips the dark beer. Flat, homemade, bitter. Thinks only of Carmen, at sea, treading water after leaping from the edge of a floating landmass. Pictures her somehow escaping the state before the drilling. He nudges the other mason jar toward Reyn. "Did you ever—?"

"Kill anyone?" Ogden says. He pours another shot. "No. Like I said, people were pretty civil about it all. Then again, word spreads, you know? People tend to wise up once they see or hear one or two go down."

"None of this happened in—" Bass pauses. "Where are you two from?"

Vitri looks at Reyn. She sniffs her beer, rotates her glass. Sniffs it some more. "San Antonio."

"Nothing of the sort there?"

"If there was, we didn't see it. Certainly didn't see anyone digging up the border."

"It'll happen," Bass says. He downs another shot. "You just wait. It'll happen. Louisiana's next and I assume they'll just keep working their way west, treating the land like it's a fucking jigsaw puzzle." He pours more bourbon.

Ogden starts laughing, but not at Bass. "First drink with the old man?" he says, referring to Reyn's scrunched face.

Vitri forces a smile, though it pains him to see how hard Reyn is trying to keep the beer in her mouth. "This is a first, that's for sure."

"How old is young Jane anyway?" Ogden asks. His crooked smile reappears.

Vitri doesn't know. He realizes he has never asked. Refuses to look at Reyn. *Has to be fifteen.* "Sixteen," he says, more for himself than anyone else at the table. Because it hits him in a painful way, what he did last night. What he's done to this girl, this kid. He looks down. Sips his beer.

"Only kid?"

Vitri nods.

"And deaf to boot?"

Vitri nods.

"Jesus," Ogden says. "Got yourself a pretty little wife though, I suppose?"

Don't fucking go there. "I did, yeah," Vitri says. He stares into the mason jar. Pictures her lying in that shallow hole, entry wound just above her ear. *Don't fucking go there.* Hair stained red, coyotes' teeth stained red, all stained red.

"How'd she go?" Bass asks.

Vitri fidgets in his chair. *Bullet.* Scratches his neck. *Suicide.* Announces as confidently as he can, "Savages. Unmasked. But savages."

"Fuckin' savages," Ogden says.

"Savages," Bass says.

They all take a drink. Even Reyn, though her reaction is delayed.

Silence.

Vitri watches Ogden lift his right arm and scratch his armpit. Inches beneath the clump of auburn-colored hair are small groupings of scars, all pink and no wider than a pen's point. He clears his throat. "This is great, guys. Really, thank you," he says. He watches Ogden and Bass nod their responses. "I think that what you guys have done here is beautiful. Beautiful work. I guess what I'm not understanding is, well, I imagine this has taken a long time. Gathering the materials, raising the walls with only three men—"

"Gonna be a while before we get it just right, too," Bass says. "River has to dry up a bit more but, when it does, we're heading north. We're heading east. We're expanding."

"Bridges," Ogden says. "Gazebos."

"Have us some plans for a restaurant, a grocery store, even a hotel." Bass doesn't bother pouring himself another shot. Swigs from the bottle instead. "I'm being rude, though. Before I cut you off, it sounded like you were going to ask us a question." Bass doesn't bother to look at Ogden. *Ask me*, his stare says. *Ask me.* "What's your question, Pete?"

"Why?" Vitri says. "Why do it?"

Despite his low, heavy voice, Bass's cackle is piercing.

Ogden has no reaction.

"I'm sorry," Bass says. "Before I answer that," he says, leaning forward, "can I ask you a few questions?"

After sipping from his beer, Vitri works to mirror Bass. Shoulders hunched, leaning forward. "Sure."

"Just looking at you," Bass says, "my guess would be that you're somewhere in your thirties. Upper thirties, mid-to-upper. But how old are you?"

"Forty-two."

"And what was it you did before this lovely continent of ours turned to shit? Did you sit in a cubicle and crunch numbers, populate the fuck out of a spreadsheet? Were you one of those 'prompt engineers'? One of them 'social media specialists'?"

"I owned and operated a store."

"What kind of store?" Bass asks, eyebrows narrowed, upset that he was off in his assessment. When Vitri points to the scarf on his neck, Bass smiles. "Still sporting your own brand, huh? Now that's dedication." He raises his shot glass to Ogden, though Ogden pays little attention, eyes flickering at Reyn every few seconds. "You build the store from the ground up then?"

Vitri shakes his head. "Parents did. Passed it down to me when they'd had enough."

"Sounds about right," Bass says. His tone says he has rediscovered comfort, a comfort that comes with a correct assessment. "See, and my guess is that you had yourself a small staff, if any staff at all, and that, by the end of the day, by closing time, you, exhausted Pete, were ready to tap out, throw in the towel. You were ready to have that fucking store demolished, am I right? I mean, just how much time were you able to devote to little Jane over there? An hour on Sundays? Maybe two?"

"Still wish I'd had more," Vitri says.

"And how about your pretty wife? How many times you fuck her each week?"

Silence.

"Never enough, right?" Bass takes another swig from the bottle. "And that's my point. Don't go feeling bad about it, because that was me, too." Another swig. "I don't do it often, Pete, and I don't do it for many, but I'm going to let you in on something, something a little more on the personal side. See, for nine years I worked construction. Had this shit boss named Thompson that paid me what he deemed I was worth to tweak strip malls, to build China Woks and Red Woks and Blue Woks and any kind of Wok you can think of. I built chicken shacks, and I built massage parlors, and, well, I built whatever else I was told to build."

Vitri notices Bass's hands then, dirt-crusted calluses along each palm, a festered blood blister on the stretch of skin between his right thumb and index finger, a large grey oval needing only a pin prick to burst red.

"By year nine, I was pretty damn good. Had lived beneath that line they call poverty all my life so I appreciated my raises, the one-percents and the two-percents, the small handouts that keep the desperate coming back. Still enjoyed some aspects of the job, too. Enough not to tell Thompson to fuck off and quit, at least. Well, one day, I get one of these handouts. Unexpectedly, no less. Just some Tuesday or Wednesday, Thompson drives out to the strip mall me and my crew were at, finds me, and says, 'You can cut out early today. You deserve it.' And, you know what? I did deserve it. I took that money, I got in my truck and I went home, thinking that, hey, tonight we'll celebrate a bit. I'll take my wife and boys out to dinner and a movie. Didn't even matter where we ate, or what we saw. Didn't make the slightest of fucking differences to me." Bass sighs. "So I go home, to the two-bed-two-bath we could afford, and what do you think I find when I get there?" Bass pauses. Refuses to blink. "I walk in and I see two men fucking my wife. Right there, on the living room sofa. And I go numb. I mean, I go can't-even-shut-the-door-behind-me numb. I just watch. But then, to my left, I hear a voice—I hear my youngest whisper, 'Dad.' So I look, and there, beside him is his brother. Both are just standing in the hallway, seeing all this. So I go ballistic. I take the ball-point hammer from my tool belt and beam one of the guys in the back of the head. The other one pulls out of my wife and proceeds to beat the hell out of me. In front of my cheating wife, in front of my sons, still hard, boner swinging all over the damn place." Bass's stare becomes distant, the memory still vivid, the wound still open.

"I'm sorry to hear that," Vitri offers.

Bass waves off Vitri's apology. "No need. Past is the past, right?" He leans in. "That doesn't mean that I didn't spend months trying to find the why. That's what we do, isn't it, try to find the why? Even if it isn't there, that's what we look for, omitting the when, the what and the how. Pointless. Dog chasing their tail kind of shit. But, with my wife, there was a why. There was a reason why she did what she did. There was a reason why she won custody. There was a reason why she moved to Missouri." Bass pauses. The reason is routine."

"Routine?"

"Routine," Ogden says.

"My routine," Bass says. "For nine years, I'd be up and gone by six to some job site, never to be seen by or heard from until seven, even eight on some nights. Did I have to do that? Did I have to work those hours? No. Hell no. I could've shortened it by at least a few, told her to find some work, enrolled the boys in a day care. But did I? Nope. I wanted her to watch the kids. I wanted to be the bread-winner. I wanted to be the lone supporter of the family. Just like my dad. Just like his dad. Blah fucking blah." Another swig from the bottle. "So what was she supposed to do? Cook all damn day? Call her friends while they were at work? No. Not a chance. Took me a while to realize that. Took getting fired. Took telling my lawyer I couldn't afford him. Took several hours spent alone. But, when I did, I started my own business. Worked whenever I wanted to, whenever I needed to, whenever I felt like it. World started going under. Last phone call I made was to Ogden."

"Came here as soon as I could," Ogden says.

"Yes, yes, you did," Bass says. He punctuates his gratitude with a swig from the bottle, which, between the two of them, is half-gone.

Unlike before, Vitri is not lost in this conversation. He just doesn't know what to say. His question hasn't been directly answered, but he doesn't know how to ask it again. He watches Bass's hand briefly. How he bounces his index and middle fingers on the table makes it seem that he is craving a cigarette.

"I'll tell you what, though," Bass says to Vitri, "that whole thing, that whole fucking mess made me a better person. You want to know why? You want to know *that* why? Huh, Pete, do you?" When Vitri still utters nothing, Bass leans in closer. "Ask me how."

"How did it make you a better person?"

"It taught me just how malleable we are. Torqued to fit a scheme some fucker thought up from his gravestone, until we don't know how to take a step back and examine the big picture, until we blindly accept that mediocrity." Bass leans back. Crosses his arms. "We're resistant only when our routines are challenged. Which makes for quite the cluster fuck in a time of crisis. 'The world's gone to shit,' we say, looking back fondly on those long ass drives to work, that shitty gas station coffee we sipped. But, really, so fucking what if the world's gone to shit? So fucking what?" Bass takes one last sip from the bottle of bourbon, then plugs the opening with its stray cork. "It doesn't for one second mean that your life has to go to shit along with it. Know what I'm saying?"

I don't. "I do," Vitri says, eyes on the cork, hoping it means that this will soon be over, that in moments Bass will rise from the table, then Ogden, and send he and Reyn on their way. "I really do."

"I'm glad you do," Bass says. "But I don't believe I've given a proper answer to your question. You asked me why, why we're doing this, you asked what the fucking point was. And though I can only speak for myself here, the answer is quite simple: as an assimilating man of a confused society, I had everything taken from me. My home, my wife, my children, my livelihood. Just gone, like snow in June." Bass leans forward. "You just wait. Soon enough we'll be out to sea, sold to goddamn Spain, Sweden, Japan, whatever other country that's been salivating since our plug was pulled. What will we have when we're being pulled through the waves? *This* is what we'll have. *This.* We're taking home with us."

Ogden breaks the silence: "Bass always says, 'Turn the world upside-down and you give the wounded man an opportunity—to shape what's left into whatever he wants.'"

Bass smiles at his own words being repeated back to him.

Vitri looks from Bass to his beer, from his beer to Reyn, who stares at the ceiling.

"Boy should've run for mayor," Ogden says.

###

Ogden locks the pub after Vitri, Reyn and Bass walk out to the road. The sky is clear, the sun high, looping toward night. Bass leads them all toward McPHERSON'S ACCOUNTING once more, where Reyn and Vitri's few belongings remain.

"If I were you two," Bass begins, without turning to acknowledge them, "I'd turn right around. Head northwest. They say Seattle hasn't been touched yet."

"Seattle? Really?" *I'm not going to Seattle. Not for a second. I'm not going west.* Whether Reyn comes along or not, he'll walk north, if only to allow Ogden and Bass to believe they'd made an impact, and then he'll turn east. Somehow, he'll cross the river, and, somehow, he'll cross into Florida, and, somehow, he'll find Carmen. He'll do it. Over an hour of wasted words won't alter his aim.

"Really," Bass says, then stops. Turns around. "You two go on ahead. We'll be right there." He steps to the side and waves Reyn and Vitri forward.

Which strikes Vitri as odd only after they have passed, when he looks back to see Ogden and Bass, halted, and whispering, words unintelligible from a dozen feet away. Vitri stops. Reyn continues, looks back at Vitri once she reaches the door.

More whispers.

As politely as he can, Vitri clears his throat, then says, "We're hoping to cover some ground before sundown."

More whispers. More. And then, as slowly as their voices heighten, Ogden and Bass start walking.

"I just think she's getting a little antsy is all," Vitri says. "Not used to this."

"Oh, I don't think Jane looks antsy at all," Ogden says, continuing toward Reyn.

"Before you two do take off," Bass says, "me and Ogden here have a proposal."

Vitri's mind jolts from one possibility to the next, from Bass asking he and Reyn to stay and run one of the stores, to Bass enlisting their help for the construction of that gazebo.

"What would that be?" Vitri asks.

Ogden steps closer to Reyn; Bass steps closer to Vitri.

"It's important to note, Pete," Bass says, "that what we want from you is going to happen whether you accept the proposal or not. The reason we're proposing anything is, well, we were just talking, and you seem like a good man, Pete, a smart man, a man who understands trade." When all Bass receives from Vitri is a squint, he continues, "What I mean to say is that, despite all that's happened to this here land, Ogden and I still believe that there's a time and a place that civility must be maintained. And this is just such a time. We believe that a father's consent is important."

"Bottom line is that neither me or Bass here have been able to take our eyes off your daughter."

Bass glares at Ogden. "What he means is that, well, women don't come through here very often."

"And when they do, they're always two days from death," Ogden says.

"Would you shut the fuck up, please?" Bass says. "You're making a goddamn fool of yourself." He returns his eyes to Vitri. "It's also important for you to know, Pete, that we have no intentions of harming your daughter. There will be no violence. You will find no new bruises on her body. You have my word."

Silence.

Vitri stares at Bass. His eyes shift from Bass to Reyn, from Reyn to Ogden. Back to Reyn. *You won't.*

"What do you say, Pete?" Bass circles. Places himself between Vitri and Reyn.

Silence.

Ogden sighs. "Come on," he says beneath his breath.

You won't. "You won't hurt her?" Vitri asks.

"Swear to God."

Vitri crosses his arms. "And what did you say about trade?"

"Jesus Christ," Ogden says.

"It's his fucking daughter, you asshole," Bass says. "It takes time to accept such a thing."

"Well if he'd been bending his cousin over a goddamn office chair for months, I'm sure he'd be a little anxious too."

Fury then consumes Bass's body. His eyes widen as he turns to Ogden. He steps toward him. Swings with a closed right fist. Strikes him in the throat with enough force to send him to the ground. His gasps for air are obstructed by two quick strikes to his chest. Bass pushes himself off of the ground. Stares at a frightened Reyn. Turns to Vitri.

"Trade, yeah, trade," Bass says. Ogden's gasping quiets. He rolls to his side and pushes himself to his feet. "We can do that. Food, weapons, you name it. Name your price."

Vitri looks at Reyn. *You won't.* "What kinds of weapons?"

"Name it."

You won't. "Rifles?"

Ogden nods.

"Available for trade?" Bass says. "Two M4s, one Springfield."

"I'll take the two M4s," Vitri says. "And ammo. Enough for Seattle."

Bass turns to Ogden. They nod at one another. "Deal," Ogden says. He extends a hand, which is not met by Vitri.

"One other condition," Vitri says.

Bass retracts his hand. "What's that?"

"I get to watch." Vitri waits for the confusion to take shape in both of their faces. "You gave me your word that she wouldn't be hurt. But I don't believe you. Not for a fucking second. I need to see it for myself."

"You don't want to watch, Pete," Bass says.

"We won't hurt her, but it'll be painful for you," Ogden struggles to say.

"You don't think I've endured pain?"

"Didn't say that," Bass says. He pulls the pistol from his holster. "Didn't say that at all. What I'm saying is that you're not going to watch. You're not going to step foot in that fucking building. You're going to stand out here, we're going to lock that door, and you're going to wait until we're done. And when we *are* done, we'll give you those weapons." Bass steps toward Reyn. "Is that clear?"

Vitri remains still. *Fuck you.* "Then bring her backpack out here."

"What?"

"Bring her fucking backpack out here then," Vitri says. "If I can't come in, if I can't be by her side, I at least have to tell her— write to her—what's going on. Otherwise she's going to fight. I can promise you that. She's going to bite, and she's going to dig, and she's going to claw."

Silence.

Stares. Skepticism. Unsure footsteps.

Ogden, to Bass: "What difference does it make? Just give him the fuckin' backpack."

"You searched hers, right?"

Ogden nods.

No you didn't.

"You're sure?"

"All that was in there was food," Ogden says. "He's the armory, she's the diner. Remember?"

At that, Bass steps past Reyn and enters the building alone, footsteps creaking across the hardwood. "Give him the backpacks then," he says.

Ogden follows.

Vitri walks to Reyn. Does not crouch. Can barely look at her.

When Ogden emerges once more from the building, he is shirtless. A thin tribal tattoo wraps from oblique to oblique. The rest is partitioned off by tan-lines, bare and white. In his hand is a backpack.

"Hurry up," he says as he hands it over.

Vitri drops the backpack to the ground, then unzips the largest pocket. He pulls out the notebook. Uncaps a pen. Writes. Caps the pen, shoves it into his pocket. Hands the notebook to Reyn.

GO WITH HIM. DON'T FIGHT. TRUST ME

She only reads it once. And, as if she were expecting it, as if she knew all along she was to be dispensable, Reyn, without so much as a glance at Vitri, drops the notebook on the ground and leads Ogden past Bass and into McPHERSON's ACCOUNTING.

"That's a good girl," Ogden says.

From the doorframe, Bass nods at Vitri, then shuts the door behind him. Locks it.

Vitri crouches to grab the notebook. Because he knows Bass is watching him from the window, he places it into the backpack as slowly as possible, as dramatically as possible. He looks to the sky as if answers are to be found there. He waits. And he listens.

"You take her clothes off," he hears Bass say.

Ogden: "I get to go first then."

A belt buckle clangs off of the hardwood floor.

"Like hell you do."

"Why wouldn't I?"

Boots are taken off, flung toward a wall.

"Because you told that shithead out there that you fuck me in the ass, that's why."

At that, Vitri re-ties the scarf around his nose and mouth, then reaches back into Reyn's backpack. Finds the sickle. Sets it aside. Locates the .22 pistol. Racks it. Stands. Turns to the door of McPHERSON's ACCOUNTING. Takes a deep breath.

Reyn lifts her arms over her head, and up goes her sweatshirt.
Once off, the bearded man folds it gently and sets it on the green-
quilted cot to his left. The other man stands nearer to the hallway,
naked, watching, working to get his penis hard. His mouth moves
but, in this dim light, Reyn cannot pinpoint any particular shapes,
any syllables. The bearded man steps back toward her, grinning. He
unbuttons her jeans. His fingers find her zipper. They find her belt
loops. And—

The floor quivers.

Again.

And again.

The bearded man's fingers stop. He turns his head. The naked
man bends to his discarded clothes, locates his pistol, and, with it
in his hand, walks down the hallway.

And then the floor is sent into mild convulsions, short but rapid waves striking Reyn's toes.

The naked man quickens his pace. The bearded man turns away from Reyn entirely. Flash. Flash-flash. Reyn watches the bearded man reach for the pistol on his hip. Flash-flash. Blood splatters onto her arms and chest. She drops to the floor. Shields her face. Coils her body.

Footsteps. More. More.

Reyn unshields her face. The bearded man squirms on the floor, jaws clenched, right shoulder slimed red. She watches Vitri shove the barrel of the pistol she carried into the man's mouth. There it stays for three seconds, four, five, the bearded man trying to speak around the barrel. And then Vitri pulls the trigger. Again, and again, and again. Blood, lots of blood. Splattered, leaking, pooling around the bits of pulp on the floor. There are ears, a sliver of an eye. His face appears more as an upside-down funnel than a face at all, jagged red cylinder leading to the skull.

Vitri stands. Walks down the hallway. Comes back dragging the naked man, places him next to the bearded man. Lets him speak. Then aims the pistol at the man's head and fires, fires, fires, fires until the pistol just won't anymore. Only then does he drop the pistol. He walks to Reyn, not once looking her in the eye, not once seeming to notice just how quickly she is retreating from him. Closer now, and closer. He reaches for her. She swats at his arms.

268

He stands her up. Buttons her pants. Once done, he searches beneath each cot. Yanks out a rifle. Black, compact, and with too many contours for Reyn to count. Still unsure of what to do—stand still, run, cry—Reyn watches Vitri rise and walk down the narrow hallway. Watches him kneel where the hallway meets the open area and aim the rifle at what Reyn, still in the bedroom, assumes to be the front door of McPHERSON's ACCOUNTING.

For minutes she watches him. For minutes she waits for him to stand once more, approach her once more, write to her once more, explain this, explain it all. She steps forward. She steps—

Three flashes from the rifle.

Vitri stands and walks out of Reyn's sight. She waits a moment before continuing down that hallway. When she does, she is met by Vitri, bent over, walking backward. Reyn backs herself against the hallway wall, allowing Vitri the room he needs to drag the skinny man neck to toe in black. On the man's chest, stitched in white: MARTINEZ.

MARTINEZ's limp right hand skids over Reyn's foot. Her eyes follow the blood streaks beneath him. Vitri does his best to toss the man toward a cot. Once he catches his breath, he starts kicking MARTINEZ's face.

###

The McPHERSON's ACCOUNTING door is still open. Night has come. The only light is the candle upon the desk, its almond scent combating the smell of urine and feces drifting down the hallway. Reyn keeps the candle close, as close as she can. Her fingers are trembling less now, adrenaline slinking somewhere other than her eyes as she watches the flame. Alongside the candle, atop the map, is the notebook, open to a blank page, an uncapped pen propped on its binding. SORRY, she has considered writing. SORRY, for being the cause of Vitri's killing of more people. Yet, in the time she has been waiting for Vitri to emerge from the bedroom, she has been unable to bring herself to do so, her heart sending the tiniest of jolts to her hand before pen can reach paper. No, she thinks it says. And she has been listening. She has been thinking. Letting it churn. *You did not cause this. You are not responsible.*

Moments later, when she carries the candle down the hallway, Reyn finds Vitri naked on the floor, his pale skin looking like wax paper in the dim light. He has stacked the three dead men in the northwest corner of the bedroom. He lies on his side, facing the opposite wall. Two empty syringes lie near his hand. A small pile of feces is on the floor, against the backs of his thighs. A puddle of urine expands before his groin. This is as close as she gets. This is as close as she wants to be. She does not want to see his face. She wants nothing to do with his eyes, or his hands. Nothing. She wants nothing of him. *Die here*, she thinks as she walks out of the bedroom. *Die right here, Vitri.*

Reyn sets Ralph's sickle on the desk and, next to it, *DEEP THROAT*. *No more weapons*, she thinks—a declaration that half of the time terrifies her. The other half? A declaration that gives her pride.

In the weapons' stead, she places more cans of food in her backpack from the plastic crate against the wall. Barley soup, stringed green beans, fiesta corn, spinach. Reyn searches Vitri's backpack for anything useful, extracting from it three more palm-sized candles, the flashlight, two and a half bottles of water, and all but one book of matches, which she shoves into her pants pocket. Into her backpack all of it goes, toppling, gravity and shape delegating where it is they'll rest. Because Reyn is leaving.

She is leaving.

She *is* leaving.

Going, gone.

Far away from here.

She is *leaving.*

Not tonight, though, not in the dark. Doing so, she thinks, will be suicide, even with the flashlight clicked on. She pictures herself mauled by some starved predator. Crossing paths with yet another man or woman she'll fail to understand. Cornered into something just like this, just as painful. She zips the largest pocket of her backpack, then struggles to slide its straps over her shoulders, the added weight enough to alter her posture. Before leaving McPHERSON's ACCOUNTING, Reyn lifts the lit candle from the desk. She doesn't think once of closing the door.

Across the road she goes, to the theatre. She carefully sets the backpack on the ground and, candle in hand, walks to the northern side of the building. Nothing but dirt, and weeds, not even a rock. On the southern side, however, sits a small pile of loose yellow bricks, two of which Reyn grabs with her free hand. Back at the entrance, Reyn sets the candle next to her backpack. She then positions herself just so—feet from the door, enough room between for her arm to wind up and follow through, for each brick to gain velocity, make a dent, an impact—and, attempting to channel as much anger as she can, offers her first throw. Though a beetle-sized shard of glass has chipped off, she has missed the mark; all she needs, all she wants is a hole above the handle, large enough to snake her arm through and turn the lock.

cH. XVii

Gone, gone, gone, she is gone, they are gone, all are gone and crack-crack, crack-crack, *the sound of glass, the sound of anger, the sound of hope shattering, falling where it belongs, where it starts, where it leads, and* crack-crack, crack-crack, crack-crack, crack-crack. Crack-crack—

Gone, all gone—

crack-crack—

you are not floating—

crack-crack—

there is no song—

crack-crack—

you are what makes it end.

When the crack-crack from across the road subsides, Vitri opens his eyes. Beneath the cot nearest him is a boy's head. No body to speak of; just his head, parallel to Vitri's, eyes aligned.

Seven years old. Eight. Grey face. Dark, disheveled hair. Violet eyelids. An indifferent stare.

"You did this," the boy says. It is not a whisper. It is not a scream. It is not his son. He has never seen this boy, in life or in dream, but he somehow knows him and trusts him.

"I did," Vitri says. He scoots himself closer to the boy. Wants to feel his cheek. Wants to find the rest of him and hold him close.

A rifle inches itself from under the cot.

"You don't belong here," the boy says.

Vitri stops. Stares at the rifle. "No," he says. He grips the rifle. "No, I don't."

And then, *like everyone else*, the boy is gone. *Gone, gone, gone.*

Once Vitri discontinues his search for the boy, he, rifle in hand, rolls onto his back. Empty syringes fracture beneath his weight. The pile of feces flattens across the back of his right thigh. He checks the safety. Off. Flips the barrel of the rifle to his chin. Rests the stock on his abdomen. Locates the trigger. Works the barrel of the rifle to the roof of his mouth.

One flash of yellow-white light rushes through MCPHERSON'S ACCOUNTING and spills onto the road, onto Reyn's back.

cH. XVIII

By the time Reyn can fit her arm through the hole that she has created in the theatre's glass door, the candle has gone out. Her forehead glistens. Her breath is heavy. After allowing herself a moment of rest, she reaches her hand through the hole, jagged glass wide enough for her to angle her wrist without being gashed, find the deadbolt and unlock the door. She retracts her hand carefully, returns to her backpack and slings it over her shoulders. Then, propping the door open with her hip, she pulls the book of matches from her pants pocket. She re-lights the candle. She enters the theatre.

Half of the floor is carpeted with what Reyn can see now are chunks of various rugs and floor mats, a mosaic as they are, when spliced together. The other half is gravel, and cold, on which dozens of posters lie, rolled tight and rubber-banded. Near the eastern wall, one projection screen hangs from the rafters, moderately sized and greyed by dust. No more than ten feet from the screen sits one row of four multi-colored seats. Black and grey, beige and red, one cloth, two leather, the last some ratty version of suede, all with gouges mended by duct tape, and armrests made of plywood, semi-wrapped in rubber tubing. Three of the four still have seatbelts, male and female ends dangling.

In the northeastern corner, at the edge of her candle's glow, Reyn spots the start of a basement staircase. She sets her backpack on one of the chairs facing the projection screen. Carefully places the lit candle on the floor and reaches into her backpack for another. Lights it; waits for the flame to settle. Then, she descends the staircase.

Ten feet down she goes, candlelight climbing up and across the nearest concrete wall. She turns right when she reaches the bottom. Dozens of weapons hug the eastern wall. A pile of pistols. Leaned rifles and shotguns. Further south are two stacks of empty duffel bags, ammunition boxes and cleaning kits between that give the towers structure. Reyn examines little here. Reaches for nothing. It's when she turns to leave that she sees anything of interest: at the edge of her candle's light, in the southwestern corner, lies what she knows to be a generator, its tires dusty, stones lodged between treads. She approaches. Crouches. Hovers the candle over CHOKE, over START, over the small engine and the pull cord. She wonders what would illuminate if she were to start it, wonders what of this small town draws its power from this stout rectangle. She pictures lampposts that have yet to be erected, neon signs that have yet to be placed. She pictures building interiors aglow, the theatre's projector flickering. She pictures wanderers along the river's shore, spooked at the sight but unable to defy their desire to approach, drawn to the light like moths. *Not yet*, Reyn thinks. *Not here. Not now.* She stands. Looks at the generator from this angle. Knows that she won't be able to get it up the stairs by herself, knows but wants to try in the morning anyway.

Back up the stairs she goes. She blows out the candle in her hand. Lets the candle on the floor burn. She sits down, facing the projection screen, knowing that nothing will play, knowing that no one will join her. And, for now, she is more than okay with that. She is content, alone in this theatre, thinking not of Vitri, not of her father, of Faye, or her mother, but of herself and of that shipwreck, of the AMERICAN QUEEN.

Before swigging from that open bottle of water and spooning chunks of soup from that pre-opened can at the bottom of her backpack, she wonders if there is a way in, a way to the deck, a ladder or rope to climb, a window to fracture and crawl through. She pictures herself standing upright in a room forever sideways, taking days to tailor it all to her liking—muscling over the tipped beds, the end tables, the nightstands. She'll read every page, every last word of the books that have flown from the shelves, scribbling notes in the margins, observations aligning with what she sees the world as. *At dawn*, she thinks. At dawn she'll start. She'll re-hang the curtains. She'll scrape the sap from whichever healthy trees remain and use it to glue the shattered lamps together. She'll come back here when she's done. Grab the generator. Wheel it north. She'll light what she can.

Reyn is at her home on LaFontaine, lying on the living room sofa, and she feels fine. Her cheek has returned to normal, as has her tongue. Nothing of her body throbs. And yet, something feels off to her. Not her body. The home.

Though she for the life of her can't remember what images were seconds ago flashing across the television, gone is the picture, reduced to black and white lines that whip like downed telephone wires. She sits up and blood dribbles down her chin.

The wall nearest the kitchen vanishes, ripped off like a scab. And through the new opening walks her mother. Her healthy mother. Back is her style. Back is her midsection. Back is her smile. And she walks straight to Reyn. Instructs her to lie her head back. Reyn does. Feels her mother's fingers caress her throat. Seconds later, her mother stands, turns, walks off.

Reyn sits up. More blood dribbles down her chin. She wipes it away. More spills from her lip. She wipes it away and then gone is the wall nearest her. In walks her father, who, drunk, stumbles toward the kitchen, doing a double-take once he sees Reyn on the couch. He stops. Smiles. Stumbles toward her. Leans down, goes to kiss Reyn on the cheek, stubbled face smearing across her chin. He smiles as he rises, blood on his lips.

After him walks Faye. Through the house she goes. Crossing her path is JOHN. Crossing JOHN's path is the old woman with the AMERICAN QUEEN shirt. Through the house they all go, past Reyn. Oblivious.

Reyn sits up once more. Blood pours from her mouth, down her chin, to her chest, on her lap. She stands but immediately feels weight on her shoulders, a force pressing down that she fights, fights-fights-fights. And then there are hands, and then there are feet, and then there are shins, and thighs. A chest. Shoulders mirroring hers. She looks up to see Vitri, eyes wide, scarf over his mouth and nose. He shoves her to the sofa. Pins her hands to the cushion. Mounts her. Thrusts. And thrusts. And thrusts, paying no mind to the same people that pass through the house once more— Reyn's mother, Reyn's father, Faye, JOHN, the old woman. Only when he is finished, only when he is face down on Reyn's chest does the roof begin to cave in.

###

Reyn does not wake at dawn, but hours after, when the shadow looming over the theatre is shifting, when sunlight leaks through the glass and onto the floor. When she does wake, it's in a panic.

That was not real. That was not real.

She rises from the two seats she'd shoved together in the night and rubs sleep from her eyes as she walks toward the glass door. It isn't until she begins pushing the door open that she sees the small boy standing in the doorway of McPHERSON's ACCOUNTING, plain blue mask on and loosely over all but his lips and eyes, the diamond-shaped holes for each glared by sunlight skimming off the plastic.

He wears no shirt, only baggy blue shorts that flare at the calf. In his lone hand he holds tight the two blue masks he'd found in the crate.

They stand like this, staring at one another across the road. For one second, for two seconds, three, and up to six before Reyn, assuming the boy to not be acting on his own, glances south. As she does so, as she shifts her eyes for but a moment, the small boy takes off. Sprints north, arms pumping but head still, legs churning, sandaled feet sending plumes of dust into the sky.

Reyn hurries through the doorway and onto the dirt road, scuffing shards of glass along. Before the boy, still sprinting north, reaches the slope she and Vitri surmounted en route to the town, Reyn sees one of the two masks slip from his grasp. But soon he is down the hill, out of sight.

Reyn slowly walks north but soon finds herself picking up speed. *He'd come so far*, she thinks, somewhere between a jog and sprint now, feeling the aluminum cans smacking her back. She feels the remaining liquid in the bottle of rubbing alcohol slosh around, jostling for position with the candles.

Reyn struggles to bend down and pick up the abandoned mask. But she does and, mask in hand, she covers the remaining yards to the crest of the hill. Looking down on the gravel shoreline, she sees the boy, two hundred yards north, veer slightly to the west, toward the treeline. To the east of him is the river, its coverage growing thicker the further north he goes, its top layer comprised of still-green grass and weeds not yet yellowed by the sun.

She focuses on the boy once more, who has begun turning his hips toward the river, his eyes, his feet following, all churning just as fast as before. At this moment, maybe more than ever, Reyn wishes she could scream, wishes she could shout, "No," and that he'd listen, and turn back, away from what she is sure are traps.

But onto the layered river the boy leaps, and sprints across, all two-hundred-plus feet, straight across loose grass kicked to the sky by his feet instead of dust.

Once on the eastern side, the boy slows eventually to a walk, either winded or bogged down by a sense of security. He then stops entirely. He turns around and holds his gaze with Reyn for only a few seconds, then is gone again, into a northeastern sprint, over the first of several small yellow-green hills.

Reyn stands, on the crest of the hill, and looks northeast, hoping the boy will come back into view. When, after moments, he doesn't, she turns her attention to the blue mask still in her hand. The inside of the mask, formed to a small nose and round cheeks, is white, save for a smear of red near the forehead. There is an indent an inch or so from the right eye, the impression no larger than what a grown man's thumb could make. Reyn flips the mask. The blue paint is uneven in spots, lighter around the jaws, nearer to purple on the chin, but for no obvious reason. Other than that, however, the mask is, like the sprinting boy's, plain, void of design, the two of them unified by a lack of identity.

Go to the boat, Reyn thinks. *Just go to the boat; that is your home now.* She walks north, cradling the mask. *Drop the mask. He'll find it. Drop the mask. Go to the boat. Drop the mask. Go to the boat. Drop the mask, go to the boat. Drop the mask, go to the boat, drop the mask, go to the boat, drop the mask, go-to-the-boat, go-to-the-boat, go-to-the-boat.*

Go. To. The. Boat.

Fifty yards later, Reyn stops. She looks again at the mask. She looks north. She looks northeast. She can't. *He had no weapon. He did not attack you. He did not beat your face. He is not Vitri. He is a boy, a boy who has been looking for something he'd lost.*

The thought, no matter how much she fights it, stays with her for another twenty yards or so, until, staring north once more, at the treeline, at the gravel, Reyn realizes that all she is walking towards, the only thing that lies ahead is the past.

If she stays on course, if she sticks to what she knows, if she walks to that boat, she'll pass Vitri. He'll be there, on the forest floor, gasping for air. He'll be there, near that pile of ash. He'll be there, and there is nothing north, nothing she can do but walk west to avoid him, travel around him, only to watch him stare once more at the AMERICAN QUEEN.

Reyn approaches the river, long stick in hand. Where she figures the small boy sprinted across, she pokes aside the top layer of grass and weeds, revealing beneath it what appears to be a thin mound of wet clay. She inserts the end of her stick into the mass, then struggles to pull it free. *A bridge*, she thinks. *Or a dam. Something made, something shaped.*

She paces north and proceeds to fling more grass and weeds aside. She sees that the clay is no more than a foot wide, with still brown water on the north and south. When she looks closely enough, she can still make out the sprinting boy's footprints in the clay; barely visible, barely felt.

For a few minutes, after easing the blue mask into her backpack, Reyn tests just how much weight the clay can hold. Backpack on her shoulders, she steps atop and stands still. Within seconds she sinks half an inch. She steps off, tries again and again, holding the backpack in different positions but knowing it won't make a difference; weight is weight.

You're too heavy. You can't run as fast. You'll sink. You'll take one misstep and fall off this shallow wall, into deeper water. Your leg will be snared in a trap. You will drown. The boy is a magician. Go back to the town. Search the alleys and theatre for a rope. Search for a crate. Tug the crate across the river as you run.

Reyn walks backwards until her heels nearly touch the treeline. She keeps her eyes northeast. Furiously, Reyn sets the backpack on the ground, unzips its largest pocket, and begins plucking cans of food from the bottom. She tosses four of the seven on the gravel, knowing someone, or something, will someday find them, will find it all and put it to use, survive if only for a few days more. Three of five candles. One bottle of water.

Reyn zips the pocket. Stands up. Pulls the straps over her shoulder. Takes one deep breath. Two. Just go.

And then Reyn takes off. She keeps her weight as forward as she can without toppling over, arms pumping, feet digging into the gravel, focusing on her line, the narrow line she must hit, and keep, stepping over the water that filled in her trial-run footprints, until she is sprinting atop the clay, across the river.

For fifty-plus feet she sprints, relentlessly, with both violence and grace, springing off of her toes. Ten more feet. Ten more, ten more. And then she loses it. Her right foot slips. Her left knee slams into the clay. She falls, taking with her into the water the topmost layer of grass and weeds and twigs.

Panic. She kicks her feet. Water splashes all over her hair, the backpack, her shoulders. Loose grass flings every which way. She digs her fingers into the clay, peeling away chunks, shoving the mound further into the water, allowing a slow current to begin in the middle of the river. Reyn feels that ball forming in her chest, forcing its way to her throat.

Forward, she thinks. *Forward, forward, forward*, and, whether or not the ball makes its way off her tongue, Reyn crawls her way along the clay toward the eastern shore. Forward, forward, forward. Forward, forward, forward. Fifty feet from shore. *Forward, forward, forward*. Forty. *Forward, forward, forward.*

Reyn's shins graze the river floor. She continues crawling until she can stand. When she does, she is up to her thighs in soggy grass, what water she'd soaked up along the way returning itself to the river with the help of gravity. And, standing there, her weight taking her and the clay an inch or so lower, Reyn allows herself to smile. She looks back at where she began and thinks it far away now. She can even see where she fell, evident by the current that continued to flow, carrying with it what its hands could grasp. Satisfied, she turns back around and steps toward shore. Twenty feet remaining. Fifteen. Ten, her knees high, feet down, water splashing around each step. And then she feels it. Some sort of hiss across her right calf. A snap in the water. She looks down, sees nothing but brown. But there is a sting in her leg, a growing sting, a throbbing sting. *Forward*, she thinks. *Forward, forward, forward.*

Once ashore, Reyn takes off the backpack and sits down on the gravel. With the amount of water that had soaked into her clothes, Reyn struggles to roll up her pant leg, grimacing with each fold. There is a gash on the back of her calf. Two gashes. Three, the first short and shallow, the second deeper, longer, the third even more so. All three bleed onto the stones beneath her.

Immediately, Reyn reaches for her backpack. Lying on her side, she unzips the largest pocket and plunges her hand toward the bottom, searching for the bottle of rubbing alcohol. She pulls it out, twists off its top and pours more than she needs over her leg. A harsher sting, a broader sting, a series of gasps.

Right pantleg still rolled, Reyn gingerly walks northeast, toward sparse groupings of trees, into ankle-high grass.

The river is no longer in sight.

She passes an empty hunting shack, two of the four walls caved in, handfuls of bullet casings left behind and rusting. She walks over patches of uneven ground she assumes to be places the blue-masked boys have dug and replaced as best they could, small footprints leading further northeast. Between two particular ridges, she spots two white-tailed deer, one buck, one doe, both sets of ears perked, their hair patchy but their frames, for the fifteen seconds they remain still, appearing as elegant as they should.

Reyn maintains her pace for upwards of an hour before her thighs and groin begin to burn—a reminder of Vitri's attack. She seeks shade beneath a wilting willow, which, thus far, having walked entirely over gradual ridges and into the sun-fried valleys between, has been difficult to find. She sits against the trunk, her left leg flat on the burnt grass, the right crossed over to examine the gashes. Dry now, reduced to slivers of pink.

Forward, forward, northeast, northeast, then northeast some more. Sun high, hotter than it has been for days. No wind. Sweat, lots of sweat, lots of steps, lots of sweat seeping into the cuts, lots of steps, lots of burning. *Northeast, northeast,* past thicker clusters of trees—oaks and elms and sycamores—past thicker knots of weeds and brush, past shade, over hearty grass, eventually back into a valley as the sun continues to arc.

Forward, forward, forward, up the steepest incline Reyn has come across, struggling all the way to the top, breathing heavy, toes dug in. Young trees, as high as her chest, trunks the size of her ankles. High enough now to see just over the crest of the hill, Reyn watches smoke eddying into the sky. *Forward. Forward, forward, forward.* Once atop, she wipes the sweat from her forehead and looks down on an old loghouse in the process of being painted light blue, two of four sides completed. The smoke comes from its center, a narrow circle in the roof. Leaning against the westernmost side of the longhouse is a bicycle. Small dark blue frame, white handlebars, white seat, evidence of its last ride able to be tracked all over the lawn, narrow trails all around the house, up and down the slope, weaving beneath trees to the north that, through its sparse leaves, appears to have taut ropes strung from branch to branch.

Reyn, weight on her heels, walks down the slope, head up and scanning for any reason to turn back, or head west. *Steel traps. Rifles. Arrows.* While she sees nothing of the sort, Reyn, unable to completely combat the doubt, raises her arms in the air as she walks toward the longhouse, surrendering before anything even begins.

Fifty yards. Closing. Arms: still in air. Mouth: dry. Sweat. The burn in her thighs easing, overpowered by nervousness. Flutters in her muscles.

Twenty-five yards, on flat ground. A blue door, uneven logs as steps, bound by twine. Windows. Blue shutters. East of the trees: glimpses of green, shin-high corn stalks, the beginnings of what look to be caged tomato plants. She doesn't tell them to, but finds her arms dropping to her sides.

Ten yards. The smell of food cooking. Meat. Fatty meat. Potatoes. Greens. She notices the window nearest her is fogged but looks anyway, albeit briefly, seeing only varying flashes of white light from the southeastern corner of the interior. She can continue this way, she knows—gawk through the windows, spy, intrude from a distance. But that is not why she has come here. Nor is she here to beat on this door, to wait for them to answer with alarm, misguided to violence.

After gathering her breath, what Reyn does is take the backpack once more from her shoulders and set it on the ground. She again unzips the largest pocket, pulling from it the pen and notebook, its pages mostly dry. She writes:

I KNOW WHERE THE POWER IS

Reyn sets the notebook on the top step, against the blue door. She places the blue mask the beside the notebook, eyeholes skyward, then reaches back in for the remaining cans of food, arranging all in a line on the bottom step and placing atop them the candle, into the heart of which she'd carved R + V.

With every intention to light the wick, Reyn pulls the book of matches from her pocket and, upon feeling their dampness, understands that there is no point in trying. It will not light. She backs away from the door and sits on the ground, pulling her knees to her chest. She hugs them tight. Curves her spine, rests her chin. She tilts her gaze from candle to door, from door to candle. This is how she'll stay, for minutes, for hours, however long it'll take to be found.

THE END

ᴀCK.

First and foremost, I'd like to thank my partner, Lindsy. You've stood by in support as I've ridden this story's varying waves of torment. I love you and I appreciate you.

I'd also like to thank my mother and my father. Many parents would've at least reached for the steering wheel upon learning of their child's desire to pursue writing, if not grab it entirely and yank. But you didn't. You encouraged me, though I'm sure it was nerve-wracking—though I'm sure that it still is. You let me chase, and explore, and find my own path. Without the freedom to do so, I don't think this novel would exist. Thank you.

To Caitlin Horrocks: if not for you saying in one of our workshops at Grand Valley State University, "It's one thing to build a world; it's an entirely different thing to tear that world down," I also don't think this novel would exist. Thank you—you remain a huge influence to me.

And finally, to Daniel Abbott, you, my friend, have seen more drafts of *And in the Dark They Are Born* than any other person, and your eyes and ears and soul have been immensely helpful throughout the entire process. If not for you, this novel definitely wouldn't be what it is today, nor would I be the writer I am. I've loved working with you over the years. Here's to many more.

ABOUT

Garrett Francis grew up on a small farm in Michigan, had a great childhood, and earned his B.A. in Creative Writing from Grand Valley State University.

In 2012, he co-founded *Squalorly*, a digital literary journal of the Midwest and served as its nonfiction editor until 2014. Two book-length projects of his were represented by a reputable literary agency from 2014 to 2016, until the relationship abruptly ended.

It was that experience that led Garrett to found Orson's Publishing in 2016, a micro press with an aim to publish "wise and approachable storytelling." He served as the press's sole editor (and designer, and publicist, among other roles) until its closure in 2020, publishing four book-length works by new and emerging authors.

In 2017, Garrett also founded *Orson's Review*, a digital literary journal that served as a companion to its parent press, publishing fiction, creative nonfiction, poetry and photography. He served as the sole editor of *Orson's Review* as well, and is proud to have helped bring the work of over 70 international contributors to life.

Today, Garrett lives in beautiful Seattle, Washington with his wife, daughter and dog. He works a day job in the field of content design and when he's not working or writing, he tries to be outside as much as he can with his family—camping, hiking, kayaking, and just generally wandering.

Subscribe to Garrett Francis's newsletter for exclusive access to his thoughtful literary fiction, creative nonfiction, screenplays, and more—including deep dives into *And in the Dark They Are Born* via episodes of author commentary.

SCAN CODE TO VISIT

www.ingramcontent.com/pod-product-compliance
Lightning Source LLC
Chambersburg PA
CBHW031057130726
47906CB00008B/701